The Melting Season

The Melting Season

CELESTE CONWAY

DELACORTE PRESS

Published by Delacorte Press
an imprint of Random House Children's Books
a division of Random House, Inc.
New York

This is a work of fiction. Names, characters, places, and incidents either are the product of
the author's imagination or are used fictitiously. Any resemblance to actual persons, living or
dead, events, or locales is entirely coincidental.

Delacorte Press and colophon are registered trademarks of
Random House, Inc.

www.randomhouse.com/teens
Educators and librarians, for a variety of teaching tools,
visit us at www.randomhouse.com/teachers

Library of Congress Cataloging-in-Publication Data
Conway, Celeste.
The melting season / Celeste Conway.
p. cm.
Summary: Giselle, the sheltered daughter of two famous ballet dancers, comes
to terms with her relationships with both her late father and her mother,
realizing some important truths that help her move forward both in her life
and with her own dancing.
ISBN-13: 978-0-385-73339-7 (trade hardcover) — ISBN-13: 978-0-385-90357-8 (lib. bdg.)
ISBN-10: 0-385-73339-9 (trade hardcover) — ISBN-10: 0-385-90357-X (lib. bdg.)
[1. Ballet dancing—Fiction. 2. Coming of age—Fiction. 3. Mothers and daughters—Fiction.
4. Fathers and daughters—Fiction. 5. Schools—Fiction.] I. Title.
PZ7.C7683Mel 2006
[Fic]—dc22
2006004573

The text of this book is set in 11-point Galliard.

Printed in the United States of America

10 9 8 7 6 5 4 3 2 1

First Edition

For Mary

ACKNOWLEDGMENTS

Thanks to ballerinas
Jenny Sui-Kan Chiang
and Svetlana Caton-Noble
for talking to me about dance
and being a dancer.

The Melting Season

Chapter 1

IMET WILL BROOKS in early spring on what happened to be Medieval Day. That's a big event at the flaky
school I go to—the Dante School for "artistically gifted
youth." We are so artistic it strains the mind. And the
Medieval Pageant is one of the most artistic, or as our head-
master, Chaz, would say, "intra-artistic" events of the year.
We really knock ourselves out with breathtaking displays of
talented giftedness.

This year's theme was "Life in a Time of Death." Which,
in a way, seemed the theme of my actual life. Of course, in
the case of Medieval Day, "Death" meant the Black Death;
i.e., the bubonic plague *(bacillus Pasteurella),* which, as
you probably know, wiped out between one-third and
two-fifths of the European population back in the fourteenth century. In keeping with the theme, all the various
departments had to make some kind of artistic contribution
having to do with how the people of the Dark Ages managed to amuse themselves and carry on while everyone was

keeling over all around them. For example, the music classes performed a bunch of songs about the plague, including "Ring Around the Rosy," which I found out was a reference to the rosy pustules (buboes) that appeared on the skin of the unfortunate victims. The part about "all fall down" really meant "die."

The art classes made a lot of gory-looking banners with pictures of dead animals on them, and the Creative Literature people delivered an original epic poem about a lark that flitted around the countryside eating berries and singing "tu-whit," oblivious to all the dead mammals along the road.

As for my department, we did some court-type dancing that was actually Elizabethan and not medieval at all. I know that from reading *A Dance Through Time*, one of the books my father wrote. Believe me, he'd have yanked me out of this school even faster than he yanked me out of nursery school. Unfortunately, it's not him but Blitz who pays my tuition, which is outrageous and obscene. Blitz is my mother's boyfriend—a subject I'd rather skip right now.

⎯⎯⎯

"Methinks 'twas the comeliest of festivals in selden a yere," said Magda, who is my best friend, as we dragged into the Michelangelo Buonarroti Parlor, where we had left our twentieth-century clothes and stuff. She had even liked lunch, the big contribution of the theater department— bread, bread pudding and lamb shank—which you ate, of course, without silverware.

"Methinks it was the goofiest," I said, yanking off my ancient Greek tunic and looking at her in the Michelangelo Buonarroti Mirror.

"Yet ye must ownest that ye verily liked the torches."

"The torches were great," I told her. I verily wished she would start talking normal again, but after an "event" it always takes a while for Magda to break character and get back to being her regular self. And it was true; the torches she designed were great. With fans and flashlights and scraps of cloth, she'd made the illusion of actual flame. She wired it all into little cages made out of twigs that she'd woven with her own two hands. Magda wants to be a lighting designer, which I'm sure she will if, in the meantime, she doesn't electrocute herself.

"Do you think Dark liked them?" she asked me next. Dark is short for Darkan, a guy in our school, an immigrant from some newly formed nation, and a cellist—one of the few music majors who can actually play his instrument.

"Of course he liked them. They were great."

"He finally knows who I am—me guesseth."

"Unless he was in a coma when Chaz called you up to take that bow."

"I wore this vest," said Magda, "so that when I bowed he'd see my tits. Eastern European guys are very big on tits, you know."

"Unlike guys from everywhere else." I stared at her chest. "It's a really great vest. Didn't your mother send you that?"

Magda nodded. "From Burma or somewhere. I think it's yak."

"Where is she now?"

"I don't know. Last week it was Lourdes. They like it there. It's 'karmic.' " By "they" she meant her mother, Fiona, and her mother's new husband, Leif. In January they went off on what was supposed to be a two-week honeymoon, and here it was April and they still had not

3

come back. A lot of people thought this tremendously funny. Like some middle-aged-crazy kind of joke. But I didn't find it funny. And Magda didn't either.

"Listen," I said, "at least they're back in Europe. Maybe that means they're on their way home."

"Who the hell cares? Who wants them back? When I think of living with Leif I die."

"At least he's not as bad as Blitz."

"Are you drunk or something? He's ten times worse. Plus Blitz doesn't actually sleep in your house—and he doesn't have a ponytail."

"He's more disgusting all the same."

"At least he has some money."

"I wish he didn't. Then maybe he wouldn't be around."

"I'll give you that. Your diva mom would never put up with some penniless slob."

She reached in her bag for a hairbrush and started to violently rake her hair, long black curls and tangles that tumble down her back. "Unlike my dear mother, who'll go for anything in pants. I wouldn't mind, I swear to God, if my mother had some standards. I'm not a maniac like you."

"What is that supposed to mean?"

"Come on, Giselle, you know as well as I do that no matter who Marina was with, he wouldn't be good enough for you. No man on earth will ever fill your father's shoes—slippers, I mean, Capezios."

"At least not Blitz."

"Or anyone." I didn't bother to answer her. We had this conversation practically every day. Who was more horrid, Blitz or Leif? And when would I come to realize that I idolized my father like a hero in a storybook?

4

"Anyway," said Magda, wrapping herself in a big black shawl (another gift from another place), "I like my life in my grandmother's house."

"The food's much better too," I said. Understatement of the year. Sonia, her grandmother, is a famous chef whom you've probably actually seen on TV. She used to own a famous New York restaurant and was still adored by her brilliant celebrity customers. She was very social even now and was always having intimate little dinner fêtes in her wonderful house near the Metropolitan Museum of Art, where Magda was currently living. She cooked for us almost all the time.

"I must've gained ten pounds on this honeymoon," Magda said. "And don't think my mother won't notice it." We glanced around the creepy Michelangelo Parlor to see if we had all our stuff; then we headed out the door.

"I think you look great," I told her. I meant it but my voice sounded weird in the echoey hall. Someone had turned all the lights off and in one of the other parlors some lingering psychos were still singing about the plague. As the day wears on our school starts to look and feel a lot like a funeral parlor (which is not surprising since a lot of people died here back in the nineteenth century when it used to be a hospital), so it's always a pleasure to leave when it starts getting late on Friday afternoons.

"So we're on for tomorrow night?" she asked as we ambled down the darkened hall.

"Of course we're on. It's Saturday night."

"If your mother wasn't psycho, we could also go out on Friday nights like the rest of the normal world. I mean it, Giselle, when are you going to take a stand?" She was talking about my mother's rule that I get to bed early on Fridays so that I'll be in shape for my Saturday schedule of ballet classes.

"I'm working on her, I really am."

"Yeah, right. Someday, you know, one of us might not be free on Saturday night. Did you ever think of that?"

"Are you trying to break some news to me?"

"Don't I wish. Magda and Darkan. Dark and Mag. But someday, you know, it actually could happen."

"It doesn't seem very imminent."

"Yeah, I know. But it's not our fault."

Anyway, we were having a pretty good time fooling around and we both felt great to be leaving our psychotic school for the whole weekend. We'd just gotten down the front steps and past the statues of the Muses when who should appear at the curbside in this really stupid antique car but my mother and Blitz. The top was down even though it was still April, and Marina was wearing one of her taller turbans. In the backseat Blitz's dog, Nipper, foamed at the mouth and barked.

"Giselle! Magda!" my mother called, waving a yellow glove. "*Vite! Vite!* We're going on a Sunday drive!"

"It's Friday," said Magda under her breath, "and *sayonara*, I'm out of here."

"Don't leave me!" I whispered wildly. "Don't make me go with them alone."

"Tell them you can't."

"Yeah, right."

"Girls! Girls!" Marina sang out. "Hop in back and hold your hats!" We went over to the car so that Marina would quit her yelling. Nipper went crazy and started jumping up and down for joy. He's one of those Chinese shar-peis, and quite fond of me. I like him too, although he is somewhat crazy.

"Hi, Marina," Magda said. "Hey, Blitz. Hey, Nipper, you nut." She would've petted him if he'd stood still for a second. "I'm sorry, but I really can't go anywhere. I have to help Sonia make *cressonnière.*"

"Sonia needs help to make *cressonnière?*" Marina said, amused.

"She likes me to chop. She hates to chop." I looked at Magda, incredulous. I had no idea what *cressonnière* was, but I knew she wasn't involved in it. She caught my eye and added, "Plus I'm really tired. Postperformance fatigue, I guess."

"Nonsense," said Marina, "you ought to be euphoric. I always was. The adrenaline is marvelous, better than champagne." My mother, by the way, is the famous ballerina Marina Parke-Vanova. I'm sure you've seen her picture. Kissing a rose or something. Or dancing with Le Hungarian, who was seventeen years her junior and endlessly in love with her until his tragic death by drowning off the coast of Corsica.

I turned to Blitz. "Where are you going, anyway?"

"On a fabulous jaunt to the wild wealds of Westches-tah."

"I've heard of that," said Magda.

"The world is our oyster," Marina cooed.

"Why are you going there?" I asked.

Marina beamed. "We've decided to fix up the terrace this year. And Yumi said there's this wonderful little garden store with all kinds of wonderful gardeny things."

"The terrace?"

"Yes. I want us to use it this summer. It's been so neglected these past few years." Since my father died is what she meant. When he was alive it was beautiful. He even grew gardenias, white as cream, delicious, with a smell that made me hallucinate.

"Sounds fun," said Magda, "but no can do." She was backing away as if Blitz and Marina might kidnap her.

"I can't go either," I said to Marina desperately. "I really can't. I'm going home."

Chapter 2

IN THE NEXT FRAME I was, of course, in the back-seat of the car with Nipper drooling all over me, as Blitz "navigated" north on Central Park West. Every now and then he would honk the horn, which made this silly *beep-beep* noise, and he and Marina would laugh themselves sick. As people turned to look at us, Marina waved one yellow glove, and I wished I could disappear.

My embarrassment turned to terror as we swerved onto Ninety-sixth Street, heading, I knew, for the West Side Highway and certain death. It was always scary to drive with Blitz. He just doesn't look right behind a wheel. He looks like he ought to be riding a horse (which he actually does quite frequently out in Central Park). He even kind of looks like a horse; like a Lipizzaner from Austria, glossy and blond with giant horse-sized muscles that bulge against his pants. Ditto for his mega-arms bulging against his mono-grammed shirts. A lot of people, women in particular, think he's a total specimen, but to me he's too massive to be from earth.

My father, being a dancer, was strong and muscular, of course, but his body was also lean and lithe. When he moved he was like an Asian monk, so graceful and light you hardly knew when he'd entered a room. I have no idea how Marina got used to giant Blitz after being with my father. But somehow she did, because here he is, Part of Our Life.

In addition to how we feel about Blitz, Marina and I do not have much in common. One look at us and you would know. She wears fingerless gloves and turbans. She wears crazy high heels, and even though I hate it, fur coats, which she says are too old to matter to anyone, including the dead ocelots' great-great-grandchildren. When teaching ballet she wears white, not black. She goes to the tanning salon and always looks as if she has just jetted in from a Riviera somewhere. Her hair is thick and blond, and overall there is something golden about her. She is fifty-eight years old.

I, on the other hand, resemble my father, a Russian. I have his pale skin and dark hair, his big, sad Russian eyes and quite luscious, I have been told, mouth. From the moment I was born I belonged to him. I will never, ever belong to Blitz.

I had been lying down in the backseat so that no one would see me. I came up for air in time to hear Marina say, "Try flooring it, *querido*. Maybe that would do the trick." We were going, I'd say, twenty miles an hour or so. Amused/annoyed drivers honked their horns as they sprinted by. Blitz managed to get the speedometer up a few notches and then, as if everybody in the world was heir to a Bavarian ham dynasty and a person of leisure like him, said,

"What's the hurry, might I ask? Just look at those daffodils out there." Marina was inspired to quote:

"I wandered lonely as a cloud
That floats on high o'er vales and hills,
When all at once I saw a crowd,
A host, of golden daffodils."

That was when I decided to lie down again and pretend to be dead. That worked for a while. Then Nipper started licking me, bringing me back to life. When I sat up, the George Washington Bridge was behind us and we were driving on a twisty stretch of road alongside the Hudson River. Across the water the Palisades, at least that's what I think they were, stood there looking like tall, dried-up waterfalls.

"The Cloisters is up there," said Blitz, taking both hands off the steering wheel and pointing at some trees. "We might consider taking a visit there before we lay the terrace out. They have a marvelous herb garden."

"J'adore les herbes," said my mother.

A few seconds later we came to a tollbooth. Nipper (I'm sure he had his reasons) started barking his head off as if he needed a rabies shot. Which Blitz didn't seem to notice at all.

"Good day, fair lady," he said in his cheery, aren't-we-on-a-picnic voice. "How much will it be to cross your bridge?"

The woman, who looked really tired and quite depressed, pointed to a huge sign that said: TOLL $2.25.

"Two dollars and twenty-five?" said Blitz. "To all points in Westches-tah?"

"To all points beyond this tollbooth," said the woman.

Blitz started going through his pocket for his wallet, which took about ten years to dig out due to his big horsey muscles bulging against his pants, as I have mentioned.

"Let's not hold up traffic," said the woman.

Naturally Blitz made a big deal of turning around to look behind us. "I don't see a breathing soul," he said. Then to Marina: "Darling, have you got any smallish money?"

"You know I don't carry money," Marina answered gorgeously.

So Blitz handed the woman a fifty-dollar bill. She looked at it as if it were a peseta from outer space. Then she said, "This is a fifty-dollar bill." Blitz marveled aloud at her powers of observation.

I could see the bill shaking in the woman's hand. I had the feeling she was about to start crying or else pull out a gun and shoot us all. I started searching through my backpack for some "smallish" money, which as a matter of fact is the only kind of money I own. Nipper thought I was playing a game with him and started biting my hand through the canvas, but at last I came up with three dollar bills. They were pretty disgusting and shriveled up, but the tollbooth lady seemed relieved.

"Thank you," she said, accepting them. She looked at me for a few seconds and even though I was pretty sure she hated me, I think she felt sorry for me too.

"Lord," said Blitz, "are we to blame if her job is *merde*?"

"You'd think she'd enjoy running into us. We're so festive and gay," Marina said as we *beep-beep*ed and took off.

"You owe me three dollars," I said before crashing down in the backseat again.

The next time I sat up we seemed to be in the wilderness

somewhere. On one side of the road were all these trees. On the other side were more trees and bushes along with a big green pond. Some ducks were floating in the water and on the banks a man was walking some kind of hunting dog. After that we got onto some other highway. We drove a bit more and after a while spotted a giant parking lot filled with cars and surrounded with flags.

"We've found it, darlings!" Marina cried. "There it is— the mall!"

The whole entire world stared at the car as we drove through the parking lot, which was filled with normal-looking cars. Then they stared at us—at big, horsey Blitz, at Marina in her deranged turban, at Nipper from China, and at me. At one point in our search for the garden store, we passed this sort of walk-through area with little shops to either side. A bunch of kids around my age were standing around a kiosk eating blue cotton candy. When they saw us they all started laughing hysterically. A couple of guys started shouting, "Tallyho!" and stuff like that. Which, of course, made all the girls start screaming like they were going to die of amusement. Someone else yelled, "Hey, can I have your autograph? Whoever you are."

"I'll autograph your tush!" yelled Blitz. At that, two of the guys cracked up so severely that they actually fell down and started writhing on the ground.

I looked at the group and my eyes locked with the bright eyes of one of the girls. Almost at once she glanced away and went back to her laughing. She was the complete opposite of me, blond and cheery and sporty-looking in her big school jacket that probably said CHEERLEADER on the back. I couldn't take my eyes off her.

I was the one who first spotted the garden store. It was

situated at the far end of the parking lot and had a big sign over it that said PATIO & POOL. It was huge and sprawling like an airplane hangar, and spilling out from some giant doors at its faraway end was a jumble of statues, white as chalk in the late-day sun.

It was hard to find a parking space. The only empty spots were for the handicapped, of which there didn't seem to be too many in Westches-tah.

Suddenly Marina said, "Look, Blitz, there's someone who'll be pulling out!" Not far away a woman was loading some huge bags into a minivan. Her two kids, already inside the van, were punching each other and screaming.

"Boys," she kept hollering, "cut it out. I mean it now."

Then the kids started jumping on top of the bags. One of them broke and heaps of dirt came gushing out.

"Judas Priest!" the woman yelled. "You've really done it now, Gerard." Then she sort of smacked him. Which caused him to scream and throw himself down in the potting soil, flailing his arms and kicking the stuff all over the place.

"Get up, Gerard," the woman said. "I mean it, Gerard. Get up."

So Gerard sat up. His wet, red face was covered with dirt, which was more or less turning into mud. Then he did this really great thing that even Tatiana, drama queen of nursery school (the one my father yanked me from), never would have done. He started eating the potting soil. Just shoveling handfuls into his mouth, then scooping into the bag for more, all the while staring straight at his crazy mother, who was practically having a heart attack.

"Stop it, Gerard! Oh God, Gerard! You're going to get a parasite!"

It was Nipper who actually saved the day. When the

mother started screaming, he started howling in reply. He's a very empathetic dog. The kid who wasn't eating the dirt looked out the door of the minivan and started jumping up and down.

"Hey, it's one of those wrinkled dogs!" he yelled. "Look, Gerard! Look, Mom—a wrinkled dog!"

Gerard forgot all about eating dirt and sprang to his feet. "Look, Mom! Cool!"

The woman, who looked a little dizzy, turned around and gaped at us. Even though I hated her for smacking Gerard, I felt a little sorry for her—kind of the way the toll-booth lady felt about me.

"I think I'd better help," said Blitz as we pulled up close beside the van.

"You're a prince among men," my mother said.

So Blitz got out and said in this very princely way, "Please, my dear, let me help you with those bags." The woman seemed totally paralyzed and just kept standing there staring at us. Blitz took over, putting the rest of the bags inside.

"Hey, mister," said the older, non-dirt-eating kid, "can we pet your dog?"

"Yeah, can we?" echoed Gerard.

Blitz looked back over his shoulder and made a bug-eyed face at us. Then he said, "Giselle, bring Nipper over for the chaps to meet."

Naturally, they hadn't brought Nipper's leash, so I started looking around for a piece of rope or something.

"Use this," said Marina, undoing the green alligator belt she was wearing and passing it back to me. I looped it around Nipper's rhinestone collar and hopped out of the car.

The chaps practically jumped out of their skin they were

15

so excited. Which kind of got Nipper going too. He put his front paws into the minivan so the kids could go crazy petting his head. Their mother, I noticed, was staring at Nipper's collar as if she thought the diamonds were real. When she looked up and realized I'd been watching her, she blushed.

"Hi," I said.

"Hi," she said. "Thanks for bringing the dog over. I was just about to lose it. I mean it."

"No problem," I said. "I know how that is." Which I did.

Gerard was feeding Nipper some Cheez Doodles he'd found somewhere amidst all the crap that was inside the minivan. Nipper was in heaven. Blitz looked weirdly happy too and the kids' mother was actually sort of smiling now. When I glanced back at our car, I saw that Marina looked happier than anyone, probably because she had never seen Blitz and me looking happy at the same time and thought we were bonding. Which we were not.

A few minutes later we were back in Blitz's car, and the lady, whose name turned out to be Lorraine, was backing out in her minivan. Gerard and his brother were waving like lunatics from the window, yelling, "Bye, Nipper! Bye, mister! Bye, lady!" Apparently they considered me to be some sort of adult.

The next thing I knew we were inside the famous PATIO & POOL. It was the hugest place I'd ever seen. It was bigger than the Metropolitan Opera House. The first department we entered was full of table-and-chair sets all arranged and set as if some happy family were going to sit down in their après-swim outfits and start eating lunch. A lot of the tables had a hole in the middle of them for an umbrella. All the umbrellas were either flowered or striped or else some very bright color. If you wanted a gray umbrella, for example, I'm sure you couldn't get one.

Even though it was stupid, I liked walking through all the chairs and tables. It reminded me of the furniture sections in big department stores, like Macy's on Thirty-fourth Street or Bloomingdale's. When I was young, my father and I would pretend that we lived in those little fake rooms while my mother was shopping around for real. "Please join me in a cup of tea," he'd say, lifting a cup from one of the gleaming tables, his pinky stuck out and wiggling.

Anyway, we somehow gleaned that the garden department was situated at the far back of the store. To get there we had to walk for several miles through hose and pool pump country, barbecue-hibachi land and a special place called lawn mower world.

"Got any trail mix?" Blitz wittily quipped. Which almost made me laugh.

In the end, the garden section turned out to be a lot nicer than the patio section. There was an actual greenhouse beyond the so-called "Tool Shed" and outside the greenhouse were all those white statues we had seen from the parking lot. Marina and Blitz decided to go outside with Nipper and amuse themselves among the deer and angels and Japanese pagodas. Alone at last, I wandered into the greenhouse.

Chapter 3

EVEN THOUGH THE AIR in the greenhouse was unbelievably humid and hot, I finally felt I could breathe again, free at last of Marina and Blitz. It was very quiet in there too. The only sound was a trickle of water, fountainlike and far away.

I started looking around at the plants, which were really quite unusual. There was one I liked especially. It had a bright pink flower that perched on top of a long thin stalk sprouting up from a base of leaves. The flower almost seemed to float, and reminded me of this girl Amanda from ballet school, whose head seems to float on her endless neck. She is almost scarily beautiful and is kind of my mother's protégée. Marina is retired, of course, but teaches at the ballet school where I take class on Saturday. Her classes are always in demand on account of her being who she is, so it's rare when she singles a student out. Amanda, however, has won the prize. She dances like a dream, of course, but Marina claims it's more than that; Amanda

18

needs protection, she says. Her mother is sick and Amanda's too young and innocent to manage all the dance world wolves. People think I'm crazy not to hate Amanda's guts. But somehow I don't. Her mother has cancer; that's reason enough.

After the Amanda plants I continued roaming around the place. It was full of strange, exotic things—tiny orchids that looked like birds, meat-eating flowers with long green teeth, and warty-looking cacti. The names of the plants, printed on little signposts, sounded like grim diseases that had no cure and would lead to death. I stopped for a while at a sea of weird Hawaiian plants. I'm sure you know the ones I mean—waxy red hearts with a yellow thingy poking out. Anyway, I was standing there admiring the flora and feeling better than I had all day, when the sound of the trickling water suddenly got close. I turned around and this person, this *guy*, was standing there holding a long black hose. Our eyes met through the red hearts, and I sort of tumbled into his. They were green. Extremely green. Like the top of a lake in summertime, when you're swimming underwater but heading up, eyes open, to the glassy surface struck with sun. His eyebrows were almost too dark for this green, and his hair was the same, a deep maroon that made me think of those reddish beans whose name I can't remember now. His neck was fairly longish and his shoulders were wide with prominent bones. I'm very partial to prominent bones. Also he was pretty tall.

"Hi," he said.

"Oh, hi." My eyes moved down from his face to his shirt. It was a red T-shirt, and on it, it said:

PATIO & POOL

YONKERS, NEW YORK

"So that's where we are," I murmured.

He folded the hose and the water stopped. It got suddenly quiet. Dead.

"What did you say?"

"I just wasn't sure where we actually were. Now I sort of know."

"I'm glad for you. It can really suck when you don't know where the hell you are."

"Yeah," I said. It was really true. I forced a smile, since he was sort of smiling at me, though somewhat suspiciously, I thought.

"So how'd you get here?" he asked me next. "And what are you doing here anyway?" He was definitely smiling now, and I increased my own without, I hoped, going overboard.

"Nothing really. Just looking at plants." I glanced at a Hawaiian heart to illustrate my point. And then I added: "It's quite relaxing. To look at plants."

"It relaxes the hell out of me," he said. Over his shoulder he glanced at a plant, then jumped as if it had jolted him. Sounds stupid, I know, but it was pretty funny, like he'd gotten some kind of electric shock.

"Really," I said, "if you actually really look at them, they're kind of scary-looking plants. They sort of look like wax, you know?"

"Zee haf a fear of vax?" he said. I laughed at that and then he got suddenly serious. "The entire arum family's weird. Calla lilies, stuff like that. My sister's scared to death of these—anthurium they call 'em—she thinks the spathes emit poison gas."

"Really?"

"Yeah. She's not too well." He was stroking one of the

20

yellow tongues, which apparently was the "spathe." It gave me a funny feeling to watch his fingers touching it, and I started sort of babbling, telling him how when I was young I had a fear of some pale blue flowers that grew near the lake at this house we used to go to. It had started with a nightmare, though I didn't go into any of that, the blue flower men and their puppy teeth. I just said that I could understand how someone could have a flower fear; that flowers were quite mysterious.

"Mysterious and alluring." He mimicked the host of a famous TV nature show.

"How old's your sister?" I asked him next.

"Six. Six. Six." You could tell what a witty guy he was.

"It must be fun to have a little Satan—sister, I mean." And both of us laughed.

"I take it you're an only child."

"It's amazing there's even me."

"It is amazing," he said and smiled. It took a few seconds for me to realize he was giving me a compliment, and when I did it gave me a case of vertigo. I took a deep breath and started counting backward in French, which was something my mother taught me to combat nerve attacks onstage. *Quatre, trois, deux, un.*

Then I said with brilliance: "So I guess you kind of work here, huh?"

"It's just a few hours after school—and every other Saturday. I kind of like it during the week. It's quiet and I really get to study the plants. On Saturdays, though, all the assholes of the world come in."

"Are you interested in botany?"

"A little," he answered. "It kind of fits in with my larger plan." He didn't go on so, of course, I asked. "Landscape architecture," he said. "Designing outdoor spaces—parks and shit, though down the line I'd like to do something more than that. Space stations maybe, oases in space." He narrowed his eyes. "What about you?"

"Me?"

"Yeah, you. What do you tend to do with yourself?"

"Nothing much. I just go to school."

"What school do you go to?"

"High school."

"I figured that—which one?" He was staring at me really hard, yet smiling too, seeming highly amused. Nipper's bark sounded in the distance and I started edging away from him.

"God," I said and looked at my wrist where there wasn't a watch. "It's really late. I've got to go."

"Where?" he said.

"I don't know . . . out by the cotton candy place. My brother's going to pick me up. He's quite deranged, he hates when I'm late."

"I thought you were an only child."

"I'm really not. I just like to pretend. You would too with a brother like mine." I was getting in deep and had no idea where this crazy stuff was coming from. It was stupid, I know, but I didn't want him to know the truth or, God forbid, see the weirdos I was with.

"Where do you and your brother live?"

"Nowhere special. Just in town."

"In *town*?" he echoed, smiling pretty severely now. I couldn't help noticing his teeth; they looked so white and organized. I was sweating like you can't believe.

"Be careful," he said as I backed away and almost tripped

over a threshing machine. Even then I didn't want to turn around. I didn't want to lose his face and those green, green eyes surrounded by all the deep red hearts. All of a sudden, from way too close, I heard Nipper's yip and bolted out.

"Darling!" cried Marina. "Where have you been? We've had such fun. You'll be so amused when you see what we've bought." I had just about smacked into her as I ran out of the greenhouse. "Come and help us choose some plants."

"I'm too hot," I said. "I'll faint if I go in there again."

"*Mon dieu*," she said, and touched my forehead as if she'd know a fever, Florence Nightingale that she is. "You'd better go out and get some air. Oh, and look at the statues. We've bought a few."

Blitz regarded me with intense concern for about five seconds. Then he said, "Perhaps you'd better take Nipper along. The heat might be too much for him." Nipper looked up at me and started wagging his pointy tail. As I mentioned, he is extremely fond of me, and likes to hang out with me whenever remotely possible.

"All right," I said and took the "leash."

I walked through the Tool Shed and out a door to the parking lot, where the statues were. The air outside felt cool and fresh—I was drenched in perspiration—and as I walked into the crowd of statues, I let it dry me off. It was an extremely weird place, the statue section, sort of like a cross between a cemetery and an amusement park. For example, there was this saint statue standing there—I guessed it was a saint because it had a flame on its head and was holding a Bible—right next to a big polka-dot mushroom with a gnome under it. The gnome was supposed to be using the mushroom as an umbrella. Nearby, a lady and a man were checking out some deer.

"Why do these deer have holes in their heads?" the lady asked this salesguy, also wearing a red PATIO & POOL shirt.

"That's for the antlers," he told her. "But we ain't got no antlers now."

"Who wants a deer without antlers?" she yelped.

"With holes in their head!" her husband boomed.

"We ought to be getting them in real soon—"

"What good is soon? Let's go to D'Amici's!" the husband said.

"They may cost more," the woman hissed, "but at least their statues are fully equipped."

I didn't stick around to hear anything else, because it really started to get me upset. I wondered if people acted like that in the greenhouse too. If they started freaking out if a leaf fell off or something—if they yelled at the green-eyed guy like that. I pulled Nipper through a cluster of birdbaths, past the angels and mermaids and Roman gods, out past everything onto the big stretch of pavement where the cars were parked. About a million miles away, beyond the last Toyota, was a stripe of green weeds and over the green was the huge blue sky. Way past that was outer space. Where the greenhouse guy wanted to make a garden.

Up till then I had never thought about outer space. Mostly I thought about inner space—my house, my room, the places where I put my things. Not many people knew this, but I had a semiproblem that had something to do with space. I could leave the house—it wasn't agoraphobia— but I couldn't, for instance, "sleep away." At someone else's house, I mean. I needed to see my toys and things. I didn't play with my toys, of course, or anything weird and sick like that; I just needed to see them sitting there. And my other things too, my souvenirs.

Magda knew because Magda knows about everything. I'll grow out of it, my mother has said for the past ten years. Actually, Dr. Sloop, the shrink I went to way back when, said it was understandable that I would tend to cling to home. It can traumatize a child, he said, when a family member goes away and then does not come back. In any event, I hadn't grown out of my complex yet and doubted I ever would. Anyway, I was thinking this stuff when Marina suddenly called my name.

I turned around and she struck a pose, pretending to be a statue. She actually almost looked like one, that's how good a mime she is. She even confounded Nipper, who tilted his head and began to whine.

"Three dollars for your thoughts," she said when we came over to her. She was probably referring to the money I'd forked over to the tollbooth lady. "You looked like someone about to take a moonwalk." As you can see, for someone so totally self-absorbed, she's often quite attuned to me. I was not in the mood, however, for any mother-daughter crap.

"Are we ready to go?" I asked her.

"Yes. Blitz is bringing the car around."

And sure enough, five seconds later there he was, sputtering up to what must have been the loading zone. I cringed as I saw the beautiful, green-eyed greenhouse guy carry out some wacko tree and put it into the back. He made several trips in and out with armfuls of giant plants.

"Come on," said Marina, taking my wrist as if I were an invalid. I resisted, but as it happened he didn't come back. I climbed into the little backseat jungle and hunkered down under the palms. I hid myself so well that the poor guy loading the statues in didn't see me and almost crushed me with a big cement pineapple. In the end, I had nothing to worry about in the Being Seen department. I couldn't even be *found* if someone were trying to look for me. As we pulled away and drove through the thinned-out parking lot, I peered through the leaves and whispered, *"Au revoir."*

In a few minutes we were back "on the road." I lay back in the seat with my cheek against a cherub's butt and, I guess, fell asleep. Because the next thing I knew it was dusk and I was very cold, and we were still driving around. I looked out and saw that we were on a tree-lined street. Streetlights shone on the nice white houses to either side. Blitz made a turn, which brought us onto another street where there were more trees and white houses and more streetlights shining. He turned a few more times, and each maneuver brought the same or similar scenery. This went on for another ten minutes or so until finally I heard Marina say, "I think we've been here before, my sweet."

"This place," said Blitz, "is a goddamn Chinese puzzle."

"Let's ask for directions," Marina cooed.

"Ask whom?" said Blitz. "Shall we ask that tree? Shall we ask that cat rooting in that garbage pail?"

"Poor dear," she said, "it's getting to martini time." Then, "Look!" she cried. "There's a person over there. Person! Oh, person! We need your help!"

So we pulled up beside this person, who was just walking along on the sidewalk, minding his own business, and Marina sang out, "Person! Yoo-hoo! Excuse us please!"

The person turned around, and it was the guy from the

greenhouse still wearing his PATIO & POOL shirt, still looking beautiful with his green eyes shining like a lake. He looked at Marina and Blitz and, of course, recognized them from all the horticultural dealings that had taken place between them while I was drying off/hiding out in the parking lot.

"Hi," he said. "Nice car."

"Why, it's you!" cried Marina. "Look who it is! Of all the people—how marvelous!" She turned to me ecstatically. "Giselle, darling, you must meet Will. We found him in the greenhouse. He's an absolute gem. He knows everything!"

I drew a breath and brushed a leaf away from my face. Our eyes met again, and again I almost drowned in his. He smiled just slightly.

"What was the name?"

"Giselle," I said and longed for death.

"Hi," he said. And, "Hi there, fella," he said to Nipper, petting his head. You could tell he liked dogs a lot and vice versa. He looked back at me, and his eyes sort of softened. Melted with pity, that is to say.

Marina started emoting again: "You're a godsend, Will! We've been driving in circles for *days,* it seems!"

"Weeks," said Blitz dramatically.

"Where do you want to go?"

"Home—Manhattan."

"East Side or West?"

My mind sort of blanked as Will (I absolutely loved his name—willpower; act of will; will to live) started giving directions. He used his hands to demonstrate. His beautiful right forearm represented the various streets, and he used his left hand, held in a karate chop position, to indicate the compass directions. It was very intense to watch. When he was done, Blitz turned to my mother and queried: "Did you get all that, my turtledove?"

To which she replied, "You know I'm hopeless with north-south-west."

"But I have to drive the car!" wailed Blitz. There was a hideous silence, then all three of them, plus Nipper, looked at me. It was utterly unfair. I would have listened if I'd known that none of them was listening. I truly would have, and that's the truth.

Will got that terminally amused look on his face again. He probably wondered how any of us made it through a day. "Look," he said, "that's my house right over there. You can all come in and I'll give you a map—my mother will freak when she sees you," he added to Marina. "She's crazy about ballet. My grandmother's even worse."

"You're an absolute darling," Marina said. Apparently she'd told him all about her brilliant career while they were picking out potted shrubs.

"A dream come true," Blitz uttered.

Funny he should mention dreams; in my opinion, things were going like a really bad one.

Chapter 4

WILL'S HOUSE WAS, I'd say, about medium-sized and was covered with whitish shingles. Around the windows was painted dark green, and the front porch, which had some old wicker chairs on it, was dark green too. In the driveway was a white car with some toys and books on the ledge in the back. And at the end of the driveway was a saggy garage with a basketball hoop nailed onto it. Blitz parked his car in front of the place, and we started piling out.

"What about Nipper?" I asked since Blitz and Marina, busy appraising the neighborhood, seemed to have forgotten him.

"Bring him," said Will. "He can play out back with Smiley."

As if on cue, some barking started inside the house. It sounded like a pretty big dog. And it turns out, it was. Will backed it away using the door so that we could get inside. Then it went really crazy, running around in circles and whacking everything with its tail. It was tall and skinny and looked a lot like the deer statues at Patio & Pool. Obviously it was quite crazy about Will and the feeling was mutual. "Hey, Smiley," he said, roughing it up. When it saw Nipper, however, it forgot all about Will and practically went delirious. Ditto for Nipper. They started chasing each other around what was apparently the living room, just to the left of where we'd come in, barking and knocking stuff over, such as a lamp, a kid's doll carriage and what looked like a homemade teepee. It was quite a chaotic scene.

At that point, a youngish woman rushed in from another room with tomato sauce all over her hands. She was wearing jeans and a huge college-type sweatshirt that said CATATONIC STATE on it, and it was hard to believe she could be anybody's mother, but she was because Will said "Hi, Mom" to her.

She froze for a moment. "What on earth—" Then, fixating on my mother, she whispered in an awestruck voice, "Marina Parke-Vanova?"

My mother glowed. "Goodness, I'm rarely recognized these days." Which, of course, was a crock; people knew her all over the place. She was constantly giving autographs.

"My God," said Will's mother, "you were an icon in our house when I was growing up. My mother still has your picture hanging on her bedroom wall—you know the picture, don't you, Will—in the silver frame, the Juliet?"

"That's her? That's you?" Incredulous, Will looked at his mother, then at mine. Marina beamed. "That was many, many moons ago. I was not much older than Giselle is now."

Will's mother turned her liquidy gaze on me. Her eyes were soft and brown and big and not at all like Will's.

"Are you a dancer too?" she asked.

I cleared my throat. "Well, studying."

"I knew it," Will murmured under his breath. Then right away he started introducing Blitz, telling his mother all about Blitz's thrilling past in Bavaria where, as I mentioned, his ham-producing family is from. I was sure Will had spent the whole day listening to those two maniacs tell their life stories.

Marina, suddenly all considerate, said, "We're so sorry to barge in like this, but we're hopelessly lost and your wonderful Will offered to show us a road map. By the way, he saved our life in the garden shop—we know nothing at all about anything green."

"He's been our guiding star," said Blitz, who proceeded to tell Will's mother how impressed they were by his knowledge of plants and also by his manners, so rare in the youth of nowadays. Will's mother looked very proud.

"I'd be lost without him myself," she said. "He's a wonderful young man." We all turned to Will, who shrank an inch and looked miserable. Who wouldn't? How can people talk like that? Then, "Please," she added, "do sit down. I'll just wash off my hands and make some tea."

"Please don't bother," Marina said. "I can see you're fixing dinner."

"It's no trouble to boil water. I'll only be a minute. Giselle," she added, "you should let Will take you out to the yard. You've got to see what he's done with it."

Will looked at me. It was obvious he wouldn't mind getting out of there. "Come on," he said and motioned for me to follow him.

"Bring the dogs!" his mother called.

31

We headed down a hallway with a couple of rooms leading off it. They were tiny rooms, like something from *Alice in Wonderland*. In one of them was a little couch with a pile of books on top of it and against one wall an equally tiny writing desk with more fat books and a lamp in the shape of a teddy bear. All the furniture was white. I figured it was his sister's room, the one who was afraid of the red flowers, but turns out it wasn't.

"That's my mom's study room," Will told me as we passed it. "She's almost done with nursing school." I didn't say anything, since what can you say about something like that? But I got the sense this was quite an accomplishment for her, considering her age and all, though I never could imagine, knowing all the things I knew, how anyone could be a nurse.

We descended a little flight of stairs. There were some shoes lined up along the steps—big ones and a few pairs of tiny ones in bizarre colors—and hanging next to the door were a bunch of leashes and Hawaiian leis and other crazy-looking stuff. The dogs, panting and snorting on our heels, burst outside the second Will opened the screen door.

"Don't worry," he told me, "the yard's enclosed."

I don't know exactly what I had expected, what I'd imagined Will's mother to mean when she said I should see what he'd "done with the yard," but I certainly didn't expect what I saw.

All around the yard, forming a large outer circle, were strange formations made of rock, some quite tall and massive, with ledges and hollows and shadowy shelves. Inside the first circle was another circle of smaller, flat rocks, which Will informed me we could sit on. There was nothing in the middle of the two circles except a sandy patch that was raked in a wavy pattern, but if you sat on one of the rock seats, which Will and I did, you realized that everything was positioned as it was for a reason. For instance, through two of the rocks you could see a single, fascinating-looking rock at the far edge of the yard. If you sat on another rock seat you could see a dead tree with a bell hanging from it, which looked very Zen and mystical and gave you the sudden urge to meditate. Through the taller rocks you could see a shimmery slab of stone and a place for birds to hang out and drink water. I don't know if you can imagine it, but it was fantastic. It really was.

"It's great," I said. "Like Stonehenge. Or La Ciudad Encantada."

"That somewhere in the Poconos?"

I cringed. "God, I'm sorry. I sound like a—"

"No you don't. It's not your fault that I've never been anywhere on earth. So tell me where it is."

"Nowhere special. Spain. It's just some rocks in interesting shapes. People didn't carve them—at least that's what the guidebooks say—they were formed by wind and rain and stuff. It took about a billion years. Anyway, Will, this place is great."

"Thanks," he said, looking away.

"So how'd you get them in here? The rocks, I mean. They're really huge."

"They didn't start off as big as that. I cemented some together after I'd hauled them in. The smaller ones I didn't really change too much. Just kind of arranged them where they are."

"God," I said. "If the kids in my school could see all

this—they think they're such total geniuses. On their life's best day, they couldn't do anything half as good. Magda would totally love this place—Magda's my friend. Her lanterns would really look great out here." Then, of course, I told Will about Medieval Day and Magda's handmade torches. Which led into a discussion of Magda and how we were best friends and had been since getting together at Dante School.

"My best friend moved to California about three years ago," Will said. "He was a great guy. George. Now I've got Nick. There are other people naturally. We hang around, but it's pretty lame the stuff we do. Most of them have never been in a museum. A bunch of philistines."

"That's better than a bunch of fake artists," I said, "which is what my school is full of. Walk in the door, there's always someone making a scene. Crying, you know, or having some kind of episode. They're all very tortured and tragic."

"The kids in my school get tortured over what's for lunch."

"The kids in my school are too tortured to eat lunch."

Will laughed. Then he said, "I knew you weren't from around this place. The minute I saw you standing there. Then when your mom and Blitz came in, I figured you were part of them. When we started talking I knew for sure. But that stuff about your brother . . . and what was that cotton candy shit?"

"I don't know. While we were driving into the mall, I saw these kids who were eating some. They started saying things to us. Making fun of us and stuff."

"Assholes," said Will.

"I don't blame them. I'd laugh at us too."

Will shook his head. "So you thought I was an asshole too. That I'd act like them if I saw you with your mom and Blitz."

"Like I said, I wouldn't blame you if you did."

"I like them," said Will. "But I understand. That's how I feel when I'm with my dad."

"He can't possibly be as bad as them."

"He's worse, believe me. At least they're fun."

At that I almost fell off my rock. After I recovered I asked, "How could someone be worse than them?"

Will took a breath before he spoke. "Well, first of all, he's crazy. I don't mean crazy like people say, 'My dad is really crazy.' My father's really sick. It's something that happened in the war."

"The war? What war?"

"God, Giselle, if you ever meet him, don't ask him that. He'll lecture you for twenty years."

"Vietnam?"

"Yeah."

"But that was a million years ago."

"Yeah, I know. He's pretty old. My mother was kind of a child bride."

"Same thing with my parents. The difference is more than twenty years."

"Really? Wow, that's a weird coincidence."

"So your father's been sick for a pretty long time."

Will looked down and started kicking some sand around. "Actually, he lost it kind of recently. He'd been just fine, like he'd gotten over everything. Then suddenly three years ago he started having flashback dreams."

"He remembered things in his sleep, you mean?"

"Something like that. Which, by the way, is pretty damn unusual. So the psychiatrist tells my mom."

"Why is that weird, I wonder. I mean, everything that happens is still inside you, isn't it? It doesn't just disintegrate."

"Yeah," said Will, "I kind of think the same as you. That somehow your brain folds swallow stuff up, then all of a sudden something shifts and it all pops out."

"And that's what happened—it all popped out?"

Between Will's feet a ridge of sand was piling up almost to his sneaker tops. "I didn't even know till then that he'd spent two years in a prison camp. They practically starved him and stuff like that."

"That's horrible."

"Yeah. You really had to feel for him. But then he got really weird with June—that's my sister, by the way— telling her stuff a little kid shouldn't have to hear. One night when she wouldn't eat her dinner, something really snapped. He started yelling crazy shit about kids in Cambodia eating dogs. He tried to stuff Smiley into the frigging microwave. That's when it happened for my mom. After that, she made him leave."

"Where is he now? Where did he go?"

"He's got an apartment nearby. A pathetic place. There's practically nothing in it, like maybe a bed and a folding chair, and I guess he eats out 'cause there's never any food around. He calls the place his bachelor pad, which is so depressing it makes me want to shoot myself. The only perk is it's right next door to the firehouse—that was his job before he got sick—and during the day he gets to hang out with the firemen. He's kind of like their fire dog."

I looked at Will, but I couldn't really see his face. He kept fooling around with the pile of sand, scrunching it up between his feet, then pressing it with his toes. We sat there awhile and nobody talked. But it was all right, it really was. You'd think we'd been friends for a couple of years. Suddenly from somewhere in the bluish dusk, a strange and puny voice screamed out:

"Enemy Statues! E-ne-my!"

I spun around, and after a second I saw her there—this skinny little person way high up on one of the rocks, frozen in a crazy pose like someone brandishing an ax.

Chapter 5

W ILL TURNED TOO. Then he stood up and shouted, "Knock it off, you nut!" To me he said: "My sister, June."

"What's she doing?"

"Enemy Statues. This thing she does when anyone comes into the yard—anyone she doesn't know. Her friends do it too, but she's the one who made it up."

"Like a ritual."

"Yeah, I guess you'd say."

"Kids do a lot of stuff like that."

"Right. Of course. It's a perfectly normal thing to do." He cupped his hands and shouted in a louder voice: "Giselle is not an enemy. Come on down and meet her."

But the weird little figure didn't move. She just stood there in profile, both arms up, like a figure on a tomb. "At least come down and meet the dog. His name is Nipper. He's Chinese."

The body stirred just slightly. "Big deal!" it hollered. "I have a beret from France!"

"That makes a lot of sense," yelled Will. "And by the way, don't be so rude. Come on down. Your arm's gonna break if you keep it like that."

"Shut up, pruneface!" she shouted back. "I'm only rude when I'm on the rock!"

"Giselle doesn't know about the rock. She probably thinks you're always rude."

"*Gazelle?*" she hollered. "That's her name?"

Will swallowed a smile, then shouted back, "Not gazelle. *Juh-selle*. Like the girl in the ballet. Giselle's a ballerina too."

"Really?"

"No, I'm lying. For crying out loud, come on down!"

"You better not be lying, Will. Or fooling around. Or anything."

"Just come on down before you fall."

"All right already," the shout came back, "but first you have to say—you know."

Will drew a breath, then hollered out: "Release, O friends of enemies!" Which must have been the Move command.

There seemed, however, to be a little problem, because June wasn't moving very much. She had dropped her arms, but the rest of her looked paralyzed. Five seconds later she started to yell, "Help me, Will! I'm stuck!"

"I knew it," he said. In a heartbeat he was at the rock. From where I stood, I could hear him chide in this fake-mad voice: "How are you stuck? Is there glue on your shoes?"

"I can't turn around!" she wailed at him.

"How the hell did you even get up there? Are you trying to break your neck?"

"Don't yell at me, Will. Just help me down."

"Who's yelling at who, I'd like to know." Then: "Don't be a scaredy-cat. Take a step. Thattagirl. Now jump!"

I watched her leap. Once in his arms, she clung for a second really tight. She'd probably been scared to death. Will patted her back a couple of times, then she squirmed her way loose and down. She started rearranging her clothes, fixing her coat and smoothing her pants. Then she bent down and wiped off her shoes. She seemed really concerned about her shoes. I think she was washing them with spit. Anyway, when she was finally ready, the two of them came over to me.

"Giselle," he announced, "may I present the Junebug? Junebug, meet Giselle."

"Hi," I said.

"Hi," said the child. "My name isn't Junebug. It's June. Just June." She stuck out her hand for me to shake.

She was a very intense little kid, not at all like her cheery mother. She had the same bottomless green eyes that Will had, which, I supposed, were from their crazy, shell-shocked father. Her hair was the same bean red color as Will's too, except that June's was longer and was full of plastic barrettes and things. There must have been two dozen ornaments stuck in there. In addition, she had on a really weird outfit—plaid pants three inches too short, a fake fur coat and a pair of green, fringed moccasins decorated with multicolored wampum beads. I could see why she was so concerned about keeping them clean. Around her neck were five or six party leis like the ones I'd seen hanging near the door.

"Are you really a ballerina?" she asked me. Gravely, like when doctors ask if you've ever had major surgery.

"Kind of," I said. "I study ballet. And it's probably what I'm going to be."

"Giselle's mom is a real famous ballerina," Will said, "and guess what. She's in the house with Mom right now."

"Oh sure," said June.

"Why would I lie?"

"Maybe you want to get rid of me." June's eyes shifted from Will to me. "Your dog is cute. What's his name?"

"Nipper, but he isn't mine. He belongs to my mother's friend."

"Her mother's friend is from Germany. From the Black Forest," Will said to her.

"But the trees aren't black. They're green," said June. "No matter what you say, they're green."

"You're no fun anymore, you know."

"Tough meat," said June but she looked toward the house. "If you're lying, you'll be sorry, Will."

"Go see for yourself. But before you go, there's still some crap on your funny fur."

June glanced down and slapped at her coat. "It's fun fur, not funny."

"Looks funny to me."

She started backing toward the house, her vivid eyes impaling us. Just before she opened the door she shouted to Will in a pissed-off voice: "It's fun fur no matter what you say."

He shook his head as the screen door slammed. "I told you that she wasn't well." Then, turning slightly on his rock: "Speaking of strange relations—who is Blitz, the guy with your mom? If it's okay to ask, I mean."

"You can ask, but I'm not sure what the answer is. At first I thought he was just some crazy fan. He used to write her letters. Then somehow he became a friend. So that's what he is, I guess—a friend."

"Not a boyfriend?"

"I don't know." Will's eyes bore greenly into mine. "All right," I said. "Maybe he is. Though if he is, I don't know how. He's nothing like my—"

"Dad?"

I didn't answer and then he asked, "Where is your dad?"

"He's dead."

"Wow. I'm sorry."

"Thanks."

"When did it happen?"

"Ten years ago. He was sort of old. Like seventy-one."

"It doesn't matter how old he was—"

"Plus he seemed much younger. No one could ever believe his age."

"What did he do?"

"He danced. That was way before I was born. Before my mother was even born. When she was sixteen the two of them met. After that he became a choreographer. He created dances just for her, and that's how her whole career took off."

"She was his muse."

"So they say."

"What's his name? I bet I can find him in a book."

"Yeah, you can. Grigori Vanov. He's really well known. He was also a dance historian and wrote a couple of books himself. He knew this system for notating dance, and whenever someone needed to know what step went where in some ancient ballet, they'd call him up for help. He consulted for companies all over the world. Even after video, people needed his expertise."

"The keeper of the flame," said Will. I nodded my head. I liked that he'd said that; and it was true.

We sat there in the quiet, and after a while I told him a couple of other things. How when I was three my father pulled me out of nursery school and let me stay at home with him. How I spent my days drawing and painting and looking at books, and how every morning I watched him do his ballet barre. "That's when I first began to dance. I started, you know, to copy him."

"Wow," said Will. "You've been dancing almost all your life. I envy you for having someone to teach you stuff. I had to find everything out myself. Things about art and sculpture. As it is, I practically don't know anything."

I glanced around at the fringe of rocks. "I know that's not true. I can see it's not." He shrugged his shoulders and looked at his shoes. And right about then Mrs. Brooks yelled out the door.

"Hey, you two! It's time to come in!"

"Notice," he said, "how as soon as June goes into the house everyone wants to leave. Smiley! Nipper! Come on, guys." The dogs cantered over lazily and we started toward the house. It had gotten dark, I realized, a dusky luminous sort of dark, in which certain objects seemed strangely bright—the daffodils, for instance, blooming along the edge of the yard, and the heart-shaped patch on Smiley's head. In this strange pale dark Will said to me, "Maybe we can get together again sometime."

Dix, neuf, huit. I could hardly breathe.

⌒

In the bright and cluttered living room, the tables and chairs were littered with open ballet books, the pictures of my mother now festooned with her swirling script. Apparently they'd had tea; there were cups and saucers all over the place, along with a plate of Mallomars, which, judging by her blackened face, June had been devouring.

"There you are," greeted Mrs. Brooks. "I finally found a map. Maybe, Will, you could mark the roads."

While Blitz and Will pored over the map, Will's mother pointed out to me the pictures Marina had signed for her. In some of them, it's true, she wasn't much older than I am now. In others she was in her twenties and far too beautiful to describe. But she was most beautiful of all, I think, in her early thirties, artistically mature by then, dancing my father's wondrous works.

Blitz grasped the directions finally, but just to be safe, Will told him to take the map along. First, however, he tore a little corner off, jotted something and passed it to me. It read: *Giselle's #_____*. My fingers shook as I took the pen. When I handed it back, he folded it once and slipped it away.

A few minutes later we were back in the car. We looked like a family of lunatics escaping from an asylum with our statues and plants and Nipper howling a sad farewell. But Will's family looked crazy too, standing there smiling and waving at us. June was still eating Mallomars. In the blurry dark it looked like her face was covered with blood. I couldn't actually see Will's eyes.

But I felt them burning into me.

Chapter 6

NORMALLY, IT'S SERIOUSLY depressing to get out of bed for my day of classes on Saturday. But the Saturday after I met Will, I woke before the alarm went off and practically bounced up. Then I started waltzing around. I waltzed into the bathroom first and stared for a while at my weird, happy face. Then I glided around from here to there—to my closet, for example, where I pulled out some pants and a half-decent shirt. To the old armoire for some underwear. To the bureau for some leotards and tights. Then I plunked down on the floor to pack my bag, humming a tune from the Black Plague fest.

"That you, Giselle?" Marina called. She must have been walking past my door or coming to check that I was up. It was pretty embarrassing to be caught singing like that, and I tried to get a grip. Her head poked in and she *bonjour*ed. She could never say "good morning" like everybody else.

"Hi," I said, looking up from the stuff I'd dumped from my ballet bag. Marina, of course, was already dressed in some chic Scheherazade-looking thing with the Black Swan makeup she wears to class to awe and terrify everyone. At the moment her grim black gaze was focused on my pile of crap. I knew what she was going to say.

And naturally she did: "Darling, you really have to empty your—"

"I know, I know," I mumbled. "I was just kind of tired yesterday."

"Yes, that was quite a day we had." She smiled in a way I hate. "Now, hurry up. Coffee's on and I've made French toast." And off she sailed with a swish of silk.

This may come as a surprise to you, but I almost always empty my bag. I'm actually quite fastidious. So neat, in fact, that Magda swears I have OCD—obsessive-compulsive disorder, just in case you've never been accused of it. That, of course, is a huge exaggeration coming from a totally chaotic nut. But I am quite neat. It's true. I got it from my father. Marina's neat too, but most of my critical formative years were spent in my father's company. He was the one who taught me at an early age to always put my toys away. Only he understood how deranging it was when people moved my things around. I still have my toys from childhood and they're still in the places meant for them on the balcony around my room. It's really a ledge but I like to call it my balcony, and it makes me feel good to see them there, all my toys, my animals, in their designated spot.

My other things are in very specific places too. Like the pictures of my father on the bookshelf in the middle just where my eyes fall, third row up. One shows my father as the Rose—that's in *Le Spectre de la Rose* where he's covered in petals from head to toe. In another, he's the Bluebird from the *Sleeping Beauty* pas de deux, flying through the air. The third is a picture of him and me on a rainy beach by an old hotel. I am very young in this photograph, but I still remember that seaside place as if it had been yesterday. Even indoors you could hear the waves and you always felt you were on a boat instead of in a place on land. Next to all the photographs is my rock from the lake. And in back of that, the mysterious bone and the feather I took on the very last day. I almost began to touch my things, but Marina suddenly called again, bugging me to hurry up.

"Okay, okay!" I hollered, climbing to my feet. I went to my hamper and tossed the sweaty dance clothes in. I packed clean leotards and tights, my old and comfortable pointe shoes and the shiny pink new ones I had to break in. I tossed in a towel and some other stuff. Then I ran a brush through my haywire hair and tied it in a ponytail. Through the window near my vanity I could see gray air and drizzle, and past the air that other window where, as usual, the three little Chinese girls were jumping on their bed. I waved to them, and they started waving and laughing so hard they almost died. I never see them playing in any other window and sometimes I wonder what the rest of their house is like. I'm sure it isn't as huge as ours. Hardly any apartments are.

I call my apartment my house because of how old and grand it is. It's even older than the house we would go to when I was young, which belonged to Otto Black, my father's friend, who was a pianist and is dead now. That was a real house. It was in the woods somewhere near a big green lake and had a fireplace with a moose's head hung over it. My house is bigger than Otto's too and very much more elegant, though it desperately needs a paint job and in some of the rooms parts of the ceiling are falling off. My father's uncle bought it back in the 1930s when things were quite cheap, which is the only reason we are here now with billionaires for neighbors. The ceilings are high and the windows are quite enormous. It was always that way. I mean, it hasn't gotten smaller as I've gotten bigger as a lot of other places have. It's just as huge as it was when I was an infant in the bassinet and my parents' friends leaned over me with their pale green drinks and cigarettes, the blue globe lamp hanging high above them, shiny as a jewel.

What's changed, I guess, is us. We no longer go into a lot of the rooms. Like my father's deep red study, and the guest room right across the hall with the giant stained-glass windows, where the Blacks used to stay when they came to town. We never go near the place we call the ballroom. It isn't really as fancy as that, but it's pretty big and that's what my father named it because that's where the parties always were.

Down the hall in the kitchen, Marina had breakfast all prepared. The little round table was set with the Montmartre dishes, which I think were meant to hang on a wall. On each plate sat a piece of French toast and six or seven raspberries. Next to my cup of coffee was a champagne flute of orange juice and three enormous vitamins.

"A horrible day," she commented, pointing a fork at the dreary sky.

"April showers bring May flowers."

"Yes, indeed." One eyebrow shot up, a perfect arch.

I swallowed down a vitamin and tried to look morose.

Then, "Will," she said, "is a lovely boy. A shame he lives so far away."

"It's not all that far if you don't get lost."

Marina laughed. "It's a good thing we did though, isn't it? Or we'd never have run into him. And you wouldn't have that *je ne sais quoi* on your pretty face."

I knew she'd start in. And there she was, starting right in. He was not only lovely, she went on, but also quite extremely bright. Wasn't it just so marvelous that he knew about plants the way he did? As for his project in the yard, she'd glimpsed it through the window, and had found it very powerful. Did I know, she asked, that he'd recently gotten an art award? And had won a scholarship to Cornell; he'd be going in the fall. He was handsome too, she noted, and a helpless smile started to creep across my face. I practically wanted to smack myself. She loves it when she makes me smile. Her Wednesday's child, the child of woe.

"Janet's lovely too," she said, referring to Will's mother. She chewed a berry and shook her head. "She's had a difficult time of it. Do you know about Will's father?"

"Yes."

"And that Janet's going to be a nurse?"

"Will told me, yes." I plopped some syrup on my piece of French toast.

"She already has a job lined up. Pediatric oncology. Sounds terribly sad and grim to me."

That's when the conversation cracked. I mean, totally cracked as it always does when the subject comes even remotely close. Oncology, in case you're lucky and do not know, is the field that deals with cancer, which is what my father died of. I don't even like to hear the word. I cringe when someone says it. And when *she* brings it up, my mother, well, I really have to get away before I come unhinged. I started putting pieces of French toast down my throat without even chewing them, like a boa constrictor. I shoved the raspberries in as well, then told her I had to pack my stuff. She glanced at the clock and let me go.

———

Ten minutes later we were out on the street hailing a cab. We zipped to the theater in a flash, neither of us saying much. At the doorway, Marina kissed me on either cheek, then ceased to look at me. Madame Skouras got on the elevator with us and all the way up they gabbed about this marvelous guy, Manolo, and his marvelous massage. It seemed like it took an hour to get up to the fourth floor on that crummy elevator, and when it finally landed she didn't even say goodbye.

She sort of has to behave like this, because I'm on a scholarship, and some of the girls at ballet school were what you might call jealous and would love to believe I didn't get it fairly; that my doting mother arranged it for me. Not all the girls were horrid like that, but some of them were, believe me—like Violetta Dinesen, Cynthia Worley and Eve (Rapunzel) Wu. Violetta, speak of the devil (which she truly was), was hanging out right near the elevator doors, and Eve Wu was not far off, splayed in a split while she combed her hair, which, by the way, came down to her knees and gave her headaches due to its weight. You really felt sorry for anyone with a problem like that. I practically tripped on her ballet bag, which was lying right in the passageway with all kinds of intimate crap spilling out.

"Hi," I said insincerely.

"Buongiorno," she replied, without even trying to look at me.

We'd arrived earlier than usual today. The dressing room was empty, which it almost never is. It's usually so crowded you can't see what a dump it is. But today I got to view the place in all its squalid splendor. A gloomy glow filtered through the skylight, giving the filthy salmon walls an iridescent quality. The floor was dank and grimy, littered with fuzzy dust balls and tumbleweeds of hair. Two huge old bins spewed lost and forgotten dance clothes—ratty, single slippers; unraveling sweaters; worn-thin tights; and dismal, stretched-out bandages. Even with nobody in the room, the air smelled of sweat and liniment. It had gotten in the walls, I guess, the way child smells linger in kindergarten rooms, and medical smells cling to the air of sickrooms even after the person has died.

I put down my bag and started to undress when suddenly I saw myself in the slab of mirror on the wall. My mother says that mirrors are mysterious. They are full of secrets and tricks and lies, and things are never what they seem. There is no one truth in the looking glass, as all the fairy stories know. An image looks different to every eye. You never see what others see when they look at you. The other thing Marina says—and she is the world's authority—is that mirrors tell you how you feel more than how you look. If you feel like hell, for instance, that's what the mirror will show to you. If you're feeling happy, the mirror will say you're beautiful. So looking at my face today, I suddenly knew this amazing thing: that I actually felt good.

The door burst open and Moira, Sasha and Liz blew in. Together, of course. As always. In the five years since I've known them, I've never seen one of them alone. Like the Gray Sisters in ancient Greek mythology who shared a single eye.

"Giselle!" they screamed all out of breath and frantic, as if involved in some great girl plot to overthrow the world.

"Guess," exhaled Sasha, "who we just saw. That horrible Amanda girl. And she gave your mother flowers—talk about kissing up."

"She's just so weird," Liz whispered. "Not your mother—Amanda Reid. Don't you think she's weird?"

"She's trying to steal your mother, you know," Moira said in an ominous tone. "And it's not like she doesn't have her own."

"Her mother's weird too," said Sasha. "I think she gets electroshock—does electroshock make your hair fall out?"

"I never heard that," said Moira.

"Well, anyway, she has no hair. No eyelashes either. Zip." They didn't know she was having chemotherapy. And possibly wouldn't care.

"Don't say we didn't warn you," Sasha pronounced, unzipping her bag.

"New bag?" I asked, though I'd seen it last week.

Sasha glanced down. "Yeah, isn't it great? My cousin bought it for me in Maine. They have all these fantastic outlet stores. Has anyone ever been to Maine?"

"Don't mention Maine," moaned Moira. "It's colder than Siberia and they hate you if you're from New York."

"That's not true," said Sasha. "Callie Levine, the one who had the nose job, I heard that she's bulimic too, has an actual summerhouse in Maine and says that it's divine."

"Well, I was there in August, *chère*. Went swimming one

day and froze to death. Had blinding headaches for a month."

"How weird," uttered Liz. "Does anyone have some talc?"

"Someday you're going to buy your own and we'll all collapse and die. What *is* your problem anyway—someone would think you were twelve years old." Moira was referring to Liz's elaborate shield-and-drape technique where she managed to totally change for class without ever baring flesh. We all used to do it way back when.

"Just because I'm not an exhibitionist like some pervert from a nudist camp." Liz was pissed and mortified.

"Do you know what it's actually like backstage," Moira said, whipping off her Wonderbra, "when you're in an actual company? You're completely naked all the time. In ten seconds flat you're out of one costume and into the next. You don't have time to worry that someone might see your tits."

I rolled my eyes at Liz. Somehow I couldn't picture my mother or Madame Skouras running around without any clothes with the stagehand union standing by. But Moira liked to act worldly. And she loved to carry on naked monologues so we'd all be impressed by how un–hung up with her body she was.

I was trying to suppress a yawn when the door of the dressing room opened again and that walking dream, that flower of the floating world, Amanda Reid, came drifting in. If you didn't know her you'd think that she was legally blind, the way she walks around the place not looking where she's going, not focusing on anything—not chairs, not walls, not even the people in front of her, of which I was the closest one.

"Hi," I said in a pretty loud voice, mainly to keep her from walking over my bag. She froze in her tracks and looked around with her doelike eyes.

"Um. Hi," she said. Then with crazy giant steps, she avoided my belongings and maneuvered into an empty space. We stared at her, mesmerized. A lot more people had come into the dressing room by then, but she wasn't fazed by the thickening crowd. She just planted herself in her little spot and, staring into the mirror, started peeling off her clothes. She never blinked the entire time, but studied herself at every phase. When completely undressed she looked at her profile, first right, then left. Then she turned around and stared into the mirror at her back. She did some stuff with her arms as well, watching the effect.

In case I didn't tell you, Amanda's body is unbelievably beautiful. She has very long legs and I've already told you about her neck. Unlike a lot of extremely fine-boned dancers, she has actual breasts, which are very nice and high and round. You can't help but notice her pubic hair, a perfect auburn triangle exactly the shade of the hair on her head, like matching shoes and pocketbook. The weird thing was, if you looked at her face, you'd know right away that my mother was right—that staring into the mirror, she didn't see what the rest of us saw. It wasn't the way Eve Wu, for instance, stared at herself, like she'd marry herself if there weren't a law. Amanda's stare was different—critical and distant, an appraisal of equipment with which she wasn't satisfied.

By now, the dressing room was really packed. If I didn't get out I would start to have one of my nerve attacks. Moira, Liz and Sasha were ready to get going too, so we gathered our stuff and tunneled out.

In the corridor, things were not much better. Bodies

sprawled all over the place, dance bags marking the parameters of personal space needed for preclass stretching. The smell of Bengay and coffee mingled with the already rising smell of sweat. I staked a place near the fire door and started my own warming-up routine. As I stretched myself out, I closed my eyes. And there was Will, smiling, his green eyes green as the summer lake.

Chapter 7

T HE FIRST CLASS that day was pitiful. I kept thinking of Will and not paying attention to what we were
supposed to do. Even at the barre, which in case you don't
know anything about ballet is the part where you do all
sorts of exercise while holding on to a barre (that's French
for bar), I stank. Then when we got to the center (the part
where you don't hold on to the barre and move into the
center of the room), I stank even worse. I was so bad that at
one point Madame Eglevsky, who was teaching the class,
actually stopped the pianist and growled in thick Siberian
tones, "Vare eez mind today, Geezelle? Eef mind not zare,
zee might as vell go back to bed."

I almost passed out. I mean it. The room closed in
around me—as if I were being shrink-wrapped—and everything began to throb. Getting yelled at like that is bad
enough with all those bitchy girls around, but causing a
teacher to halt the class, well, that's as bad as it can get. I
could sense the whole class staring, but I couldn't really see

56

anyone—except, of course, for Madame, whose nostrils seemed suddenly huge and black like terrible gaping holes. I swallowed what felt like a lump of glass and whispered a faint "I'm sorry."

"Vhy apologize to me?" Madame threw up her hands. "Eet's not my class. Eet's yours." I thought she was going to spit on me. From the row in front Nicola O'Donahue, an Irish girl I hardly knew, passed me a sympathetic glance and I thanked her with my eyes. As for my so-called actual friends, they seemed to be somewhat enjoying things. Sasha's eyes were big as Marina's Montmartre plates and Moira, I'd swear it, smirked.

Madame Eglevsky was right, of course. I was totally off. As in not really there. You can do that in other places—school, for instance, and sitting over dinner at some restaurant they drag you to—but in ballet class you can't zone out. No wonder I'm tired all the time. Then another thought (also fatiguing) came into my mind: what if Madame told Marina how bad I was. Then I'd have to deal with *that*. This thought alone was enough to make me get a grip.

It wasn't easy. Really. Whenever I stopped moving, Will's beautiful face came floating back. And once it was there I fell into his eyes and began to drown. I tried Marina's counting-backward-in-French technique—*dix, neuf, huit, sept, six*—which is very boring but seems to help in a way I couldn't explain to you. You should try it some time when your mind is going out of control.

By the end of class I'd more or less redeemed myself. In my opinion anyway. My little jumps were fast and neat and my *grand allegro* (giant leaps across the floor) dripped with verve. Last but not least, I hammed it up in my *reverence*. But Madame wasn't buying it. "Too little, too late," her expression said as she turned on her tiny, slippered feet and exited the room.

One of the worst things about ballet schools is that there's nowhere to go to be alone. There are bodies everywhere you look. Even the bathrooms are totally booked, including, of course, the shower stalls. So if you ever have to cry, you just do it in front of everyone. It isn't at all unusual; someone's bawling all the time. Not that I really wanted to cry. I just desperately wanted to be alone. I managed to evade the Gray Sisters, who'd gone off together to get a drink, and made my escape through the fire door.

Mercifully, the dark, disgusting stairwell was uninhabited today. There's almost always a couple of people smoking there, so this was really a stroke of luck. Even though the stairs were pretty filthy, I plunked myself down and leaned my cheek on the chilly wall, closing my eyes and breathing deep—"centering," Marina would say. My center to me is like the lake. I imagine it inside of me, a place that never changes and was there when I was born. Once I find it I'm okay. Then I can do what I have to do. But when I lose it I'm a mess. You wouldn't think I'd find it today, what with Will's face floating all around, but after a while there it was, my quiet, shining place. I swore I'd keep it with me. I'd keep my focus. The calm inside. Next class was Madame Skouras, and I swore that I'd be good.

And I actually sort of was. In center, Skouras made me demonstrate my cabrioles, which she said had "great alacrity," a good thing, I guessed, from her tone of voice. She also did a quirky thing with pirouettes that almost no one in class could do, and I was one who could. As she tiptoed out, she turned to me and said, "Nice work."

In Marina's variations class after lunch (which consisted

58

of a banana and a granola bar eaten on the crummy floor), I was pretty decent too. I'm usually good in this class because I kind of have to be. As I think I may have mentioned, there's a lot of competition just to take Marina's class. How bad would it look if her daughter got in but danced like a moose? I did several quadruple pirouettes with my stiff new pointe shoes on, and thirty-two decent fouettés. I could tell Marina was impressed, though she didn't say a word to me.

Back in the dressing room, Sasha said it was like *The Three Faces of Eve* how much I had changed from class to class.

"Thanks," I said, as if that were a compliment.

"So, where are we doing coffee today?" Moira veered from the subject of me.

"Diner," voted Sasha. "I want a piece of that chocolate cake."

"Negative," said Moira, "they don't have cappuccino there."

"Like you'll shrivel and die without it."

"Café Europa then," said Liz.

This time Sasha shook her head. "You can't really hang around in there. They expect you to eat and, you know, leave."

"What's your vote, Giselle?" asked Liz.

"Actually"—I was already dressed in case they hadn't noticed—"I have to get home this afternoon."

Sasha snapped up from the crude first aid she was giving to a bloody foot. "But you *have* to come. It's after-class tradition."

"Yeah," whined Liz, "we need you there."

"Sorry." (Lie.) "I have plans with Magda, my friend from school."

"Personally," said Moira, staring at Sasha's torn-up toes, "I'm losing my appetite anyway. Are you a hemophiliac or what?"

"Shut up," said Sasha. And then to me: "Just a cappuccino. *God.*"

"Don't badger her," said Moira, dropping her towel and acting like she didn't care. "We can talk about her if she's not there." Everyone laughed, but of course they really would. They'd talk about Madame Eglevsky's class, savoring the memory like icing on their mile-high cake. I grabbed my bag and made a beeline for the door.

"Have fun wherever you go."

"Diner," said Sasha.

"Europa," said Liz.

The last thing I heard was Moira's voice—"That's totally revolting!"—as I closed the door behind me and started down the hall.

I was almost at the stairway when all of a sudden the floor started shaking under me. Looking up, I realized that the children's class had just let out. A herd of frenzied little girls was barreling toward me crazily—toward the water fountain really, a few yards past the place where I stood. I wobbled as the wave swept by, smelling of little child sweat, animal-warm yet pale as their sky blue leotards. It seemed to me impossible that I used to have sweat as sweet as that; that I used to be one of those laughing girls.

"You should skip, not run," my father used to tell me when he'd come to pick me up from class. I must have been five years old back then. He'd crouch down low beside me so his plum-colored eyes were right near mine: "How were your pas de chats today?" He was the most elegant of all the fathers, always in something silky black. The modern-day fathers are nothing like him in their jeans and sneakers and baseball caps. But neither were the fathers then. There was no one like my father. Men like him were all extinct, gone from the earth forever like a species of exotic bird.

The swarm of little girls blew by. I'd almost reached the door when I noticed a crowd gathering outside Studio 4. I thought someone famous might be inside—Angel Corella maybe, who sometimes came to practice there. But drawing close and craning my neck, I saw that it was Marina. She was coaching Amanda for *Romeo and Juliet*. It was the scene where Juliet, who is really still a child, is teasing her nursemaid with a doll. Amanda wasn't quite getting it, so Marina put the music on and took the role of Juliet. It was amazing. It really was. My mother is almost sixty, yet suddenly she wasn't. Suddenly she'd become a girl—in her body language, her energy, even the the way she used her face. I heard a sigh from one of the dancers watching, and I couldn't help it; my eyes filled up.

I never thought my mother ever really wanted a child. She was forty-two when I was born and was back onstage within six months. As soon as it was legal she signed me up for nursery school. It was a French-speaking nursery school—*L'Ecole des Sauvages,* my father called it after he came to pick me up one day while Jacques Feldman was having a French tantrum—*"Je vais vous mettre en feu!"* ("I am going to set fire to all of you")—and cross-eyed Tatiana was throwing up crayons.

The day I was yanked out of nursery school was the happiest day of my life. On the way home my father took me to the Russian Tea Room, where I had a cherry-filled *blinchik* and he had several glasses of clear liquid that I knew was not water. There was a big silver samovar in the window of the restaurant, and on the way out he picked me up and we looked at our funny, bulging images in its shiny belly. He told me to make a wish, and I wished, of course, that he'd take me away—just me alone—to live near the lake at Otto's house; that he'd never go away from me. He laughed out loud, his musical laugh, then scooped me up and carried me all the way to the park, high atop his shoulders, over the hats and tall men's heads, and into the warm, dark taxicab that smelled of candy Easter eggs.

After that, I spent every day with my father in the big, shadowy, wine red room called the study. I loved it in there. It was full of books and soft chairs and old tables with odd things on top of them—mysterious boxes, lamps that looked like jewels and hardly gave off any light, statues of people dancing and playing tambourines. There was also a big statue, almost as big as my father, of a Russian bear. My father would hang his scarves around its neck, the bear that we called Ivan. The scarves were so long they reached the floor and splattered into pools. Still, the room was a serious place. In those days my father was working on archives of obscure dance notation. I wasn't allowed to make a lot of noise, and for the most part had to amuse myself. But that was easy because there was so much to do in there.

I could spend whole hours just sitting in this one big chair. It was covered in a tapestry that had a scene of ladies swinging on swings in a woods somewhere. When you ran your fingers past them, you'd come to some groves of dark green trees and a herd of grazing sheep. There was a path too and if you followed the path you came to a house. In front of the house was a garden and in the garden, a fountain. If you moved your finger farther still, you would come to the swings all over again and so on and so forth up the chair. Every day I pretended I was in the scene. Always I would get away from the ladies on the swing. They seemed like idiots to me. Instead I would walk to the cool, green grove and I would disappear.

On rare, wonderful days, if I was very quiet and didn't jiggle around, my father would let me sit on his lap as he worked on his notations. I hardly breathed. I thought that would make me weightless and he'd somehow forget I was even there. He was so comfortable and nice to sit on, even though he was not large. He always wore a silky happy coat that smelled like the woods near Otto Black's and his skin smelled like the soap he used, that black soap from Italy.

At dusk when the sky through the slats of the old wooden blinds grew purplish, he would gather up his papers and put them away in big leathery folders. He would never rush and would bind the folders with thin gold cord tied in a slipknot I could never understand. Then he would let the tape recorder play, and as we listened to the music he would stroke my long hair. I knew, of course, it would soon end and Marina would come in and take him away for a damn cocktail. *Tup tup*, her slippers would say and there she'd be, flirting in the doorway in some lounge lizard outfit from Zanzibar. I would try to be stiller than ever then.

It was during those last few moments before Marina came in that my father would tell me how utterly wonderful I was. How lovely my mouth. How soft my hair. How smart I was. And good as the day is long. How much he loved me and how always, forever, his love would be a part of me. He needed me, I really believed, even though I was just a child. I needed him too and could not understand why, when he got sick, Marina sent him away to die.

I turned from the door of the studio, not wanting to watch her anymore. The music echoed in my head as I slowly ambled home.

When my house is empty it's like a big old museum closed for the Christmas holiday. You can actually hear the emptiness as you drift around from room to room or stand in a doorway to take a breath. I like how it feels and I love the way it smells. Like gin and camphor and wafting smoke. Sometimes in the quiet I imagine I hear party sounds—clinking glasses, laughter and faraway, faint piano keys. I imagine I see those slender guests, transparent now, talking and drinking cocktails, eating ghostly, see-through shrimp.

When I was small my parents' friends were always around. They were dancers and musicians, and every single Sunday they'd come for drinks and dinner after the matinee. Children are quite exotic to dancers since a lot of them don't get around to having any, so you can imagine what a great treat it was for them to stare at me, lying there doing baby things in my tulle-draped bassinet. I was the real-life Sleeping Beauty (I still can't believe my name is Giselle and not Aurora), and every Sunday night my worshiping fans paid homage. They smelled of tobacco and gin and liniment, and the scent of them merged with the rosemary smell of Jocasta's roasts.

I remember them all. Mostly I remember how, like the fairies in *The Sleeping Beauty*, each had a colored aura that tinted the air around the face looming over my bassinet. Carla, for instance, was lilac-toned. She had purplish eyes and wore clothes to match. Yvette was a kind of evil green like poison or chartreuse. It thrilled me when she leaned over my crib, staining the tulle mosquito netting with her envy color. Le Hungarian was the color of chicken paprikash. My mother says I couldn't possibly remember him, but I can still see his mad eyes and wildly crooked teeth and hear his demented "ga-ga"s. Even as a baby I knew he was in love with my mother. And that is why I didn't like him, as I liked Blue Edgar and Tawny Frank and all the rest of those long-gone people I miss so much.

If I ask Marina where they went, she says that my father pushed them away. That he didn't want to be seen by them once he got sick and began to fail. Don't I remember, she sometimes asks, and she looks at me intensely as if trying to pierce right through my head. But I knew it wasn't the way she says. I think the friends all went away because nothing was left when he was gone.

The telephone's shrillness startled me, jarring me harshly back.

"Giselle," said the voice on the other end. "It's Will. You know, from yesterday."

For a second I froze. Completely. And then I began to burn—that melting, shrink-wrap thing again. *Trois, deux, un*—I started to count and somehow managed not to pass out. Shortly thereafter I eked out a hi.

"Is this an okay time?" he asked. "You're not doing something important, I mean."

"Me? God no." That was the truth.

He laughed a little. And then he said, "I hope it's not too soon to call—too soon from yesterday, I mean."

"I can't believe it was yesterday. It feels—I don't know . . . much longer than that."

"Yeah, I know. Like a month or two. Anyway, I'm calling

65

from work. I'm on a break." He cleared his throat. "So how'd you do in ballet class?"

"That depends on who you ask."

A second of silence, then he said, "I know it's not much notice, but you said that you have Sundays off, and I'm not working either and tomorrow's Sunday, as you probably know. So I sort of wondered if you'd like to go to the art museum and maybe have some lunch. I just didn't want to wait a whole week. So wouldya maybe . . . want to?"

My heart was making so much noise I was sure he could hear it over the phone. I covered the receiver, but he probably heard it through my hand.

"That would be great," I think I said. I couldn't hear myself, I swear.

"So I'll pick you up—is twelve okay?"

"Twelve is great."

"So where exactly do you live? I mean, what's the specific street and stuff?" I gave him the address and described the way my building looked.

"Okay," he said. "So I'll see you tomorrow at twelve o'clock."

"Twelve," I echoed. "Great."

"Till then."

"Yeah. Bye."

And then with a click he was suddenly gone. I put down the phone and stood there like a zombie. Like that woman in the parking lot whose kid was eating the potting soil. God, that was also yesterday. A lot had happened in twenty-four hours. The telephone rang again. This time it was Magda.

"I'm sorry," she said instead of hello. "I know I putzed out of that car trip thing. But I just couldn't deal with Marina and Blitz—especially her in that mushroom hat. I'm a horrible friend, I know I am."

"Forget it, Magda. That's more than a friend should have to do."

"But you've done horrible things for me."

"Really, Magda, it's all right."

"So where'd they end up dragging you?"

"To this garden shop in this crazy mall."

"You went to a mall? Oh my God! If I'd known you were going to a mall—"

"We only went to the garden shop. You really would've hated it."

"I don't get it," Magda said. "What's with this sudden garden kick? It's not a Marina kind of thing."

"It's Blitz's idea. Part of the invasion plan. Anyway, they bought a lot of plants and stuff."

"Maybe I'm glad I didn't go."

"Actually, Magda, something else did happen. Something really big."

"What?"

"I kind of met a guy."

A huge stunned silence filled the air. Then breathlessly she whispered, "Grab a taxi. Get over here."

"I have to take a shower first."

"Well, hurry up. Don't wash your hair. Hold on a second, my grandmother's yelling something—wait." For a few seconds I heard their muffled shouting, then Magda was back on the line again: "She wanted to know if you wanted to stay for coq au vin. I told her no 'cause we're going out. Plus two of her crazy friends are here and they've already started on the *vin*."

"Good," I said. "Want to go for Mexican? I don't even care about calories."

"Oh my God. This is really serious. Get in the shower. *Hurry up!*"

Chapter 8

IF YOU WERE ever walking around in New York City and came across Magda's grandmother's house, you'd want to go in and take a nap. It's that kind of house, a storybook house, skinny and tall and scrunched between two ordinary buildings. In the tiny, odd-shaped windows the light glows red and golden through diamonds and ovals of colored glass, and when Magda is there—as she was tonight—there's an amber porthole half hidden with leaves, way up high just under the roof.

I went to the door and rang the bell, a tiny black knob on a mound of gone-green copper that always reminds me of somebody's breast. The walls are so thick you never hear the ringing sound, nor Sonia's heavy footsteps as she comes to let you in; just the snap and swirl of the peephole grate and the quick unbolting of seven hundred dead-bolt locks. Then there she is, short and wide and soft as a couch. Tonight she was swathed in a huge white apron spotted with sauce.

"Giselle!" she cried, drawing me in, glancing past my shoulder on the lookout for loitering "creeps." Sonia always calls criminals creeps, from litterbugs to hit men. ("That creep Charles Manson," "Jack the Ripper, that British creep.") A cloud of delicious, wine-soaked smells floated past me out the door. Which Sonia shut and bolted before clasping my hand and pulling me down the shadowy hall into the sudden bath of light, which was how her kitchen always felt, especially with a fire lit, as it was now.

The cooking smells deranged me, so at first I didn't see the two old ladies sitting in Sonia's cushioned nook under the hanging pots and pans. They were all dressed in evening gown–type outfits, and one had a flower in her hair like she might jump up at any time and start to do a flamenco dance. As Magda had reported, they were into their second bottle of wine.

"Giselle, dear," said Sonia, "these are my friends Audrey and Babs. I think you may have already met Babs."

Believe me, if I'd met Babs I wouldn't have forgotten. Not even if I wanted to. With her fuzzy pink hair and beak-like nose, she looked like a flamingo. A jumble of charms dangling from one narrow wrist, thin as a flamingo leg, made a deafening clang whenever she moved.

"I know who you are," she told me. "You're Magda's dear best friend. And I know your parents also. You favor your father, rest his soul. And your mother is a goft of Gid—gift of God." She turned to Audrey, the one with the flower in her hair. "Have you any idea who her mother is?"

"Of course I know who her mother is. Do I look like a hermit from out of the West? Listen, my dear, I know what it's like to have a famous mother. My sainted mother was

D. K. Lloyd, author of the mystery books. All my life people were always asking me, 'So when is *your* book coming out?' It nearly drove me out of my mind. And explains, I think, why it took me nearly sixty years."

"Audrey wrote *The Essential Celtic Potpourri*," Babs informed me proudly as if she'd written it herself. "It's doing very well."

"And becoming a series," Audrey said. "Number two is *Potpourri of the Holy Land*. All sorts of scents mentioned in the Bible, though of course it's not a religious book."

"Illustrations by Milton Fu," Babs said confidentially, "who's a barrel of talent, I happen to think. What Andy Warhol did with shoes, Milton does with seeds and pods."

"Are you going to stay and dine with us?" Audrey asked excitedly. Sonia, as if to tempt me, lifted the lid of the cooking pot. "A peasant dinner. Coq au vin. With little artichokes to start."

A lot of people, including peasants and also Blitz, would think we were crazy to turn down Sonia's cooking. But for Magda and me Saturday night means freedom. Plus, Sonia cooks for us all the time. We had lobster Wladimir just last week.

"Why would they want to hang around with a bunch of old potatoes like us?" Sonia said with a sniff of the air.

"Old spuds," agreed Babs, and she squawked like a bird before dipping her beak to the glass of wine. "What do young people *do* these days?" she asked me, leaning forward. "We used to get all gussied up and go to the hotels to dance, though I don't suppose you do that now."

"Not really," I said.

"Is there someplace you go—someplace where all the young things go?"

"Magda and I just usually go and eat somewhere."

"If you call that food," said Sonia. She was almost never critical except when it came to the food we ate. She thought we consumed a lot of junk and were ruining our tender taste buds before they had a chance to bloom.

"Have you and Magda been friends for long?" Audrey asked through a sip of wine.

I told her the story of how we'd first met at the age of five in the pediatrician's waiting room. Fiona and my father talked and I caught Magda's chicken pox. We didn't see each other again till nine years later at Dante School. Weird as it sounds, we recognized each other at once. Even that day when I was five, I somehow knew we would meet again. Once I even dreamed of her, her wild curls entangled and her gypsy face all spotted with pox.

"That's how it was with my husband," said Babs. "The first one, Hank. We met out sailing. His boat went zipping past our own—I was with my sister, Geraldine—and he waved at us and I instantly knew: there goes Mr. Right for Me."

"Enough!" said Sonia, coming to my rescue. She whispered to me, "Magda's up in her hideaway. Escape while you have the chance." I told the old ladies how nice it had been to meet them and I hoped they'd enjoy their meal. They assured me they would, and Babs made a racket with her charms as she waved a fond goodbye.

I was pretty relieved to find myself free and climbing the stairs toward Magda's room. Along the way I glanced at the sea of photographs covering the stairwell walls. Pictures of

Sonia with all kinds of famous people—like Margaret Thatcher, King Hussein, Itzhak Perlman and the Pope. When I got to the landing I took a rest—mostly to inhale the scents, the lavender and linen that always lingered in just this spot. Even more than the smell of cooking, these upstairs scents to me were the essence of Sonia's house. I breathed in deeply, then passed through the tiny dollhouse doors that led to the attic stairs. In the blurry dark lit by the faintest yellow sconce, I could just make out the tiny paintings of vegetables in their ancient and elaborate frames. Loud, disturbing music was seeping out of Magda's room, but somehow she sensed my presence and opened the door before I had finished climbing the stairs.

"I see it," she said like a psychic with a crystal ball. "Something happened. Something big."

"You're crazy," I said, though I knew she was right. She pulled me into the attic room, which looked as if marauding Vikings had recently made a raid. She shut the door and locked it, then stood a ways back to look at me.

"Tell me everything. *E-ver-y-thing.*"

"I will," I said, "just let me sit down." I looked around. "This place is a wreck. There's nowhere to sit."

"Of course there is," said Magda as with one great shove, she swept a pile of clothes and books out of a nearby chair. "This place is too small for who I am. Now just shut up and talk."

I sank down into the tiny cleared-off armchair. "I don't know where to start," I said.

"Start with his body, you idiot!"

"You're such a perv."

"I take that as a compliment." Magda flopped down in

the pile of crap camouflaging the chic chaise longue, aka her bed. "Come on already. Is he tall or short? Fat or thin? What was he wearing on his feet?"

"His feet?"

"Type of shoe is critical. If his shoes are goofy, chances are he's goofy too."

"I think he was wearing sneakers. I know they weren't goofy shoes. Yeah, sneakers—I'm sure. I remember them from when he was helping June down."

"Who the hell is June?"

"June's his little sister. She got stuck on the rock thing in his yard."

"His *yard*?" she screamed. "What were you doing in his *yard*?" Then, leaning forward breathlessly: "You better start at the top, my dear."

And so I did. Beginning with the cotton candy eaters. And crazy Lorraine and her crazy kids. Lawn mower World. Hibachi land. Then at last the greenhouse and Will coming out of the red wax hearts. Magda uttered a breathless "wow."

After that, she made me describe the way he looked. It was really weird and awkward; I kept smiling like an idiot. Not that Magda tried to make it easy with all her goofy quips. When I said he was lean like a beautiful tree, she said that was due to his working in the greenhouse. Then when I described his hair, how the color was like those dark red beans I didn't know the name of, she told me they were lima beans. I looked for something to throw at her—some sweatpants, as it happened—and aimed them at her head. Then I got serious again as I tried to explain the rock construction in his yard. She was totally intrigued by this, asking why he built it and what it meant. She is very intrigued by large creations of any kind.

For a couple of seconds we didn't talk, then she said, "I have some pretty big news as well." She shifted on the chaise longue, picking up the sweatpants and twisting them in her hand. "I might be leaving town," she said.

"What do you mean?"

"I mean I might be moving. To California with my dad. My mother isn't coming back." She flipped a postcard over to me. I looked at it and groaned. This time it was elephants. With big gold covers on their tusks. I turned it over and there was Fiona's large, loud script:

The Ganges. Golden thingies everywhere. And little Legless Beggar Boys.

From a Mat in the Ashram,

Me

I looked at Magda. "What is that supposed to mean?"

"It means my mother's in India and living with monks and isn't in Switzerland anymore."

"What about Leif? Did she drop him over a mountainside? And what are 'golden thingies'?"

"How should I know?" Magda said. "I'm writing to my father. I can't stay here forever. I'm very expensive to feed and keep."

"Don't be ridiculous."

"Maybe he would want me there. I could babysit the baby. I could earn my room and board."

"Right," I said. "Your stepmom would really go for that."

Magda scowled. "Have you ever seen her vomitizing photograph? It's why Fiona lost her mind and decided to marry Leif." Before I could answer, she started digging through the place, under the piles of paper and clothes, not that she'd ever find it and not that it mattered anyway since I'd already seen it a hundred times—Agrippina ten months pregnant in a leopard-skin bikini. The picture wasn't recent, since the famous baby, Marcus Something Aurelius, was already six months old.

Magda's father, by the way, isn't just your average jerk. He's far above average at being a jerk. Even Sonia thought so and she's his mother, which says a lot. Nobody really knows how Magda turned out normal, what with both her parents being out of their minds. (Her other grandmother, Loli, is crazy too, and spends her life traveling the country competing in tango tournaments.)

"Listen," I said when she finally stopped throwing stuff around, "how long do you think Fiona's going to sleep on a mat—if she even did for an actual night? She's just trying to be—colorful." I passed the postcard back to her and she shoved it in the scrapbook with all the dippy postcards and spaced-out letters and weirdo stuff that her mother stuck into envelopes—fibers from a coconut (like we couldn't get coconuts in New York), a fish tooth from South America (like fish in New York didn't have any teeth). At first it was quite amusing, but now it was pretty sad, since the book was getting fat.

"She'll be back," I promised. "And in the meantime, just stay put. This house is great. And Sonia's great."

"Yeah," said Magda. "Sonia's cool. She knows my dad's

an asshole—though she told me not to use that word; that 'jackass' was more respectful. Of course, she loves him, she just can't help it, but Sonia knows that I know what he is, and she doesn't pretend it's otherwise."

"And knowing all that, how could you think of moving to California?"

"I'm crazy, I guess. An idiot. I'm happy here with Sonia and her batty friends."

"And what about *me*? What about *your* batty friend?"

"Oh please," said Magda wearily. "You'll be with Will from here on in. That's what always happens. You can say it won't, but I know it will."

"That's a really horrible thing to say. What kind of friend do you think I am? Plus, how would I live without you? I *need* you, Magda, you lunatic!"

Magda cracked a semi-smile. "That's true, I guess. You'd turn totally compulsive without my screwed-up influence."

"That's right," I said. "Plus my heart would shrivel and then I'd die."

This seemed to cheer her up a bit and she kicked the scrapbook under the bed. Then she stood up and started searching around the room—for her shoes, I guessed, or her pocketbook.

"You look great, by the way," I told her, watching her move around the place. Her curly hair was gathered back with a very ratty but great-looking scarf. One earring was a blue half-moon, the other was a silver sun. Her dress was black with some shiny parts in the shape of leaves, and around her neck were a bunch of silver necklaces. She kind of jangled when she moved, though she was no competition for Babs downstairs.

"Oh sure," she said, responding to my compliment as she pulled on a pair of high black boots. Then: "Here you are!" she greeted her shoulder bag.

"You do look great," I said again, and she made a face as if I were mental and out of my mind.

Then we went down the stairs with the vegetable art, to the landing and lavender laundry smell, then past the famous people shaking hands with Sonia in their shiny wooden picture frames. On the lower floor, the old ladies had just sat down for dinner. We could hear the clink of silverware and the murmur of their voices floating from the dining room.

"Sorry," said Magda, "but I have to say goodbye to them."

We followed the clinks to Sonia's cozy dining room. There's practically nothing in it, just the heavy, massive table and a sideboard for holding dishes and the giant candelabra. On the wall is a huge and priceless painting by some very famous Dutch guy—*Harvest Roadkill,* Magda likes to call it, which amuses Sonia out of her mind—of dead pheasants, rabbits and ducks draped on a mound of raunchy-looking vegetables. It's all very dark and varnished, and in the candlelight looks wet.

The old ladies were having a first course of some artichokes that were so small they looked like brussels sprouts. But they forgot all about their food when they saw us. (If you ever want to get a lot of attention, just hang around with old ladies. They really think you're great.)

"Magda, angel, how chic you look!" This from Audrey, touching the flower in her hair. "Isn't she the chicest thing, like a page from that Italian *Vogue*!"

"The pair of them!" gushed birdy Babs. "Pity the boys with those two slaybabies on the loose!"

"We're lethal all right," said Magda, going around the table to kiss each one, and Sonia twice.

"I'll ask once more," said Sonia, "just so you know it's genuine." She rose from her chair and lifted the lid of a fabulous hen-shaped serving dish. The coq au vin glistened, luminous as the roadkill scene, and the smell of it made my stomach growl.

"It looks delicious," Magda said. "But you know us, we gotta bust out."

Sonia nodded and the others looked understanding. "Just promise me you won't eat those wretched hamburgers, all aswarm with E. coli germs."

"We're doing tacos," Magda said. "Tacos are healthy, aren't they?"

Sonia rolled her eyes. "There's money in the flour jar. If you won't let me feed you, at least let me take the two of you out. Now off you go, our artichokes are getting cold."

"Have a marvelous evening!" Audrey called.

"Pity the boys with you two slaybabies on the loose!" Babs decided to say again, ringing her charms like violent bells.

"Take cabs," said Sonia. "Cabs." She was terrified of the subway because once about three years ago in Grand Central Station two "creeps" knocked her down and stole her purse—and it was a real Chanel. Not only that, they broke her nose.

As we headed out I looked back at the old ladies. They'd returned to their little artichokes and Sonia was pouring a dinner wine. They looked happy and peaceful like people on the other side of life, when most of the things to do are done. And they seemed sort of glad—like they wouldn't want to do them again, all the things that Magda and I hadn't even begun to do. I was thinking this as we plunged outside and the cool night air rushed into my mouth and made me feel loose and wild inside.

Chapter 9

T HE MINUTE WE stepped onto Fifth Avenue, this
lunatic taxi cut across the traffic lanes and screeched to
a halt in front of us. It was quite satanic really, how it came
out of nowhere and practically mowed us down. But we
got in anyway and told the back of the guy's head where we
were going. He was wearing a turban and didn't say anything, just jammed on the gas and lurched away, throwing
us back against the seats, which struck us as very funny and
made us start laughing hysterically. We often get quite
hysterical over practically almost anything.

This guy was a true maniac, however, and we could
hardly breathe what with laughing so hard and having the
wind knocked out of us. At one point, he violently braked
to avoid a bus, and Magda's head crashed into the Plexiglas
barrier.

"Hey, buddy!" she yelled into the money slot as if it were
a microphone. "Why don't you go a little faster so we can
all crash and burn!"

"My name's not Buddy!" shouted the guy. He whipped off his turban and swiveled his head to look at us. The turban came off in one piece like my mother's crazy turban hats, not that I know how an actual turban really works, though I think it might unwind. He was really young though totally bald, and his blue, blue eyes were severely pale with little black pupils like peppercorns. It seemed like an eternity that he kept his head swiveled around like the possessed child in *The Exorcist,* though it was probably only for a few seconds. Long enough for him to say in a singsong voice: "My name is Decker. My dad's name is Diver. We come from Deats Avenue, and we sell death."

I knew then what people meant when they said that their blood ran cold, because that's exactly what happened to mine and everything else inside me. I heard Magda gulp, but almost at once she changed her course and started acting cocky as she always does when anything harrowing happens to us.

"We saw that movie, Dicker," she said. "I mean Decker, Docker, whoever you are."

"Yeah, what movie?" yelled the guy.

"Like you don't know. Like Robert De Niro's not the hero of your life."

"De Niro's Italian!" he hissed at her. "I'm more like Mickey Rourke."

"In a *turban*?" Magda practically screamed.

"That's just a thing I like to do."

"What do you really want to be—an Indian or Mickey Rourke?"

The guy explained how sometimes he wanted to be Mickey Rourke and at other times he wanted to be an Indian. While he was busy talking, he tended to drive more slowly, almost at seminormal speed, which gave me the chance to read the name on the license thing posted on the plastic shield that separated the front seat from the backseat. I poked at Magda to make her look.

Bruce McGinty? She mouthed the name and both of us started to laugh again. Meanwhile, the crazy guy was telling us that his actual name was Al, and as a matter of fact, he wanted to be an actor. He had just joined some acting workshop in Carnegie Hall, and one of his exercises was to pretend to be somebody more or less his opposite, but he had gotten carried away and had pretended to be a crazy person (Decker) who was pretending to be an Indian. Magda told him that I was a performer too and that my mother was a world-famous ballerina and that *her* mother was living in an ashram in India.

"Way cool," he said, adding that although I was pretty quiet we were both cool chicks, not like the chicks from Deats Avenue. Wherever the hell that was. He said that he'd like to see what we'd be like in about ten years. Magda said it would be pretty interesting to see what *he'd* be like in ten years too. He told us some other wacko stuff, and somehow she kept him talking till we landed safely at the curb in front of the Mexican restaurant.

"*Adiós,* Bruce," she said as she slipped him a wad of Sonia's dough, and yanked me from the car.

He looked at the money, then smiled at us. "Cool chicks," he repeated. "Very cool." Then he howled like a werewolf and hit the gas. Leaning out in the street, we saw him slap the turban on.

"Psycho," I said. "And he doesn't look old enough to drive." I took ahold of Magda's arm, but her eyes went trailing after the car.

"I've got to find out just who he is."

I opened my mouth to scream at her, and she pulled me into the restaurant, where a nervous guy with a bunch of dog-eared menus came zipping over, yelping, "Two?" Before we actually answered him he steered us to a table, smacked down the menus and zipped away. It was pretty crowded being Saturday night, but by some strange luck we got our favorite table right in front of the giant cactus sculpture. It always felt secluded there—like the cactus was really a cactus god, protecting us with his big green arms.

After a few seconds our waitress came over and said hi and what would we guys like to drink. We ordered a couple of fake blue margaritas and some nachos and guacamole. The stuff came pretty quickly and Magda went back to the subject of Bruce.

"I think he's really fabulous. So uncool and *out,* you know? Can you imagine where he lives? Some squalid row house, maybe in Queens."

"And what about that is fabulous?"

"Don't you see? He isn't like those wimps from school. He's one of those warped creative minds that come out of wasteland places where you thought imagination was dead and art could never rise."

"First of all, you have no idea where he lives," I said.

"Well, I can find out. How many cab companies can there be?"

"For God's sake, Magda—"

"Ditto, Giselle. Don't you think I can tell the difference between a lunatic creep and a guy making theater out of life?"

It was funny that she used the word "creep" like Sonia, who, by the way, was the one who found out about the last

84

theater-life guy Magda had been attracted to (it was around the time her father married Agrippina) and reported him to the police. There was nothing to actually charge the guy with since nothing had actually happened yet, though he was a mature adult postal worker of about thirty-five and that was bad enough. Magda tended to do things like this when she got mad at her parents. Which, as you know, she was right now.

I steered the subject away from Bruce.

"Whatever happened to Darkan? I thought you had a thing for him."

"Darkan doesn't care about me. I've been practically throwing myself at him." She jabbed a nacho into the guacamole. It broke and part of it got stuck in the bowl, which added to her pissed-off mood. She was digging it out when our waitress suddenly reappeared.

"What'll it be for you guys?" she said. She was like a parka model from an L.L.Bean catalog, wholesome, clean and oozing cheer. Rolling her eyes, Magda ordered a chimichanga combo plate. I ordered a salad, which really pissed Magda off.

"You're having a salad—*here*!"

"It's a South of the Border salad," I said.

"They're really quite huge," the waitress said, exaggerating the *h* in huge.

"Oh, a really *h*uge salad. That's different," Magda said.

I felt bad for the waitress and said something very New York and urban about Magda's shrink being out of town and how tense that always made her get.

"No *problema*," the waitress said, then asked if we guys would be wanting more chips. I told her we would, and she went away.

Meanwhile at the table right behind us, a man and a guy who was a few years older than us sat down. Right away the man ordered a vodka martini straight up with three olives and "a Perrier for my son." They way he said "my son" you could just tell he hardly ever saw the kid. Magda heard him too since the back of the father's chair was practically touching the back of hers. She gave me a fishy, dangerous look.

"So what should I wear tomorrow?" I asked her since clothes was a subject Magda adored. Her attention shifted back to me.

"Are you really asking my advice?" And before I even answered: "It's high time you did, I want you to know. Tell me, why is it that dancers are always one of two types—the chic ones like Marina and the ones like you who dress themselves like mental patients on weekend leave?"

"Very funny."

"In your case, however, it might actually have to do with Flamboyant Mother Syndrome or FMS as it's sometimes called."

"Dare I ask?"

"It's simple. Flamboyancy in females skips a generation. Look around at practically everyone you know, and you'll realize I am right. In your case it's even more glaring than usual since your world-famous mother always looks gorgeously beautiful."

We stopped talking as the cheery waitress came back again. As we started to eat, I could hear the father's weary voice: "Bobby, hey, Bobby, do you think I was born yesterday?" It was about the third time I'd heard him say that.

"I just want to go and see for myself," Bobby replied, reaching over and taking a big swig of his father's martini.

"Do you think," said the father, "that your mother and I have never heard of the damn third world? Bobby, hey, Bobby, do you think we were born yesterday?"

"I don't think he was born yesterday," muttered Magda. "Or even within the last millennium." I made a face to tell her to keep her voice down. We could hardly hear the soft responses of the son, but it seemed that he wanted to join some kind of Peace Corps–type organization and ship off to Rwanda or Uganda or someplace to work on a plumbing project.

I got that idea when the father said something extremely weird about how they weren't going to sit calmly by and watch the fruit of their loins get himself killed building toilets for Bantu warriors who'd rather pee in the bushes for Christ's sake anyhow. And then something about how he wouldn't be getting airfare to the Dark Continent or any other *tercero mundo* pisshole place, nor airfare back if he managed to somehow get there without parental funds and contract terminal diarrhea. Or words to that effect.

He was a pretty brutal guy, as you can see, beneath his dry martini exterior. I was really worried that Magda might start mouthing off, so I started talking clothes again. Did she remember those black palazzo pants I had? Should I wear them tomorrow possibly?

"You actually still have them? I thought you might have thrown them out on account of how good they look on you. And what about that nipped-in jacket you also practically never wear?"

"You mean the one Marina bought?"

"The only decent one you own."

After that we talked about shoes. Then we turned to hair. I had to wear it down, she said. The tied-up ballerina look made guys nervous and insecure.

"And don't eat stuff that'll stick in your teeth. Or anything plain disgusting like egg salad or chopped liver. And order dessert. It shows how sensuous you are; I read it in *Cosmopolitan*." And then to prove her own great sensuality, she ordered flan when our waitress came by to collect our plates. I ordered some banana thing.

It was nice hanging out with our desserts. The father and son had finally gotten some food, along with a bottle of red wine, and weren't arguing for the time being. The father was having what looked like some kind of Tex-Mex stew that a cowboy might eat out on the prairie and share with his dog. He had spread a bunch of pamphlets on the table in an obsessive-compulsive fan shape, but I couldn't tell what they were actually about. Things went okay for a while, then Magda asked for the check and dispensed some more of Sonia's money. When we got up to leave, we saw that the pamphlets were college brochures. The father was pointing out some great feature about one of the schools, probably a football field.

Magda walked around to the other side of their table so she could look the stew-eating slob in the eye. Then she said in a very calm voice that was quite polite: "You ought to let him do what he wants. It's his life, not yours."

The father looked pretty stunned at first. Then after about a half a second he put down his fork and smiled at us. It was a really nasty smile, and you could just tell he couldn't wait to start in on us. If I hadn't hauled Magda out of there, like pronto, we'd have really been in for it. As for Bobby, I think he was too plastered to even see us, let alone be grateful for our emotional support.

"What a bastard," I said to Magda out on the street.

She shook her head. "Just like my father. Digital Dad. He's either totally ignoring me or trying to run my life."

"At least your dad doesn't eat dog food," I said.

"He would," she said, "if Agrippina told him to."

I hooked my arm through hers. "I'm not really sure that Bobby would make it in Africa. Do they even have martinis there?"

Magda laughed. "Ole Bobby's not going to Africa." She squeezed my hand and we started walking arm in arm. We went clear through SoHo and into Greenwich Village. It was really fun, talking and walking, and pretty soon we'd gone all the way to midtown. Just for kicks we went into Grand Central Station.

It was pretty empty on account of its being Saturday night, and it looked so peaceful bathed in white and golden light. In front of us the expanse of floor glimmered like a frozen lake, and Magda and I started pretending to skate on it. She did a figure eight, and I skated backward for a while. Then because there was so much open space, Magda told me to do some kind of big leap or something. I don't usually go around making a spectacle of myself like that, but because of how lousy she'd been feeling, I decided what the hell. I started doing some tour jetés and then some grand jetés in a huge circle. It was really fun, and some people buying train tickets to suburbia started applauding, and one guy yelled, *"Bravissima!"* Magda went hysterical laughing, and we skated out onto Vanderbilt Avenue into the bright night.

"Sonia would freak if she knew we were here," Magda said when we finally stopped fooling around. "Let's take a cab the rest of the way."

"Yeah, cabs are so much safer," I said, and we started laughing all over again.

Our new cabdriver was some kind of genuine immigrant. He was young and small and sad-looking, as if he

deeply missed his remote village in the foothills of wherever. I remembered seeing pictures of Kurdish people, and I
wondered if maybe he was a Kurd. His sadness floated from
his black eyes and filled the whole car. Magda lay back
against the seat and rested her head on my shoulder. Her
curls felt ticklish, touching my jaw. Light from the street
rolled through the car in intervals, even and smooth with
soundless thumps, and I had the strange sensation that we
were being bar-coded by light.

Then Magda started talking in a sleepy voice about how
nice it would be if I stayed over at Sonia's with her. How
fun it would be to just hang out and talk all night. I didn't
say anything and a few seconds later she moved her head
from its resting place.

"Don't worry, Giselle, I know you can't. Sometimes I
just wish you could."

"Yeah, me too," I told her. But the truth of it was that
even if I were normal, as in not neurotic and able to sleep
away from home, I would still want to be alone tonight. I
needed to get ready. I needed to find the lake inside. I had
to be calm for my date with Will.

"You'll call me, right?" she murmured.

"Of course I'll call."

"And you'll tell me everything."

"Everything."

The cab pulled up to Sonia's house and Magda gave me
a quick, hard hug. Through the window of the taxi, the
house looked warm and cozy, and we knew that Sonia was
waiting upstairs, pretending not to worry, pretending to
read a book.

"Don't ever leave this place," I said.

"Yeah," said Magda. "I guess it's all right." She passed

me a clump of money. "Sonia's orders. Oh, and let's not mention dancing in Grand Central—she'll totally freak out. Have a really beautiful time with Will."

"Thanks," I said, and kissed her goodnight. I watched her as she ran to the house, all flying curls and swinging purse. At the doorway she turned and shouted, "Call!" and then she disappeared.

After that the sad, possibly Kurdish driver took me home across the park. He probably thought we were fabulously fortunate Americans on account of the fabulous places we got to live in, but I wanted to tell him it wasn't that great. I bet that in his village, mothers didn't take off on endless honeymoons leaving their children without a thought. And I bet that in his village when someone got sick, the family made soup and gathered around and kept him close till the hour of his death amen.

Chapter 10

WHEN I WOKE the next day I just lay there in bed as my slowish senses started to work. I eased up in the pillows and suddenly it all came flooding back to me: today was Sunday. My date with Will. Loopy sensations started in my stomach and spiraled to my throat. I dropped my head to the pillow again and stared at the ceiling high above. The deep blue globe shone like a big, suspended gem in soft, unreachable cobweb mist, and for just a moment I wished I were a child again. Drawing a breath, I pushed myself out of the warm cocoon.

It was chilly in the world outside, and I threw a ratty sweater over my ratty nightgown. I went to the window, then snapped up the shade and looked across the courtyard. But the little girls were not in their room. They were probably already at the park, flying their fancy kites. I saw them once, big, bright fish and boxes you wouldn't think could leave the ground. There wasn't much wind, however, and though not quite bleak the day was sort of overcast with weak, pale sun straining against a wall of clouds.

I went to my bathroom and took a shower. I washed my hair and prayed to the saints of beauty that it would look all right today. As always, I weighed myself with a giant towel around my head so that if need be, I could take away an ounce or two. There was no need. It always said ninety-eight these days, except if I had my period, which was not very often lately; something to do with fat cells, which dancers often tend to lack.

Lucky for you I'm not going to describe how I looked in the mirror naked or tell you stuff about my face. I weigh ninety-eight, so you know I'm thin. In fact, I was in such primo dancing shape that the famous palazzo pants drooped down around my hips. (I realized I might have to use a safety pin, that mortal sin of the best-dressed set.) I put on the Chosen Shirt, which was pukey green yet quite attractive with its squarish neck and just-below-the-elbow sleeves (a convenient length for eating food).

I dried my hair with the hair dryer, then tossed it around like Zora, the world-famous model who goes to our school. I put a little mascara on and some lip stuff flavored like passion fruit. I still didn't look too great. Then I put on the French jacket—the "nipped-in" one, as Magda says—and things improved. That's not my ego talking; it was totally the jacket's fault that all at once I went in and out, not just up and down. I gazed at myself and admired certain parts of me, which didn't include my hair. I just wasn't used to wearing it down and it made me feel weird and not myself. I tried to recall what Magda had read in *Cosmopolitan* magazine, but I couldn't remember what made guys feel threatened, tied-back hair or eating dessert. In the end, I just rolled it into the usual knot I always wear. I had bigger things to worry about, like my pants falling down around my knees.

I put on my good jade earrings next. Marina had also given me these. Big and round, they dangled down, making my neck look semi-long, though not in league with Amanda's neck. If I got my pants to cooperate, I might almost look halfway passable. I went out to the kitchen to get a pin from the drawer where we keep that kind of thing. Marina was there, a coffee cup in front of her.

"Thought I'd let you sleep today in honor of the big event." She was wearing one of those sexy-looking peignoir sets, ivory-colored with matching slippers, feathery puffs from some poor dead duck fluttering at the toes. She poured more coffee, then looked at me more closely. "Is that the jacket I got you in France? And are those the earrings—" Her voice cut off; I guess she found it moving that whenever I tried to look half good, I ended up wearing all her gifts.

"The only problem now," I said, opening the jacket, "my stupid pants are falling down."

"Let me take a look," she said. Her fingers clasped the waistband. They were warm, not cold as I always expected them to be, marble-smooth beneath her glittering diamond rings. "Goodness, darling, you've lost some weight. Quite a bit from the looks of it." For several seconds she pondered this. Then, "I can fix this. Come with me."

I followed, of course, and we headed toward her bedroom, a place I hardly ever go. As a matter of fact, I hardly go anywhere in my house except for my bedroom, the kitchen and the room that's just inside the door, the one we call the reading room. It made me nervous to follow her. I started to think that there might be telltale signs of Blitz. What would I do if I saw some personal thing of his—like maybe a sock, or something worse? But when we got there, everything looked normal. Her bed was made, the pillows in a dozen different shades of white piled at the headboard, the tulle tied back in bunches around her Cleopatra tent. There were no empty glasses lying around, no three-legged coolers, no popped-off corks. The one and only sign of Blitz was a bowl of ivory roses, fat and pale and echoed in the mirror's glass.

I stood beside her writing desk while she opened a drawer in one of the antique bureaus. There was all kinds of chichi stuff inside—shimmery scarves and silky things, poufs of velvet and gold lamé and unidentified furry fluff. She rummaged a moment, then pulled out something snaky and black.

"Believe it or not, this once belonged to Martha Graham." She wrapped the thing around my hips. It was stretchy and firm yet softer than elastic. It felt really snug and looked quite good. I turned from the mirror to tell her thanks, and my eyes plunked down on a notebook lying on the desk. At the top of the page above some notes was the single word "Amanda." My face must have changed, though I think I'm a sphinx, because right away Marina said, "She's auditioning for Chicago Ballet."

"Really? Wow. Do you think she'll get in?"

"I think she could. If she weren't under so much stress. You know her mother is very sick."

"Yeah. I heard."

"And then there's that man—"

"Amanda has a boyfriend?"

"I hope it hasn't gone that far."

"I just can't picture—"

"Yes, I know. She's like a child." She fussed a bit with the knot of the sash. "That happens with dancers sometimes. Our lives are so sheltered, we're slow to grow up. Some man comes along—of course he's decades older—and wants to be your mentor, your guardian angel, your everything."

"Amanda has some guy like *that*?"

"Let's just say he's trying. He wants her to move to Denmark. He wants her in his company. And to lure her in he says he'll bring her mother. That he knows some famous specialist."

"Why is that bad?" I stared at her fingers, touching the sash. "It sounds like your life, doesn't it?"

"Yes, it does, as a matter of fact."

"And everything turned out great for you."

"Is that what you think?"

"Well, didn't it?"

"My career has been quite wonderful, and I loved your father very much. But think about it, darling. Try to imagine it for yourself. You're sixteen now, as I was." She waited a moment; I felt her gaze seeking my eyes. "Imagine a man nearly forty years old—"

"I really don't think I can do this now."

"I thought perhaps you could."

"Well, I'm sorry, I can't."

"All right, Giselle. But just so you know—so you understand—that's Amanda's predicament. And I can't stand by and watch this man co-opt her life. Things have changed since I was young."

I took a step away from her. Suddenly I didn't want her touching me. I wanted to run right out of the room. This was nothing new with us; it happened all the time. Just when things were going all right—she'd be lending me something to wear, like now, or telling a story about ballet—and she'd say some creepy thing like this. As if my father did something wrong by completely falling in love with her, by making her the star she was. Sometimes I think she hints at things to make an excuse for what she did. But there is no excuse, there will never be, for sending him off to die alone.

I started to leave, and as I did the house phone rang. Its gong seemed to hang in the empty air.

"Will must be here," Marina said. "Stay right here. I'll let him in." I opened my mouth to protest and she coached me in a low hushed voice, "Don't be too anxious. Let him wait." Turns out it was Blitz, not Will. I found out moments later when Nipper barged into Marina's room and started jumping all over me. He chomped at my heels as I headed to my bedroom to take a final look at myself and throw some stuff into my pocketbook. Then I went out to the reading room, the closest base for exiting. Marina and Blitz were already there, deep in some kind of tête-à-tête. Blitz looked up as I came inside.

"You look splendid," he muttered as if in shock. Which led me to wonder just how bad I normally looked. I mumbled thanks and started petting Nipper's head. I noticed that there was a big fake-looking picnic basket on the coffee table, a road map (which I guessed was a joke) and a giant bunch of flowers. I also noticed the air in the room. It wasn't just the flower smell, though that was pretty powerful. It was something else—a kind of heat that hovered around the two of them and gave me the crawling creeps. I was just on the verge of gagging when once again the house phone rang. I glanced at Marina and didn't move. I didn't need any more advice about how to look like I didn't care.

"Nervous?" asked Blitz when we were alone. I told him no, why should I be. He asked if we had a vase around and picked up the bunch of flowers. They weren't normal flowers but weird green orchids that looked like frogs. Interspersed was some hairy-looking swamp grass that must have come from the black lagoon. I opened a closet and pulled out a suitably hideous vase. Blitz stuck the flowers into it and pretended to arrange them there.

We could hear Marina, gushy and effusive and not giving Will a chance to talk. Then, finally, I heard his voice. I didn't exactly catch the words, though he might have said something like, "Sure. All right." It murmured, his voice, deep down low inside me, soft and easy and just as I remembered it.

Then there they were standing in the doorway. My mother became a splotch of white as my eyes homed in on the sight of Will. I looked straight at his face, and he looked back. Our eyes locked tight like that very first moment of first-locked eyes in the dripping greenhouse among the hearts.

"Hey, Giselle."

"Hi."

Nipper, who had gone to the door with my mother, was nudging his hand and running around in circles, trying to make him play with him. Will didn't seem to mind at all. "I think he smells Smiley. Don't you, boy?" I looked at him while he fooled around with that maniac. He was wearing jeans and a black jacket. The jacket was unzipped and under it was a black shirt that was like a T-shirt but fancier. I knew it had long sleeves even though I couldn't see them. He was wearing sneakers that were whitish and not that clean, and there were blue parts on them that were almost black. (Magda would ask about the shoes.)

Meanwhile he inquired about the plants they'd bought, how they were doing and stuff like that. Blitz suggested he come and look at the terrace himself.

"We haven't really done anything yet. All ideas are welcome," he said as if the place belonged to him. "Come," he added, urging Will into the hall with him. Marina followed and motioned for me to come along. Only God knew how much I didn't want to go. I hadn't been out on the terrace in years, nor into the room from which you reach it, the one we call the ballroom. But suddenly, horribly, there we were, and Blitz was on the threshold, inviting us in like lord and master of the realm.

"Wow," said Will, looking up, then out. Light poured through the floor-to-ceiling windows that wrapped around two sides of the room and made it feel suspended like an air balloon floating over Central Park. But looking around, I was shocked by how much it all had changed. Everything had faded—the carpets and drapes, the velvet on the old French chairs—which of course made sense with all the sunlight flooding in. Still and all, it startled me and made me feel like the room had been drained of all its blood. Even the walls were paler; the papered scenes of frolicking lords and ladies hazy now as if shrouded in mist. The only unchanged features were the cherubs' disembodied heads afloat above each window and the egg-sized jewels of the chandelier. Blitz opened one of the terrace doors and a gust of air came rushing in. It felt like an insult, that fresh cold breeze. Nipper barked and we went outside.

Will caught his breath at the sight of the panorama

below, the big green splash of Central Park and the city sprawling to either side and past it, endlessly unfolding in paling blocks of gray. Nipper seemed pretty impressed as well. He put both front paws on the thick stone rail and yelped into the wind. As Blitz described his urban-Eden dream to Will, my eyes wandered over my father's long-abandoned place.

Wind, intense and mournful, rattled through the dried-up stalks and made papery sounds in the withered weeds that straggled out of broken pots. The statues and plants they'd recently bought were clumped together, looking depressed. In a corner of the terrace flush against the building were the square wooden pots, half rotted now, where the dense gardenias used to grow. For an instant I smelled them, truly, their drowning white essence making me lose my balance. Will looked at me then from far across the terrace. It was just for a second really, maybe even less than that, then everything snapped back again and Marina was reminiscing about just how lovely it once had been, with the table and chairs and the sun umbrella that came, she said, from Bangkok, orange and magenta with long gold tassels that caught the breeze, tinkling tiny bells.

Will said it sounded beautiful. They could bring it back, he told them. They could plant a million different things. He mentioned some shrubs that thrived on wind, and offered to make a landscape plan. Marina was thrilled and Blitz declared how "flat-out marvelous" that would be, acting again as if it all belonged to him. Then he glanced at Marina and acted like *she* belonged to him, whipping off his sweater, which he wrapped around her like a shawl.

"Thank you, darling. We'd better go in." Will seized the moment and said that we ought to get going too. We stepped inside and closed the doors against the wind. It was suddenly very quiet. Marina leaned on one of the chairs. She didn't sit down or seem to want to stay there.

"Have fun at the museum," she said. "Soak up lots of Beauty and Truth."

"And Truth and Beauty," suggested Blitz.

I was starting to get extremely tense. Nipper was too; he realized, I guess, we were leaving him. Not that I could blame him. It's a testament to his inner strength that he hasn't already come unglued. Anyway, finally, miraculously, we managed to get ourselves out of there. A few more rounds of torture—elevator small talk with some mogul neighbors from Tokyo, Q and A with Paki, the weekend doorman from Pakistan—and Will and I were finally alone, out on the street in the cool spring air.

Chapter 11

A s u s u a l I apologized for Marina and Blitz being lunatics.

"I like them," said Will. "And your house is unbelievable." He glanced back at the open doors where Paki stood, still watching us like some crazy doorman-uncle in his braided jacket three sizes too big.

"We've been there since forever," I said. "It belonged to my father's family a hundred million years ago."

"Well, it's really great. And the terrace, God. You could really do awesome things out there. You could plan it out so that all year long there'd be something in bloom."

"That's what my father used to do. Even at Christmas the most amazing flowers grew."

"It must've been great."

"It was. He planned it all out on a special chart that he did with colored pencils. It looked like something out of a book—like an aerial view of all the plants with their Latin names written real tiny next to them."

"Wow," said Will. "Do you have it still? I'd love to see a thing like that."

"It's somewhere, I guess," I mumbled, though I knew exactly where it was, folded in half and once again, pressed in a book on a high-up shelf in my father's room, which of all the rooms I didn't go into ever, was the major not-go-into one. Will waited a second and then he asked, "Do you want to walk or take a cab?"

"Let's walk," I said. "The air feels good." Not that I'm any fresh air fiend, but sometimes I think I'll suffocate for no apparent reason, which would definitely happen now if I stepped inside a taxicab.

We crossed the street and entered the park. "Blitz doesn't care about plants," I said. "He just wants to weasel into things."

"What do you mean?"

"I mean our life."

"I want to do that too," said Will, nearly causing me to trip. I tried to come up with some woman-of-the-world reply, but nothing tumbled out.

Will went on, "They seem like a pretty good pair to me. Your mother likes him a lot, I think."

"What if she does? It doesn't mean she should let him come in and start taking over everything."

"What's he taking over?"

"I told you, Will, the terrace was my father's. For all these years we haven't even stepped foot out there—"

"Which is really a waste, I happen to think. What's wrong with fixing it up again?"

"It's not that simple, believe me, Will. He wants to erase all signs of him."

"I kind of think nature took care of that."

"That's what's supposed to happen."

"Like suttee of the plant world?"

"What?"

"Suttee, you know. When the Hindu widow throws herself on the funeral pyre. The plants had to die when your father died?"

"They died when he went to the hospital. If they mattered to Marina she would have taken care of them."

I could feel Will looking hard at me even though I was facing front. "I guess," he said in a quiet voice, "I'll feel the same when my mom starts going out with guys. Especially if the guy starts changing things around like he's planning on moving in."

"You will, believe me. You'll hate it too."

We passed a sign that was tied to a tree with a bunch of bright balloons. JESSICA'S PARTY →, the message said, and Will steered the conversation off. "When I was a kid we used to have fabulous parties. Mrs. Gramerson—that was George's psycho mom—used to go really overboard. The year he turned eight, she made an Indian party. She stuck a canoe in the middle of the living room and we sat inside it, all decked out in feathers, eating corn nuts and crap."

"That sounds really nice," I said. He told me then how bad he felt that June's childhood wasn't as great as his had been on account of their father losing his mind. He kicked a rock that was lying there.

"By the way, we went to see him yesterday."

"How'd it go?"

"Exquisitely. The way that activity always goes. First we went up to his 'bachelor pad.' June ate a couple of Mallomars and then we went down to the firehouse. The guys always fuss all over her and yesterday someone gave her one of those whistle lollipops. She sat on one of the fire trucks, ringing the bell like a maniac and blowing the stupid lollipop while my dad and the guys talked about some big explosion somewhere. My dad has one of those police-band radios so he's up to date on all the big disasters. The firehouse guys are nice to him, especially this old guy, Joe. You can tell they know he's crazy and really feel sorry for June and me."

"I know how that is. That's how people feel about me."

Will laughed. "Who the hell would feel sorry for you?"

"Lots of people. Take my word for it."

Up ahead there was a softball game going on. It wasn't any big deal or anything, just some fathers playing with their sons and a couple of daughters too. Will asked me if I could tell which father belonged to which kid, and I started matching them up. A couple of them were easy, like the one black kid and the one black father, but some of them were tough. The girls, of course, were the hardest. When I was little anyone would've matched me with my father, I told Will. He said that he'd like to see a picture sometime of the two of us together. So I told him about my photograph, the one of us at that seaside hotel. I found myself talking about that place. How it always rained when we were there, and how cozy it was in the dark and oaky dining room, the tall, wide windows fogged with salt like the windows on a boat. "Funny," I said, "I remember all that just looking at one photograph."

"Pictures can sometimes fool you, though."

"What do you mean?"

"They don't always tell you what's going on. Underneath the surface, I mean." I didn't answer and he went on. "Just the other afternoon June and I were looking at some photographs. We found this one where she's sitting in a high chair, blowing some birthday candles out. We're wearing those stupid party hats and smiling like idiots. Suddenly my mom walked in. She looked at the picture and said to me, 'That's the day it started.' That's all she said because June was there, but later on she told me that my father's flashbacks began that day. Who the hell knows what set him off, but the first of the nightmares came that night." I looked at Will and he squinted into the pale, weak sun. "All this time I thought we were having the world's best day. My dad cooked hot dogs on the grill and we turned the garden sprinkler on. It was hot as hell, Junie's birthday, August fourteenth. Anyway, what I'm trying to say is that sometimes pictures lie to you. They show a scene that looks great when really it was shit."

Some chilly air seeped up my sleeve and I crossed my arms in front of me.

"I'm sure that's true, but it's not like that with my photograph. Everything was wonderful. No one was sick. We went inside and had lobster soup."

We walked for a while not talking. On the pebbly path our feet made a goofy crunching noise, and I tried to walk in synch with him to cut the sound in half. There were other sounds you couldn't block out, squirrels scurrying and stuff like that, and tweeting in the branches, cheerily swishing overhead.

⌒

The sun burned bright on the Temple of Dendur's huge glass slabs as we reached the back of the museum. When we got to the front the wall of clouds had cleared away and tons of people were sprawled all over the big white steps.

There were so many people sitting there, you had to wonder if anyone was inside the place looking at the art. There
was a clown-type guy performing on the sidewalk and
gathering money in a hat. When anybody serious or
dignified-looking went by, he'd run up behind him and
make fun of how the person walked. At first you didn't
want to laugh, but after a while you kind of couldn't help it.

When we got inside Will paid for our tickets. He stuck
his little metallic entrance button onto the neck of his shirt,
then fastened mine on me, which was, God, so sexy I almost died.

"Let's go this way," he said to me next, and motioned to
our left. We passed through the giant lobby, then down a
hall toward the Michael Rockefeller wing. We walked
through a room of African art and another filled with Mexican gold, everything chilled in cubes of glass, then into a
place I knew I'd never been before. It was huge and spa-
cious and full of light, the kind of space where sleek, modern sculpture might be displayed. But the room was filled
instead with primitive artifacts encased in glass or sealed in
huge clear cubicles.

"That's Michael," Will said, pointing to a black-and-
white photograph on the wall. "You maybe know all about
him. Like how he disappeared and stuff."

"Actually I don't."

"It happened a pretty long time ago. In 1961, I think.
He'd already graduated from Harvard, where he'd studied
anthropology. He was all intrigued with South Pacific cultures, especially the Asmat, a tribe from New Guinea who
happened to be cannibals."

"They look so friendly," I commented, gazing at the picture of the large black men sitting with Michael, smiling.

Michael looked like a brainy geek, small and pale, wearing horn-rimmed glasses and chuckling along with them.

"Anyway, on this one expedition to bring back artifacts and stuff, Michael and another anthropologist—I think the guy was Dutch—set off in a boat with two native guides. Along the way, the tides got bad and the boat was swamped. The guides decided to swim for shore, and after drifting around all night, Michael figured he'd try it too. The Dutch guy who stayed with the boat was saved, but Michael was never seen again."

"Don't tell me the cannibals got to him."

"No one knows. It could have been that. Or crocodiles. Sharks. Or maybe he drowned."

"But that's the end? That's the last they heard of him?"

"Yeah," said Will. "His father, who was governor of New York back then, mounted this giant search but nothing was ever found." He added as we moved away, "See what I mean about photographs."

Suddenly he touched my back. It was such a light touch but it buzzed like a shock.

He was guiding me now with this light but burning pressure through another doorway and into a much larger room. Then, leaning close so that I felt his breath against my hair, "This is what I brought you to see."

We had stopped in front of a totem pole–like structure cut from the trunk of a grayish tree. Carved in the wood from bottom to top were strange-looking figures of little men with humongous penises that looked like the rudders of boats. At either end of the looming pole was a hollowed-out hole, and way at the top another gigantic rudder thing. Will eased me closer to read the information plaque. The

Asmat, it said, would carve the poles when a villager died. They believed that death was balanced out by another death, so when somebody died or got himself killed they'd go on one of their headhunting trips. If they caught somebody on their land, they would cut off his head and stick it into the hollowed-out hole for everyone to see. They'd do the same if they were trying to claim new land and captured some poor indigenous slob. Imagine, said Will, coming across a pole like this in a quiet jungle paradise. Imagine the shock when your eyes moved up the length of wood to the bloody human skull.

An awful thought. Just awful. But he hadn't moved his hand away, and all that I could focus on was that fan-shaped burn against my back. I could hardly breathe, let alone feel sympathy for the sorry tribesmen who'd lost their heads. Soon I gave up even trying to read. I just let my eyes roam up the poles, over the little naked men, to the shadowy, pit-like groove.

"Let's go somewhere to talk," he said. "I want to explain why I brought you here." Dumbly I let him guide me out, back again through the rooms full of spears and clubs, through the Mexican gold and African masks, into the swarming corridor. "Let's go to the cafeteria." Gently he pushed me thataway. Already, you could hear the hum of voices and noisily clinking silverware. The smell of museum food, damp and disillusioning, wafted on the air. As we reached the entrance, his hand dropped softly from my back. I guess it seemed weird to keep it there forever, but my back felt orphaned suddenly. We joined the line of people waiting to get a table.

After about a million years, an exhausted-looking waiter

led us to a café table in the bar. Will took my coat, hung it over the back of my chair, then stood there waiting till I sat down. As I probably don't have to tell you, hardly anyone behaves like that unless they're old and were born in Europe. Or unless, I guess, their father was a soldier and a fireman and is now crazy. He even ordered my lunch for me. Then, leaning in close so I could hear him over the noise, which, by the way, was pretty intense: "I wanted to show you the mbis poles because I used the idea for some sketches I did to get into Cornell. Aside from the academic stuff, they asked us to come up with some kind of monument idea. Something we'd build if a city or somebody financed it. I'd always been drawn to totems, but the mbis poles were something else. And after I saw them I got my idea."

"Tell me," I said when he didn't go on.

He cleared his throat and looked at the table as he spoke. "As you probably know, totem poles have a bunch of different meanings. First of all, they serve to identify your tribe, kind of like a coat of arms. They can also function as homages to ancestral spirits and gods and stuff. They're burial markers and also territorial ones—I think of the mbis poles as both.

"Anyway, I started thinking about the poles and how I could use them in my work. They had to have a meaning, though, and not be decorations like totem poles in Disneyland. A meaning for now, this time that we're in." He shifted around and pulled a little notebook from the pocket of his jeans. It was all beat up, covered in worn brown leather. He slid his chair over another inch and opened to a dog-eared page. It was covered with tiny drawings, cryptic and mysterious, which you almost had to squint to see. He

110

flicked to a page toward the front of the book and my gaze dropped down to a minuscule sketch of a totem pole. It was only about three inches high, but exquisitely drawn and detailed, with tiny notes scribbled on either side of it. He flipped the page to other tiny drawings, each showing a detail of the totem pole.

"Here," he said, pointing to the upper part, "I'd put the world's protecting gods—Allah, Christ, Science—all the things that people believe take care of them. Farther down, say right about here—though no two poles are exactly alike—here's where I'd carve the victims' names."

"The victims?"

"Oh, yeah, I forgot to explain. The pole's an AIDS memorial." He turned the page to an eerie sketch of a modern-day city, drawn in brownish ink. Between the high-rise buildings a single mbis pole loomed up. The wings at the top made me instantly think of vultures waiting for something sick to die. Off to the left I spotted the second totem pole.

"That's the warning part," he said. "The mbis poles as counters, multiplying like headstones in a graveyard, so everyone can see." He stopped talking, and I stared at the beautiful drawing. Then gently I took the book from him and worked my way through the rest of it. Every drawing was so complex that the book itself, worn and thin, felt like an ancient book of code. I looked up from the page and saw that he was squinting again—wincing, I mean, the way he does.

"It's so small and so big," I whispered. "My mind doesn't really think like that."

He let out a breath and took back the book. His fingers brushed softly over my hand.

"Thanks," he said. "Thanks for looking. I mean it, Giselle."

"Thanks for showing it to me."

At this profundo moment, the harried waiter reappeared. We smiled at the timing and looked at our food, plates of panini sandwiches that hardly fit on the tabletop. The panini bread was really hard and when Will bit in, the entire sandwich fell apart. I bit mine and it fell apart too, only mine was a little messier due to its having watercress. Some little kid at the next table saw us and thought, I guess, that it looked like fun, but when he tried to do it his mother got mad. Will crossed his eyes and made some faces at the kid behind the mother's back. I loved watching Will laugh. And not laugh too. He looked so good whatever he was doing, just sitting there in his nice black shirt. Every time I looked at him something welled up inside me. It almost felt like nausea, though of course it wasn't that at all. I wondered if I could eat.

Turns out I could. After the kid and his mother left, we reassembled our sandwiches and tried to eat them normally. I told him about how Magda had advised me about not ordering anything too difficult or disgusting and how she would've gotten a kick out of our falling-apart sandwiches. Will laughed, but then he said, "Do you really think I'd care if some watercress got stuck in your teeth?"

"Is that a rhetorical question?"

"No. That's a real question. Do you? 'Cause I wouldn't. I'd just tell you, 'Hey, Giselle, there's some watercress stuck in your teeth.' "

"Is there?"

He laughed. "No. But you'd still be pretty if there were." The waiter flew by to pick up the money Will put down.

Then we gathered our coats and headed out of the restaurant. I told Will I wanted to go to the ladies' room, which was right nearby.

The first thing I did when I got inside was to look in the mirror at my teeth. It was true, there was no watercress there, or anything else that I could see. I leaned on the sink and closed my eyes. The words came sailing back to me: "You'd still be pretty if there were." I got drunk one time in my life when I was six. It was at a dinner party and, of course, it was an accident. I thought the champagne was ginger ale. Anyway, I felt the same sensation now, as if everything were dancing around the way the chairs had danced that night—the paper towels, a woman's purse on the edge of the sink, the tampon dispenser on the wall. And my face in the mirror, my pretty face.

Chapter 12

W HEN I CAME OUT Will was standing there holding our coats.

"So what do you want to do?" he asked. A couple of ag-
gressive art lovers went by, banging us with their museum
shop shopping bags, and I told him that I wouldn't mind
getting out of there.

"I was hoping you'd say that. Weekends are a zoo in
here." Then, taking me lightly by the wrist (setting me on
fire again), he pulled me through the crowded hall, everyone streaming the opposite way, back through Pompeii and
ancient Rome to the teeming, roaring lobby and out the
huge brass doors. Chilly air blew up the steps and hit us in
the face.

"You better put this on," he said, referring to my coat.
He made a big comedy routine about helping me into it,
missing my arms and stuff like that. It was pretty funny.
When I got it on I was still cold.

"I hate spring," I told him, looking around and shivering. You couldn't even feel the sun.

"Yeah, me too. What happens in spring? Just Easter. Passover if you're Jewish. Matzoh balls and purple eggs."

"And everyone gets all cheerful like life's worth living suddenly."

"All that rebirth crap. I hate that shit."

"When I think of spring, I think of mud."

Will nodded. "Spring sucks eggs. Of the purple kind." With his head he gestured toward the park.

"Okay," I said, and down we went, stepping around all the crazy lunatics sunning on the stairs.

"I have to *be* Spring in our end-of-year performance at school," I told him when we got to the bottom and started to walk. "Talk about miscasting."

Will chuckled. "Tell me more."

"Well, the ballet's called *Snegurochka,* which in some ancient Slavic tongue means the Snow Maiden. She's the daughter of Moroz, alias Frost, and Vesna-Krasna—Spring. Which explains, I guess, why she's so confused."

"I can understand—with a name like Snotsgurachka."

I laughed and pulled my jacket close. It was really cold as we entered the park. Budding branches with tiny, vivid, spring-green leaves shook against the hard blue sky, now totally cleansed of clouds.

"So tell me the story."

"Really?"

"Yeah." I glanced at him to see if he was serious.

"Go on," he said. "I want to hear."

"When the story begins, Snow Maiden—or Snegurochka—lives in her father's kingdom, the Realm of

115

Ice. Though she's sort of like a prisoner, her father, Frost, is really just protecting her. Which is fine with Snegurochka until she hits a certain age."

"Then she wants out."

"That's right. What sets her off is the sound of some people—the Berendeys—celebrating Mardi Gras. She goes to the party and meets the merchant, Mizgir. He's betrothed to this girl, Kupava, but when Snow Maiden wanders into their midst, he forgets about Kupava and falls in love with her. Not that it matters anyway since in the end Yarilo melts Snegurochka down."

"Yarilo?"

"Yeah. The Sun. Snegurochka's major threat and her father's bitter enemy. Yarilo, the Sun, is jealous of Frost and likes to melt his handiwork whenever he gets the chance. Snegurochka is safe from him as long as she follows her father's advice: Keep your heart as pure as snow and cold as ice."

"But she doesn't, of course."

"There'd be no story if she did."

"So when does Zaroolo nuke her?"

"Yarilo," I said, and smiled at him. "Remember the merchant, Mizgir? Well, Snegurochka likes him too. She lets him melt her icy heart, and Yarilo gets his chance."

"And where does Spring come into things?"

"That's the other element. All along, Frost and Spring, Snegurochka's parents, disagree about how to raise their daughter. Frost wants to keep her frozen and safe, at the cost of having an actual life. And Spring wants her to live it up, even though it could cause her to die."

We walked for a while not talking, then he asked, "So

how do you play your character? I mean, how do you act when you're being Spring?"

"Flighty, sort of. Self-absorbed. I'm in love with my own creations—the flowers and sparrows and puffy clouds. I'm constantly showing off." I shrugged my shoulders. "I relate much more to the role of Snegurochka. My early childhood was just like hers."

"Imprisoned in the Realm of Ice?"

"Well, not in any realm of ice. And not imprisoned either. But my father was a lot like Frost. Not grim or cold, but very protective. I told you how he pulled me out of nursery school because everyone was crazy there. And how after that, I stayed with him at home."

"It never got boring without other kids?"

"Not at all. We were busy all day. First we did our ballet class and then he'd start his work. There was always music playing, and I'd draw or paint or look at books. Every so often he'd take a break. He'd tell me stories and teach me things—Russian words and manners and how to walk with a book on my head."

"Sounds pretty nice."

"It was. I never got sick of being there. And he never got sick of having me. Marina was always sick of me. All the same, I don't think she wanted me there with him. She didn't like to share him, and in the end she totally took him away from me."

"What do you mean?"

I dropped my eyes. I hadn't planned to say that. It just sort of tumbled out of my mouth. "Never mind. Forget it."

"No, tell me, Giselle. I want to know."

"She sent him away is what I mean. When the cancer got

bad"—my voice sounded thin and cracky—"she stuck him in some hospital. Some horrible ancient Catholic place where people go to die."

"Like a hospice or something?"

"I don't know. I only know that we should have taken care of him. *I* would've taken care of him."

"You were just a little kid, Giselle."

"It doesn't matter. He could've stayed home. Lots of people stay at home. Sometimes it makes them better. There are lots of studies that say it does."

"But maybe the doctors told her—"

"That's Marina's story. That the doctors told her he had to go. That he needed equipment and stuff like that. That he'd be a lot more 'comfortable.' "

"And why don't you believe that?"

"It happened too fast. It didn't make sense."

"Sometimes people get suddenly worse—"

"He didn't get worse. He was just as sick as he'd been for months. We were staying with some friends of theirs, Otto and Jacinta Black. Marina couldn't handle things and Jacinta was a nurse. They had this house somewhere in Connecticut. It was really peaceful, right on a lake. Nothing was different from before."

"But maybe they knew something was *going to* happen soon. Something they wanted to shield you from."

"Why are you sticking up for her?"

"For who?"

"Marina."

"What?"

"Everyone does it. All the time."

"I'm just trying to understand, Giselle." He paused for a

second, then asked in a slightly softer voice, "How long had he been sick?"

I opened my mouth to answer, then realized that I didn't know. "I was six when he died," I told him, though that wasn't what he'd asked.

"I bet he was sick long before you knew it. Maybe you were three or four when he first found out what was wrong with him. And I'm sure your mother always knew and was dealing with this thing for years, probably trying to shelter you. How long did he stay in the hospital? Didn't you go to visit him?"

Things were jumbling in my head. Of course, he was right. You don't get cancer and instantly die. He must have been sick for a while, at least. Maybe he'd had treatments like Amanda's mother was having now. I didn't remember that part of things, though I knew, of course, that something had changed. Sometimes he'd get angry. Sometimes he would cry.

Will and I lapsed into silence for a while. We passed a group of old people in pale gray jogging suits practicing tai chi. It was like a dream of old people floating in a green sea, and it soothed me to watch them. We had slowed our pace without even really meaning to, and Will took my hand as the path began to widen and slope. Through the thin new foliage, fine as feathers on a hat, we could see the West Side buildings and lights coming on in windows, and people doing things inside.

"Are you all right, Giselle?" he asked.

"Yeah. I'm fine."

"I hope I didn't mess things up. My mom says I push—"

"No, it's all right. I guess I don't know how long he was

sick. Or how long he was in the hospital. I visited once. Maybe twice. It was horrible there. Everyone was dying. Some of them looked already dead. She never should have put him there, no matter what any doctor said."

"Yeah, okay. I'm sorry."

"You have nothing to be sorry for."

"Well, anyway, I am."

I smiled at him; I tried, at least. "No matter what, it was nice today."

"Really?"

"Yeah."

"Good enough to do again?"

"Yes, of course. I'd like to."

"Next time I won't talk so much. We could go to a movie or something like that. Or eat some sort of actual food."

"Anything," I told him. "I wouldn't mind doing anything. Or even nothing. That'd be great."

He kicked a bottle cap lying there and it scudded off, catching the light on its silver edge. Then he put his arm around me, and we walked like that all the way to my building. Paki had gone off duty and Simon, the oldest of all the doormen, who is probably ninety-five, opened the door with a curious smile.

"Hi," I said.

"Good evening, Giselle." Simon has known me since I was a baby, so I always feel self-conscious when I do something mature in his presence, such as walk around with a guy's arm around me. Tomorrow he would probably say something about how very handsome my "young man" was. Will and I rode up in the elevator. There was nobody else in it, but we didn't talk anyway. It was terrible to waste time missing him while he was still with me, but I couldn't help it. I kept thinking how in just a few minutes he wouldn't be there anymore and it would just be me all over again. We got out on my floor and stood there looking at each other, smiling really stupidlike.

"I'll call you," he said.

"Okay. And thanks."

He started backing up toward the elevator, which was still waiting there. When he got inside he stopped smiling and just stared at me. The doors started closing and suddenly he held them open with his arm and came out again. I guess I must have moved forward too, because all at once he was kissing me and I was also kissing him. Which I didn't know I knew how to do.

Chapter 13

I STOOD IN THE HALL for a really long time after the elevator left. It was quiet there with the dusty chair and table and hundred-year-old rubber plant. The elevator's humming dimmed, and now I could feel a humming from inside myself, which must have been my blood and heart and all my wild cells. I dug for my keys and let myself into the dim foyer. Weird how I knew, the moment I crossed the threshold, that something wasn't right. A slab of light from the rediscovered ballroom fell across the hallway floor, and a figure stepped into its shining pool. It glided toward me soundlessly, seeming to levitate off the floor.

"Darling, hello." Marina drew close and looked at my face as though she could tell it had just been kissed. "Did you have a good time?"

"What's going on?"

"How did you know? There is bad news." She lowered her voice. "Do you remember Carla? She used to dance with the company." I nodded. Of course I remembered Carla. I remembered every one of them. "Then, of course, you also remember Frank?" I nodded again. Ditto for Frank. I used to call him Tawny Frank for his catlike golden eyes.

"Well, I'm sorry to tell you, Frank is dead. Carla is here. She came to bring his ashes back."

For a moment the news did not compute. Pictures of Frank rolled into my brain—balancing cocktails on his head, tangoing on a tabletop. Before I could speak, crazy Nipper burst from the room, his toenails scraping the rugless floor as he skidded down the hall. It really made no sense to me how every time he saw me, he lost his mind with joy. Now Blitz appeared—I recognized his massiveness—a silhouette in the slanting light, stepping aside so a woman could pass.

The woman came quickly toward us. But when she was there, her face revealed in the hallway's light, it was no one that I recognized. Instead of Lilac Carla with blossoms of softly clustered hair and purple eyes and cool, blue skin, a dark, old lady stood there, leathery and gaunt. A wide, slow smile creased her already well-lined face. When she hugged me, however, in two amazingly strong thin arms—well, it *was* Carla after all. And when she let go, drawing back to look at me—"God, if you're not Grigori's own!"—I caught a glimpse of something, some flash of amethyst in the eyes, some passing purple shadow that told me I hadn't dreamed the face.

"It's grand to see you again, Giselle." The same low, husky voice, as well. She touched my cheek as if to test for realness, then gathered my hands in hers. I needed that proof of realness too. "Let's go sit down and talk," she said, and we drifted toward the spilling light. Blitz hovered massively at the door like a big, fat angel of death.

"Hi," I mumbled as he stepped aside to let us pass.

In the ballroom the chandelier was blazing, and I noticed at once that the furniture was rearranged. (I suspected Blitz: step two in the invasion plan.) It looked like a hotel lobby now, dotted with clumps of tables and chairs, one of which Marina led us over to. I studied her as she posed herself on a rickety Louis-the-something chair. She was wearing dark green velvet pants, a matching tunic and a rope of pearls. The green made her hair seem even more golden than usual, or maybe it was giant topaz earrings glittering through the swept-back waves. On her gorgeous feet were some brocade booties trimmed with mink.

I glanced from her to Carla and felt a little ill. It wasn't just her crazy hair, which was long and gray with spots of black that made me think of hyena fur. In the too-bright light you could see each line on her sun-aged face—she and Frank had lived in Puerto Rico—and the veins in her neck like thick, brown strings. But worst, believe me, were her eyes, the whites so pink it stung my own to look at them. She was wearing some dark red scary pants and a beige top with a drawstring neck. I won't even tell you about her shoes. Looking at them together, Carla and my mother, you knew that Magda's theory was right: Carla, like me, was the mental-patient dancer-type.

"Shall I make manhattans?" queried Blitz. He hadn't sat down and was floating around us, butlerlike.

"That would be grand," said Carla. "Maybe it will help me sleep." She glanced at her watch. "It's almost twenty-four hours now."

"You'll sleep tonight," Marina said. "After we feed you and ply you with wine."

Blitz disappeared, and Carla turned her painful-looking eyes on me.

"I'm really sorry to hear about Frank." My voice sounded stupid and insincere.

"It's really a pity, isn't it? It's a truly hideous disease."

I glanced at my mother.

"It was AIDS," said Carla. "He was positive for many years. But he stayed quite well till recently." She attempted a smile but ended up more like grimacing. Then, taking a breath: "Lord, Giselle, I really can't get over you. You were six years old when I saw you last. A tall, skinny thing with a long black braid. So what's been going on since then?"

I smiled and shrugged. "The usual stuff. School and ballet. Ballet and school."

"Your mother tells me you're dancing wonderfully these days."

"She has the lead in her school's performance," Marina announced from her delicate perch. She looked as if she were sitting for a portrait, one languid arm draped across the gilded back.

"It's not the lead—"

"It's not the title role, Giselle. But Spring in *Snegurochka* does some of the loveliest dancing parts."

"You're doing *Snegurochka*? I'll have you know that *I* played Spring—when was it? Eons ago at one of those summer festivals. Vesna-Krasna, I loved the role. My little Snegurochka grew up to be Marissa Kent. She was just fourteen and magnificent." Suddenly Carla sprang from the chair. Tapping her forehead with her palm, she began to

125

mark one of the variations, where Vesna-Krasna dances with her winter child. "Brisé volé, pas de bourrée—and of, course, I am waving my flower wand. God!" she said with a breathless laugh. "I haven't thought of that in years. I'd fall on my skinny derrière if I actually tried brisé volé."

A few seconds later Nipper announced the cocktail hour, and Blitz minced in behind him, bearing a quaking tray.

"You're an angel of mercy," Carla said. She took a glass that was big enough to swim in and settled back in the faded velvet loveseat. "Does anyone mind if I have a smoke?" Of course we said no, we didn't, and she pulled out a pipe, which she filled with dark tobacco from a worn-out leather pouch. Blitz, Mr. Suave, conjured a silver lighter and held the flame as Carla sucked in and out. It seemed sort of weird, her Indian pipe, his silver Dupont. The tobacco smelled good, like woodsmoke and fall, and seemed to calm her down. Blitz went back to his butler's tray. He had filled a sherry-sized glass for me, but Marina hijacked the drink midair.

"Nice try anyway," Carla said, winking at Blitz through the curls of smoke. He pulled out his cell phone and started to dial.

"I'll make the reservation. Four of us in an hour, say?"

"Not me," I said, maybe slightly too fast. I turned to Marina and forced a yawn. "Tomorrow's school. And I'm really tired." A lame excuse, as you've probably gleaned from what I've told you about my school, but Marina went along with it, signing to Blitz with a waggle of dainty fingers that there'd only be the three of them.

"We'll catch up tomorrow, okay, Giselle?" Carla said with a smile at me. Then, glancing down at her mental-patient pants and shirt, "I suppose I ought to change for this."

"If there's anything you need," Marina offered softly.

Carla briefly closed her eyes. I thought she might say that she needed a dress and maybe also a pair of shoes, but instead she said: "I just need to be here and not alone."

"And so you are," Marina soothed. "We're going to help you through all this."

She turned to me. "I've given Carla Otto and Jacinta's room."

I nodded. That was the room with the giant stained-glass windows, which the Blacks used to call their own. Carla could stay there, I didn't care, but I'd never visit her in that room; I'd never go near that place right across from my father's den. There were two other rooms where guests could stay, but maybe Carla wanted to sleep in the Blacks' old room, which felt like a tiny church.

The two of them got up to change. I seized the moment to make my escape, so as not to be alone with Blitz. "I'll keep an eye on Nip," I said as the happy dog scampered after me out the door. It was weird how small Blitz suddenly seemed, standing alone in that big huge space under the chandelier.

In my room, I collapsed on the bed without even looking for the Chinese girls across the way. Nipper got all excited and leaped on the bed beside me, licking my face and slobbering as if I were a bone. After that, he started digging in the quilt. I tried to get him to knock it off, on account of its being some Amish antique, but when dogs start digging they lose their minds and don't pay attention to anyone. Finally, when he'd formed it into a suitable mound, he plunked himself down in a velvet heap. I patted his rump, hoping he would fall asleep.

Then I closed my eyes and pictured Will. Will walking

127

backward through the elevator doors. His face as the doors began to close. The way he stopped them with his arms and stepped out into the hall again. How we fell together, the both of us . . . The humming sensation started again, soft at first, then more intense till I felt as if some weird little engine had been installed high in my stomach under my heart. Nipper must have felt it too; he suddenly toppled onto his back and started to paw the air. He was smiling, the grin so wide I could see the roof of his shiny mouth, a lattice of pink and black. I was just like a dog, I realized. Grinning and ecstatic regardless that Tawny Frank was dead. All I could think of was myself. Myself and Will. My hand reached out for the telephone; I needed the sound of Magda's voice.

"So," she breathed, "how was it?"

"Great."

"How great?"

"Extremely great."

"Did he do it?"

"What?"

"You know what I mean."

"Yeah, he did. Affirmative."

"Where?"

"In the hallway."

"Don't be cute."

"He did it where you're supposed to."

"Yes!" she whooped, and I sensed her toppling over in a mound of wrinkled clothes.

"But when I got home I found out that a friend of ours had died. A guy who danced in the company."

"He must've been old."

"Not really."

"Then AIDS, I bet. Dancers are always dying of AIDS."

"Yeah, it was. The woman he lived with is at our house." I drew a breath. "So Frank is dead and Carla's a wreck, yet all I can think about is Will. What kind of—"

"Listen, dahling," Magda broke in, in the tone she reserves for giving advice, "all through history people have felt the way you do. Like in *Dr. Zhivago*—remember that film? The entire world was falling apart, people were getting massacred, yet Omar Sharif thought about Lara all the time and Lara thought about Omar Sharif—"

"That was a movie, Magda!"

"Well, the same thing applies in actual life. If you stop your life because someone dies, well, you might as well be dead yourself. Even your mother's getting on."

As if sensing her cue, Marina appeared at my bedroom door.

"Listen, Magda, I've gotta go."

"Madame Marina?"

"Affirmative."

"Catch you later."

"Yeah."

Marina tiptoed over. "Do you really need the dog on the bed?" She said the words, but didn't actually seem to care. As she sat beside him, Nipper sidled over, nuzzling her hand.

"Did you have a good time today?"

"Yeah, I did."

"I'm glad. I'm sorry it didn't end so well."

"It's sad about Frank."

"I know." She reached out a hand and touched my left

jade earring, making quivery chills run up my neck. "We may be out quite late tonight. We have to get Carla to sleep somehow."

"Maybe with some food and wine."

"Let's hope that works." She rose to her feet and crossed the room. In the doorway she paused and asked me, "Will you be seeing Will again?"

"I think so, yeah."

"I'm glad."

⁓

A little while later I heard them in the hallway. The door fell shut behind them, and soon after that the elevator's rumble told me they were gone. I stayed where I was on the rumpled bed till Nipper began to snore. Then I got up and dragged a chair to my balcony. Climbing up, I reached for Hugo Junior, the small stuffed monkey Frank had brought me from India when I was four years old. I smoothed his gauzy gathered pants and touched his golden cap. Tiny oval mirrors glinted on his sequined vest and ricocheted light to his garnet eyes. I brought him back to the bed with me and lay there in the pillows, stroking the fur around his face, smelling the sandalwood incense smell that clung, indelible, to his clothes. But all the while I was thinking of Will and not of Frank, only of Will and his long, deep kiss.

Chapter 14

ELICIOUS SCENTS—onions and spice and things you might smell in Sonia's house—woke me in the morning. For a second I wondered where I was. Then, falling from bed, I shuffled barefoot down the hall. In the kitchen I found Carla, stirring things in a frying pan I didn't know we owned. She turned when she heard me.

"Hi, Giselle."

"Hi," I said. "Wow, that smells good. But why are you cooking?"

"It calms my nerves."

She didn't look very calm to me. She looked, in fact, like a total wreck. In the light of day you could see the strain lines in her face, along with a lot of other lines I hadn't noticed the night before. Her eyes looked pinched and shrunken—you could tell she hadn't slept at all—and something pulsed in the side of her neck. As for her clothes, they were pretty dismal too: a faded plaid shirt and the same red pants as yesterday. An apron/dish towel dangled from the waistband, gathering spots of grease.

"It's really good to be here," she said, glancing back at the frying pan, where onions and green peppers danced around. "I think I'd go mad being at Casa Rosa now."

"Your and Frank's house?"

She nodded. "It's pink, you know—Frank's idea."

"How long did you guys live there?"

"Almost twelve years. Which is hard to believe. Before that we lived in Old San Juan, like all the North Americans. We had a little studio, even a little company."

"Really?"

"Yeah. We did *Nutcracker Suite* at Christmastime. Everyone came to see the snow." She smiled at the memory. "Anyway, it wasn't making money and soon we decided what the hell, let's retire for real this time." I sank onto one of the kitchen chairs and watched her whack the food around. "We started to look for a place to buy. We ended up in the center of the island. Utuado, it's called. An Indian name."

"I remember my parents visited once. They left me with the Blacks."

"Yes, that was fun. The good old days." She began to beat some eggs in a bowl. "Then all of a sudden everyone started getting sick. Sean and Larry and Harold Palm. And then, of course, your father, though he didn't have what the rest of them had." With her one free hand, she reached for a glass of orange juice and took a long, slow sip. "Did you know, Giselle, that Frank found out he had HIV the very same week your father's cancer was diagnosed?"

"No one told me that Frank was sick."

"I guess they thought you were too young."

"How old was I then?"

"Maybe four or five." She swallowed another gulp of juice, then turned back to the stove. "Anyway, it gave them a kind of comfort to know they were in the same doomed boat." A vicious hissing rose from the pan as she trickled in the beaten eggs. "They used to laugh about who'd die first and who would make the more beautiful corpse. They thought it so daring to joke like that. Like spitting in the eye of death. Of course, they were partly serious. They cared very much about how they'd look."

"My mother's always saying that. Not about Frank. But she tells me how vain my father was."

"Narcissus was his middle name. We all adored him just the same."

"But Marina says—she says he drove their friends away. That he didn't want them to see him sick."

"That was later. When things got bad."

"It's true then?"

"Yes." Quizzically she peered at me. "Why do you think I'm the only one left—out of all those hordes of people? It's only because we were in Puerto Rico while Grigori was driving the world away. If we'd been here, he would have done the same to us." She flicked off the burner and wiped her hands on the crummy towel. "People really wanted to help. But Grigori wouldn't let them. If someone came to visit, he'd shout at them or say some awful, insulting thing." She sank into the chair across from me. "I understand to a certain point. To Grigori life was a form of art. Perfection, beauty, physical strength—he made these part of every day. And maybe that's not vanity. Maybe that's respect and pride, and absolute love of life. Let me tell you, Frank was angry too at first. I remember his rage the first time he couldn't get through a barre. He screamed at me as if I were the one responsible for the awful thing that had happened to his body." Her blood-tinged eyes seemed to be seeking something out. "You, of course, know more than I on the subject of that."

"What do you mean?"

"Oh come, Giselle. You don't remember the way he'd get?" I didn't answer, and after a moment Carla said, "Memory's strange. The mind selects and keeps what it wants. Of course, you were very young back then."

"I remember he got angry—" My voice sounded weird, defensive. I felt I was being patronized. "I also remember how sorry he felt."

"Yes, of course. He was terribly sorry afterward. After all the damage was done. And then, guess what, he would do it again. I loved your father; he was brilliant at everything he did—except at being sick. He made Marina's life a hell."

"She wasn't exactly the ideal nurse."

Carla's pink eyes widened. "How can you say a thing like that? She tended him like a mother. Like a mother would tend a dying child."

"She never stopped dancing all the while."

"Grigori wouldn't let her. It would kill him, he said, if she stopped for him. He liked to be the martyr too. But she never traveled, she wouldn't do tours. And later on, she just defied him and stayed at home. By then he didn't care."

"She was already old."

"She could have danced for another year. Remember, Giselle, she'd already lost that other year in order to have you."

"I'm sure that wasn't her idea. My father probably begged her to."

"Your father *what*?" She laughed out loud. "You think he

wanted children—*him?*" I must have looked stunned because right away she added, "He adored you, of course,
once you were here. He worshipped the air you breathed.
But dear Giselle, he was totally shocked that he felt this way.
He thought a child would ruin their life." I'm sure I looked
really stupid, my mouth half open with nothing to say. I
knew my father loved me. I was sure of that, I had no
doubt, but it came as a shock—I mean, if it were true—to
know that he'd never longed for me.

"How old are you?" Carla asked me next.

"Sixteen."

"That's old. I mean, old enough to know some things.
Like your father wasn't perfect. And your mother made
some sacrifice."

"I want to know about that," I said. "About my mother's
sacrifice." I wished my voice sounded more adult, instead
of puny the way it did. But Carla had really jolted me. "If
my mother was so wonderful—if she really wanted to care
for him—why, in the end when he needed us most, did she
send him to that awful place?"

"The hospital?"

"Yes."

"Are you serious?" She was staring again with those
wide, pink eyes, but she seemed confused, uncertain now.
"Come here," she said, though I was only about a foot
away. I didn't move, and she leaned in close over the
kitchen table. Then she did this really weird thing. With
one of her hands she cupped my chin; the other went roaming through my hair. "Where is it?" she mumbled softly, her
mouth almost touching the side of my face. It was then that
I caught the scent of gin floating on her breath. I was too
freaked out to pull away.

A splotch of light appeared in the door, and I looked to find Marina there. For the first time maybe ever I was actually glad to see her. She glanced from the ticking clock to me. "You should be getting dressed for school." And, "You, dear Carla, should be in bed." I climbed to my feet and she moved a little to let me pass. There was silence for a moment, then Carla's quiet, slurring voice: "You're crizza, Marina. Crazy. I just found out that—" Her words cut off with the closing door.

—

I met Magda at the corner where we always meet. As usual, she was eating a giant cookie and gulping down cappuccino.

"There you are!" she hollered, postponing a bite to look at me. "I was worried sick. Love and death are very big things. Here, have some cookie. Sugar is a drug, you know." I bit the cookie she shoved in my face, its sweetness making my jawbone ache.

"Let's get the death part over with. I'm sorry, of course, but until last night I'd never even heard of him—Frank, you said? And his girlfriend brought his ashes back?"

"She's not a girlfriend. Frank was gay."

"But his ashes are actually in your house?"

"I don't know. I didn't ask."

"Well, that's totally creepy if they are." She dropped the cookie into the bag. "Anything else you want to say? Before we change the subject, I mean."

"Try not to be so sensitive."

"I'm sorry, Giselle, but the concept of death just turns me off. I just can't handle the whole idea."

"Yeah, I know. On top of which, Carla's weird. She was

drinking gin at eight o'clock this morning and she said some real weird things."

"Things like what?"

"I don't know. Stuff about my father. Things about my memory."

"What about your memory?"

"That maybe I don't remember things. That maybe my brain blocked things out when my father was sick."

"Yeah, so what? That isn't bad. You know enough already."

"She said that my father didn't want to have me."

"That's crazy, Giselle. He was nuts for you."

"Yeah, I know. When I was born. But according to her, I wasn't really in his plans."

"I'm sure I wasn't either. You know, in *my* father's plans."

"It's just kind of weird to think of."

"Yeah," said Magda, "considering all the stuff you thought." She pulled out the cookie to take a bite and mulled things over for a while. Then she said, "But the way I see it, it's all good news. Your father didn't want you—at least he didn't think he did—but once you were born, he adored you. You forgot some stuff from childhood, but yeah, so what—you're probably much better off." She stared at me over her Styrofoam cup. "I mean it, Giselle, you're lucky. Forget that stuff that happened a million years ago. Tell me what happened *yesterday*. I want to hear what happened with *Will*!"

"I already told you, didn't I?"

"Actually, no. Thanks to your mother barging in, you told me practically zip."

I reached for her cappuccino and took another sip. I hadn't finished talking about the other stuff, but she clearly didn't want to hear. It still felt weird to think of Carla's fingers scouting through my hair. I shook it off, and started to describe Will's shoes. I was still talking when the pointy green roof of Dante School came gloomily into view.

You might be quite surprised to learn that an artsy "alternative" school like ours could have such a lousy atmosphere. But Dante really does. It has a lot to do with the clientele, but it's also because of its hospital past, which I think I mentioned to you before. They can fill the place with statues, hang ten million etchings on the wall, but nothing will change the karma. You can practically hear the sick old ghosts retching tuberculosis globs. Magda and I got quiet as we climbed up the stairs and entered Dante Dungeon, where depressed-looking people walked around ignoring us. One of them was Zora, the model. She looked exhausted, worse than us, though probably for totally different reasons; jet lag, for example. Tahiti-LA-New York is tough. Two "plastic arts" people went by carrying a big, hideous construction of chicken wire and beat-up wigs. Magda said hello to one of them, and he said, "Yeah, right."

She looked at me. "And so begins another glorious week of school."

"Yeah, right," I said and we tried to laugh. Then I turned left in the direction of the dance studios and she went off the other way where the horrible hairy thing had gone.

As always, I somehow managed to do the day. Most of the time, except when I was dancing, I ended up thinking of Will, replaying the scene when we said goodbye. A hundred times he held the elevator doors. He pulled me close a hundred times and a hundred times I kissed his mouth. I never got tired of thinking it. It never lost its drama and the humming inside me never waned.

After classes Magda and I met up again and walked together to *Snegurochka* rehearsal. We barely got a chance to talk because for once rehearsal began on time. Mrs. Turock, who was directing the ballet, was trying to get the dancers more attuned to the story's nature element; how primitive "peoples" (she always called people "peoples") went around anthropomorphizing everything. In our characterizations we were supposed to imagine how the ancient Slavic peoples might have visualized a Sun-God-Man, a Spring-Mother-Woman, et cetera.

I didn't think about any of that. Actually I thought of my Vesna-Krasna in very modern kinds of terms. The truth of it is, a lot of mothers I happen to know seem very Vesna-Krasna-like. Just look at Magda's mother, running away with the guy who used to dye her hair. Vesna-Krasna would do that too, just flit away and disappear, never mind that Snegurochka might need her there. Another thing I thought about Vesna-Krasna was this: if one of her sparrows fell out of the sky, she wouldn't do much of anything, such as try to nurse it back to health. And even if she gave it a try, she wouldn't be very good at it. Caring for creatures was not her forte. Her forte was being beautiful. Anyway, I guess my interpretation worked; at least Mrs. Turock seemed convinced. When we stopped for a break, she clasped me in her clammy grip and announced to all that *someone* at least had a grasp of the pagan peoples' minds. On the way home Magda and I chuckled over that one, but were too exhausted to give it the laugh it really deserved.

When I arrived at my house, Marina, Blitz and Carla were having drinks in the reading room. Nipper was also there with them, which is always quite enjoyable if you feel like getting licked to death.

"Dinner's at eight," said Carla, lifting her glass and spilling a splash on her clownish green-and-white-striped pants. It's hard to describe how bad she looked. Every time I saw her she looked a little worse.

"You cooked again?" I tried to sound like I disapproved.

"Just a little lasagna thing. Cooking really relaxes me."

Marina, who must have come in quite recently because her mushroom turban was still on the chair, told me to have a seat. Blitz offered me a cocktail; i.e., ginger ale, decrepit cherry afloat on top, and they told me about the memorial they'd be having for Frank on Saturday.

"And afterward," Marina said, "we're having a reception here. Courtesy of Blitz." We all turned around to look at him and he waved us off as if to say 'twas nothing at all. "It will just be Frank's family," Marina said, "and whatever old friends we can dig up here."

Carla nodded over her drink. "There are lots of people I'd like to see. I think I can help you track some down." Then, turning to me, "And I hope you'll also invite your friends—to the party, I mean, after the memorial. Magda, of course, and I'd love to meet Will. Some fresh young faces to cheer us up." I almost choked on my ginger ale. The idea of us cheering anyone up. It was obvious she was drunk again.

Chapter 15

W HEN I TOLD MAGDA about the reception she
said it sounded truly sick and if I had even half a
brain I'd forget about asking Will.

"I'm dying to meet him, you know I am. But I'm willing
to wait for the sake of the relationship. A wake's no place
for a second date."

"But Carla really wants him there."

"Just say he has to work that day. Or make up some other
decent lie." She looked at me across the lacquered table and
over the single orchid stem. (We were having lunch in a
Japanese place on Broadway.) "I worry about you sometimes. What would you do if I weren't around?" She
stabbed her chopsticks into a California roll and shuddered
at the thought.

After lunch there was more school. It didn't ask too
much of my brain, but made me tired all the same. Mr.
Lenox, our World Civilizations teacher, spent the whole
hour talking about mummies. Supposedly, he was some

kind of billionaire who taught school just to amuse himself. But he didn't dress like a billionaire and he had this habit of pulling his underpants way up high so they stuck out above the waistband of his trousers. He tucked his shirt inside his high underpants, which fortunately were in dark colors like forest green or navy blue. He wore a moth-eaten tweed jacket over the whole mess.

Anyway, he was some kind of expert on Egyptian burial rites—the rites of other cultures too; he was totally obsessed with death and today the topic was mummified pets. Opening his jacket so he could move his arm better and we could all see his maroon underpants sticking out over his dark blue regular pants, he made a little drawing on the blackboard of a mummified mouse. The mummified mice, he told us, were put into the tomb for the mummified cats, which were put into the tomb for the mummified human beings. A kid named Vincent Falco, who's in the rock band Flinch, said they should have put in some mummified bugs for the mummified mouse and so on and so forth down the chain. Mr. Lenox played along and drew a picture of a mummy scarab beetle, but said that we should ask St. George, our biology teacher (yes, his parents actually named him that), if mice in fact "ingested" bugs. It was all extremely enlightening. I was sure I would go far in life armed with information like this.

After classes was the usual *Snegurochka* ordeal. Magda showed up with her underpants—silk boxer shorts patterned with Hawaiian scenes—pulled way up near her chest. She held up a drawing of a mummy mouse and asked everybody to guess who she was. Mrs. Turock said we would all be better served if Magda channeled her creative energies into her lighting responsibilities, but you could tell she was having a hard time keeping a straight face.

This afternoon we worked on the part in act 2 where I urge Snegurochka to get out in the world and enjoy herself. We had to stop about a million times because the sparrows kept going in the wrong direction, crashing into the water nymphs, who were off the music a little bit. Mrs. Turock helped further alienate me from my peers by saying again how I was the only one in the entire cast who actually knew her part. Which got Walter D'Amici, who played Mizgir, really pissed off since he hadn't even gotten to dance. He started going around punching the scenery and acting all tortured and thwarted like some thwarted, tortured genius. By the time it was over everybody in the whole place was pissed off. And exhausted. Magda was especially unnerved on account of having gotten an electric shock while plugging in some crummy cable. We hardly even talked as we dragged ourselves out of the wretched place.

The rest of the week was more of the same. Except that on Thursday the sparrows had a breakthrough and finally started going in the right direction, and I actually started having fun with my part. The girl in the Snegurochka role had begun to play off my interpretation, I noticed. The more flighty and irresponsible I behaved as Spring, the more susceptible she seemed, as if patterning her mother's ways. According to Magda's flamboyant mother theory, this would actually never happen, but it seemed to make sense in the ballet. If Snegurochka were the opposite of her mother, she'd be like Moroz and wouldn't want to ever leave the Realm of Ice, and then there'd be no plot.

That night Will called me again. We had finished dinner,

delicious bouillabaisse Carla had made, and she, Marina and Blitz were discussing the reception and trying to round up guests. When the telephone rang Marina quickly answered it. Surprised at first, she then got very gushy. I already recognized the tone, and now as I listened, gritting my teeth, I heard her invite him for Saturday.

"A little reception, really . . . so good for Giselle to have you there . . . well, of course, she wants you. I'll put her on." Smiling, she offered the phone to me.

"I'll take it in my room," I growled. I was so enraged I went legally blind. I only found my bedroom by clawing along the walls. When I picked up the phone, Marina was still talking to him.

"I'm here," I said, trying for an icy tone.

"He's all yours, darling. See you, Will, on Saturday." And then she was finally gone.

"I'm really sorry," I blurted out. "She shouldn't have pinned you down like that."

"What do you mean? And by the way, hi."

"Hi, of course. I meant to say hi. She gets me so crazed when she acts like that."

"Like what?" said Will. "She asked me to this cocktail thing."

"Is that what she called it—a cocktail thing? That's not what it is—it's a funeral thing. And she should have let me ask you myself."

"You don't want me to come?"

"It isn't that. It's how she asked—so you had no choice."

"I had a choice and I chose to accept. I thought you'd maybe want me to."

"I did. I *do*." Which was actually true, I realized, never mind Magda's Japanese lunch advice. "But it isn't going to

144

be much fun. A bunch of burned-out dancers, everyone all depressed and sad."

"I can do depressed and sad. Magda's going, isn't she?"

"Magda has to. It's her job."

"Because she's your friend?"

And when I didn't answer: "What the hell am I?"

"Okay, okay. Just don't say I didn't try to warn you, Will."

After that, we talked about various stupid stuff, such as what went on in school that day and what we had for lunch. He asked what I had for dinner too, and I told him about the bouillabaisse and how Carla cooked for us every night and never went to sleep.

"I guess she's pretty stressed," he said. "Maybe it takes her mind off stuff. By the way, I know what that is—bouillabaisse. I'm actually taking French."

"C'est vrai?"

"Yeah, *vrai*. I'm not that bad at reading, but my accent really sucks."

"I can't read, but my accent's great. It's from hearing my mother carry on."

"We should talk in French on Saturday."

"That would be fun. 'The boy is tall,' 'The car is red.' " Then, "Listen, Will, if you change your mind, if you think it over and don't want to come—"

"I'm not going to change my mind, Giselle."

"Okay. All right. Till Saturday then."

"Au revoir, mon petit chou." His pitiful accent made me smile.

I didn't want to be anywhere Marina was, so I headed for the kitchen instead and started cleaning up. Carla came in after a while with a pile of empty plates.

"You don't have to do that," she said to me.

"Neither do you." She gave me that line again about how doing dishes helped her relax. What a joke. In four days she seemed to have aged about forty years—ten years for every day. I guess it was the lack of sleep; you could hear her walking around all night and then you'd smell whatever she was cooking. Not that she ate very much of it. She was skinny as a beanpole, especially her neck, and even if she washed a million dishes or cooked a lake of bouillabaisse, I doubt it would make her look relaxed.

"So he's coming then?"

"Did he have a choice?"

"Actually, yes, he did. And so did everybody else. We've been making calls all evening and everybody wants to come—all the old crowd we danced with. They're very sad about Frank, of course, but everyone's glad to hear Marina's voice again." I looked at Carla's exhausted face, and suddenly I wondered if part of the reason she was going along with this "cocktail thing" was to help Marina get back with her friends. Maybe, I thought, as she pulled out a tiramisu she'd made in the middle of the night, all she really wanted to do was curl herself into a ball and cry. That's what I would want to do. Later that night I woke to the smell of chocolate, and knew that when I saw her next she'd look another ten years older, and that somewhere in the kitchen I'd find a plate of brownies or a seven-layer torte. Plus another dead-soldier bottle of gin.

Chapter 16

FINALLY IT WAS FRIDAY. We had no *Snegurochka* rehearsals, and for some mysterious reason—possibly a bomb threat, the theater department's specialty—school shut down at two o'clock. Magda got the burning urge to zip across town to try on hats in Bloomingdale's, and even though that store tends to give me a nerve attack, I went along to be nice to her. A half hour later, as she peered out from under a chic yet witty polka-dot fedora, she told me that she wanted to come to Frank's memorial so I'd have some decent company. She owed me, she said, for not going in Blitz's car that day. I told her, of course, that she didn't owe me anything, but in truth I was glad she was going to come. We made the plan that she spend the night at my house and go together straight from there. Then we headed for cosmetics to try on some of the sample stuff.

We spent a while squirting ourselves with perfume and testing out the wrinkle creams. Then Magda let some bulimic-looking Bloomie's girl give her a free makeover. It was pretty interesting to watch, and she looked about twenty-nine when she was done. On the crosstown bus as we headed home, our mélange of fragrance filled the air. People edged away from us, and one dramatic passenger had some kind of allergy attack.

Back at my house, things were pretty crazy. People I'd never seen before were zooming around, whisking glasses and plates and stuff down the hall to the ballroom where, of course, the reception was going to be. There were more of them in the kitchen, where we also found Carla, Marina and Blitz, and some glamorous, unknown woman in a blindingly bright red suit. They were talking in solemn voices about canapés and hot hors d'oeuvres.

Marina was sporting a huge white apron that must have belonged to the caterers, which of course was who these people were. With a little checked scarf around her neck, she reminded me of someone in a magazine advertising pickled snails or a high-tech wine rack from Milan. Funny how even in an apron she looked fancier than anyone. Carla, on the other hand, looked another ten years older— a hundred and forty-five or so. Nonetheless, she was the first to say hello.

"This must be Magda. Hi!" She set down the glass that was in her hand and clasped her in a hug.

Magda explained that she didn't usually look how she looked; that she'd been remade at Bloomingdale's. Then, "Sorry about your—Frank," she said.

"Thank you. A shame you never got to meet."

"But I heard about him from Giselle. And I saw that monkey-thingy gift."

"Ah, yes," said Carla. She squeezed my shoulder and smiled at me. Since that morning in the kitchen, she'd been pretty normal and nice to me and hadn't gone poking through my hair.

"Hello, darlings," Marina said. "Sorry for the bedlam here." Then, sniffing the air: "Quite a mishmash, don't you think?"

Blitz, who'd been standing at the counter, which was covered with open bottles of wine they'd apparently been tasting, introduced Ms. Panton, the manager of the caterers. He called me "Miss Parke-Vanova's daughter, Giselle" and he referred to Magda as my "cohort." Ms. Panton shook our hands. It seemed to me she had overdosed on perfume too, but of course, I might have been smelling myself. Bright gold jewelry beamed on her hot tomato suit. She didn't seem to like dogs too much.

After a few minutes of chitchat, I told everybody that we were going to go wash our arms and necks. We had almost escaped when Blitz announced they were going out to dinner. He beamed a big Bavarian smile. "And I hope you girls will come along."

Magda's heel dug into my foot and I stammered out a semipolite refusal, something about how tired we were from our grueling day at school. Marina didn't seem to care as she whipped off her crisp apron. There was silk underneath that rustled as she turned to him. "I guess we'll be *à trois* tonight." Carla nodded, not rustling at all in a gray wool skirt that looked like a prison uniform.

When they were gone Magda said we should put on pajamas early like people in a nursing home. That sounded relaxing somehow, so I found a nightgown she could wear and put on my rattiest, oldest one. We took off our shoes and put on giant winter socks, then shuffled to the kitchen to dig out some of the caterers' food. Nipper came along with us and we fixed him a plate of canapés and a pile of pâté. It was pretty nice just sitting there with Blitz and Marina nowhere in sight, and we talked about stuff that was going on—stuff about school and stuff about *Snegurochka,* which Magda pointed out to me was four short weeks away.

"That can't be true," I blurted. But she swore it was, and to prove her point ran to fetch her agenda book. ORGAN-IZER, it said on the front, which was such a joke you could almost laugh. What she'd do in this book was scribble over each day that had passed. I mean, scribble out the entire page, even the date at the very top, which, according to her, kept her from "looking backward," a very destructive thing to do, which caused one to destroy oneself. She made me watch as she flipped the pages forward, halting grimly at May twenty-fourth.

"Hell," I said, and she nodded her head. This realization kind of ruined our festive mood, and after a while we cleaned the kitchen more or less, then headed for my room. On the way, the telephone rang. I took it in the hallway, my light "Hello" echoing loudly off the walls.

"Hey, Giselle." As he always says.

"Hi. How are you?"

"I'm okay. What ya doing over there?"

"Nothing much. Magda's here and we're hanging out. How 'bout you?"

"I'm just sitting here in my hellhole room trying to get inspired to go to this sort of party thing."

"Not in the mood?"

"Not really. On the other hand, there's really nothing else to do."

"You could stay at home and study French."

"Yeah," he chuckled. "That'd be fun. Anyway, I'm glad

that Magda's with you. I'm looking forward to meeting her. What time should I be there, by the way?"

"Like five or so."

"Okay. And hey, good luck. You know what I mean, at the funeral thing. Don't let it get you sad and stuff."

"Yeah, okay. And thanks."

"Thanks for nothing. I'll see you then."

"Bye," I said and then he was gone. I stood there awhile, still not believing that Will could be true; that he was in my life.

Back in my room, Magda was standing at the window.

"Look," she whispered as I came in. As if the girls might hear her, clear across the courtyard, through all the panes of glass. I looked too and found them in the nightlight's glow, sound asleep in the huge white bed. A feeling of longing swamped me as I stared across the dark. Magda must have felt the same. She turned away and headed for the bathroom. A couple of seconds later, I heard the water blast on full force.

When we got into bed, Nipper jumped up and dug around, then settled at our feet. For a while we just lay there, quiet on our separate sides.

Then Magda said, "You were really lucky meeting Will."

"Yeah," I agreed. "Stuff like that never happens in my life."

"Not in my life either. Usually stuff that happens by chance ends up being shitty. Like Fiona meeting Leif while her hair color guy was out of town."

"Like Marina meeting big old Blitz at some opening at ABT."

"And what about Frank? He probably met some guy one night. I'm sure the guy was clueless too."

"Yeah," I said. "Stuff that happens usually sucks. It's nice to know that good things actually happen too."

"Though it's better not to count on that."

"That's for sure."

"Remember those guys in the Mexican restaurant that night? People might think when they first walked in: Look. How nice. A father and son. Then that bastard started in. Like one life wasn't enough for him. He also had to live his son's."

I murmured, "Yeah, he wanted control of everything."

"You know what I wish," said Magda.

"What?"

"I wish my father had died like yours when I was a little kid like you. Because then I'd still think the best of him instead of the horrible things I think."

"It's not because of how young I was—"

"Whatever," she said in a whispery voice. "Keep thinking all those things you think. Even if they aren't true and no one alive could be that great. I mean, what's so good about knowing the truth if it only makes you feel like hell?"

There was nothing I could say to her to make her understand. She wouldn't believe me anyway. I reached my hand across the bed and tangled it in her hair.

———

I woke the next day in a panic attack. I thought I'd forgotten to set my alarm and would end up late for Madame Eglevsky's ten o'clock class—though that, of course, would never really happen. Not with Marina in charge of my life. Then I saw Magda lying there, her hair splayed out across the rumpled pillow, and remembered slowly what day this was. I climbed from the bed carefully so as not to wake her (Nipper had been retrieved by now), and went to the window to look outside. It was rotten and cloudy, a day designed for the sort of thing we were going to do. In the window across the courtyard I could see the little Chinese girls playing with dolls on the floor of their room. They were so absorbed they didn't even notice me. I decided to take a shower, and when I came out Magda was sitting up, awake.

"Hi," she said, "or should I say *bonjour*?"

"Marina was here? What did she want?"

"Something to do with breakfast. I wasn't completely conscious yet. What time is this shindig anyway?"

The "shindig," as Magda called it, began at three o'clock. Somehow or other, we filled the hours in between. There was breakfast, of course—Carla hadn't really slept and had baked croissants during the night—then Magda and I went out for a walk. We bought lukewarm tea in Styrofoam cups, which we drank on a bench in Central Park. It was dreary as hell and drizzling, and it didn't help that our bench had a dedication plaque nailed onto one of its dark green planks. FOR ARTHUR, it read. A FRIEND TO ALL. When we got back home it was time to dress.

Magda, who as you know is a fashion queen, just threw on her clothes from the day before and managed to still look good. I dug out my Laura Ashley dress, a velvet thing with a little lace collar and matching cuffs. It seemed just right for a wake, I thought, but Magda said I looked eight years old and mentally ill.

"Change," she moaned, but there wasn't time. Blitz had shown up, and with him a troupe of caterers. They were very intense and focused, like people on a bomb squad, and

you knew they wanted us to leave. I told her I'd change when we got back home.

———

Nobody talked much as we crossed town in the limousine Blitz had hired for the day. Carla looked really awful—exhausted, strained and as old as the bride of Frankenstein. She was nervous too and kept grabbing onto Marina's hand, which you wouldn't think would calm one down. I was really glad that Magda was there.

The outside of the funeral parlor looked like someone's house. There were curtains on the windows and a couple of flowerpots next to the door. A lion's-head knocker hung on the door though I doubt you could actually make it knock. As we stepped inside, a guy came out to welcome us. He was shiny and smooth like a rubber doll with slick brown hair that looked painted on. In quiet tones he began to speak to Marina and Blitz, not seeming to know that Carla was the loved one. Or maybe he took one look at her and decided there'd be no point. Her face looked bad and her outfit was awful too—an ugly green dress, ugly flesh-toned stockings and ugly beat-up shoes. Marina, on the other hand, looked tragically sad and gorgeous in a gorgeous and tragic little black suit with a few gold accents here and there. Blitz looked very tragic too in a pin-striped, glossy way.

Magda and I hung around looking at photographs of the various generations of the family that owned the place, while the three of them mumbled with the man. When the mumbling was over, he escorted us to a nearby room. I started to think of my father's wake and all the people that came that day, half the world, it seemed to me, though I hardly saw a face I knew. In *The Daily News* was a tiny inset picture of me, looking totally confused. How had it happened? It didn't make sense. He was here one moment, then suddenly gone. Afterward, the only ones who came home with us were Otto, Jacinta, Carla and Frank. They had cocktails in the ballroom, and Frank and Carla did a waltz in honor of my father. I think that night was the last time we ever used that room. I went to bed and Marina came in to kiss me goodnight. I remember she said, "Don't be sad. He's dancing," and I wondered with whom and where.

⁓

"This gives me the creeps," Magda whispered close to my ear. "And why the hell do they call it a wake? It seems like just the opposite." I managed a smile and looked around. The room was on the smallish side with cool blue walls that were edged in white exactly like a Wedgewood plate. A bunch of chairs in even rows slanted toward a Doric-style pedestal on top of which the urn was set. The urn looked weird and tiny on the big dramatic pedestal, and huge bouquets to either side (so big and ostentatious they had to have come from Blitz) dwarfed it even more. Carla went over and touched the thing. Then, turning to us, she said, "Please sit." She said it again: "Sit down—relax." Magda and I sat down in a pair of heaven-colored chairs.

It was weird just sitting there all in a row, as if waiting for a show. Then one of the funeral guys came back and whispered into Marina's ear. A few moments later the music from *Apollo,* one of Frank's most famous roles, came floating through the vents. It's really achy music and it seemed masochistic to play it now. Marina's eyes got instantly wet, and Carla began to rock. Blitz put his arm around the backs of their chairs in a gesture of protection that made me think of the cactus god in the dark of our Mexican restaurant. I turned away, and that's when I noticed the photographs—groups of them arranged on tables around the room. They were pictures of Frank dancing, his silhouette unmistakable in elegant, long-lined arabesque and arching, airborne *temps de poisson*.

"That's him," I said to Magda, pointing out the photographs.

"God," she whispered, "at first this seemed more weird than sad. But now I feel sick and I'm going to cry." She took my hand and clasped it, and we sat there staring into space as the other mourners began to arrive.

The first were a pair of very tiny women, one of them clad in a leather jacket and matching beret; the other dressed in a Spanish-looking riding suit that must have been chic a hundred and fifty years ago. Marina and Carla greeted them, and they hugged and kissed and had a big reunion in front of the teeny urn. It was weird to watch Marina. In the early moments she almost seemed shy. I had never seen her look like that. Of course, I had to meet the ladies too. They were also former dancers—Flor Something and Stella Finch. They made a fuss like you wouldn't believe, going on and on about what a gorgeous thing I was and how much I resembled my darling, gorgeous father, whom they missed, even now, unbearably.

While they were still talking, another midget appeared on the scene, a man this time, in a sky blue suit that matched the walls. On seeing the women he burst into tears, then like a magician pulled from his pocket an endless scarlet handkerchief into which he dunked his face. Some normal-sized people also came in: a mysterious guy with huge dark glasses thick as bowls; a bone-thin woman extremely white; and someone in a fuzzy-looking warm-up suit whose gender wasn't clear. They were all limping or at least hobbling on their turned-out, ducklike dancer's legs, and half of them used canes. Magda didn't have to open her mouth for me to know what was on her mind as the room filled up with crippled wrecks.

Of course, I had to meet them all, and they *ooh*ed and *aah*ed just as they had when I was that rare creation lying in my bassinet. The weepy man, whose name was Michael, wept some more—if I wasn't my "father incarnate," he said, and wasn't time a thief. And the lady in the riding suit stroked my face and sighed. The weirdest part, however, was finding out that the all-white woman was Green Yvette. Even her eyes were gray, not green, so I knew there was something wrong with my brain in the part that houses memory.

A short while later Frank's family arrived: a brother who looked a lot like him with a wife and several children, and a dazed old man who must have been the father, who I knew was still alive. There were other nondancer people too, relatives and family friends and a dark-haired priest, who after a while got up to talk. He said a bunch of stuff about Frank—they were cousins, turns out—like how funny he was when they were kids in the old Italian neighborhood; how his crazy pranks had them in trouble all the time. Then he described the night that Frank discovered ballet. He was sick in bed and Nureyev was on TV. After that night, he was never the same; something had gotten into him. When the fever broke, he began to dance around the house, doing "Cossack jumps" and striding about in a bedsheet cape. No one in the family had the faintest clue about ballet ("Italian boys played baseball") and it took a lot of broken lamps before his parents crumbled and let him take a ballet class. Eight years later, said the priest, he saw Frank dance at the Metropolitan Opera House and was totally moved to tears. He cleared his throat and said some stuff about Frank's being gay. How it took Sean's death and the death of Aunt Rose to make them accept the *whole* of Frank, even the parts the family didn't understand. He mentioned a couple of other things about Frank's great life and how much they were going to miss him—his joy and spark and stuff like that. Then he mumbled some prayers and made a blessing over the urn. We all stood up, except for Frank's father, who couldn't move. A couple of men took hold of him, while the brother's wife collected her children and ushered them out. Then the whole thing was over and that was that.

"I need a drink," said Magda, as we shuffled out on the Wedgwood-colored carpeting into the late-day glare.

Chapter 17

WHEN WE GOT BACK HOME, the manic caterers were gone. Slightly calmer waiters now roamed about with trays of champagne and wine. I saw at once that the ballroom had been transformed again. A Persian rug that wasn't ours (not before today, at least) spread over the newly polished floor, and piles of pillows that looked Chinese camouflaged the couches, somehow matching the French-style paper on the walls, the scenes aglow in the pineapple sconces' half-assed light. Through the high, wide windows the sky was a wash of violet blue.

Right on our heels, groups of guests began to arrive. They seemed to be in a pretty good mood—you wouldn't think they'd all just come from a funeral home—laughing and talking loudly, gushing over our gorgeous house, which according to them hadn't changed a jot. I watched as Michael, swollen-eyed, swept a glass of champagne from a passing tray and drained it in a gulp. Flor, still in her leather jacket, clutched at another waiter as Stella grabbed drinks and passed them around to their fluttering friends. A scent of mothballs, faint but unmistakable, floated from their sailing sleeves.

Magda suggested, "Let's get some bubbles while we can," and we beelined for a cocktail cart that hadn't been discovered yet. As we sipped our drinks, the man in the thick, dark glasses, whose name I had forgotten, drifted by talking to a woman in a mile-high feathered hat.

"Will you ever forget dancing on the Acropolis with that *globular* orange moon?"

"That was swell," the woman agreed, "but the absolute high point of my life was dancing for the queen."

"The queen? What queen?"

"Of England, ducky. What queen do you think?"

"I bet your mother wants her hat," Magda said as they floated past. "By the way, does it seem to you that there's more of them here than over at the funeral home?"

"I noticed," I said as another cluster came into the room, squinting as they scanned the scene. Already, Marina seemed much more at ease. It seemed, in fact, that she'd slipped back into the hostess role as if ten empty years had never passed. Magda said that it must have made the guests depressed to see how unchanged and gorgeous she was while they all looked so pitiful in their weird, old, mental-patient clothes. She glanced at her watch, and I grabbed her wrist to see for myself. When I looked up, Will was coming into the room. He was talking to Blitz, his head turned slightly, a flicker of candles on his cheek. He was wearing a dark jacket—black or blue, I couldn't tell—and a dark, dark tie on a bright white shirt.

Magda swallowed. "That's him? Oh God. He's totally hot."

By now he'd found me in the crowd. He started moving across the room and we met in the middle somewhere.

"Hey," he said, his mouth in my hair. "How the hell's it going here?"

"Weird, that's how. You'll see for yourself."

His fingers touched my shoulder. "I like your dress. You really look nice."

I glanced down to refresh my memory. Oh yeah. Wait'll I tell Magda that.

"I guess," he said, "I ought to say hello to your mom. And to Carla too—which one is she?" I searched the room and found her with Yvette and Flor. Marina was not too far away, standing near a mirror so you saw her like a statue, front and back and dark and light. She took a step forward to kiss Will's cheek.

"So good of you to come to this. How's your mother? And little June?"

"Fine and crazy, respectively." He glanced around. "The place looks great."

"Candlelight hides a world of sins."

I cleared my throat. "Will wanted to meet Carla."

"Yes, of course. She's over there—and looking like a fright." Marina wasn't kidding, and when you got close she looked even worse. Her face was pale and shimmery with sweat. She lost her balance slightly as she reached to take Will's hand.

"What a pleasure to finally meet. So h-happy you could come." Her hand withdrew and for several seconds froze midair before suddenly jittering back and latching on to Will's lapel. Then, ever so slowly, in weird successive stages, she started to go down.

161

"She's fainted," he said as I sank beside him on the floor. He touched her face with the back of his hand and instructed me to loosen her clothes, directions I half remembered from a first aid chart at ballet school. Her dress was of thin, worn corduroy with a matching belt all frayed at the holes. The way she was lying there all exposed, it struck you how really bad she looked. Those crummy shoes I mentioned before, and the fact that she needed to shave her legs. She was greenish white, like one of her marvelous fish fillets marinated in pesto sauce.

"Good Lord," said Marina, suddenly there. Then Blitz's I'm-in-charge-now voice, urging the hovering guests to move and "give the patient air." From the back of the crowd someone passed some smelling salts, which Will waved under Carla's nose. Almost at once, the pallid eyelids fluttered, then slowly opened up. She looked around as if to pinpoint where she was and why she was on the floor. Then, turning to Marina, "They're all still here," she whispered. "I told you, Marushka, didn't I?"

Marina nodded, her slender fingers smoothing beads of sweat away. "Yes, my dear, you told me."

"They knew you couldn't do a thing." Faintly, weakly, she shook her head. "They always knew it wasn't you." She suddenly pinned her gaze on me. "You're the only one who doesn't know."

"Shhh," said Marina.

But Carla slurred on: "Sweet sixtin but like a child. Someone ought to tell you. Tell her, Marina, so she knows." Will glanced at my mother, then turned to me. I looked at her too.

"She's delirious, darling, don't you see? Let's get her into bed."

Blitz and Will each took an arm and eased her to her feet.

Yvette appeared with a giant fan like something from Kabuki, and started whacking air around. Carla wobbled in the wind. I turned my head and there was Magda, staring at Will over the rim of her champagne glass.

"I'm Magda," she told him.

"I'm Will," he said.

"Later, darlings," Marina suggested wearily.

I probably should have offered to help, but I truly couldn't do it. I couldn't step foot in that faraway room. I couldn't go anywhere near that place. I'd be sick if I did—or something even worse than sick. I just knew I couldn't, don't ask me why. Yvette, thank God, volunteered her services and, swinging her fan, headed out the door with them. Moments later Blitz and Will returned, alone.

"Everything okay?" I asked.

"Yeah, I guess. They're getting her to bed."

Magda opined, "She was starting to look like a day-old corpse." There was a moment of silence, also corpselike, then she said to Will, "You and I will have to work out a schedule. Up to now, Giselle and I have always gone out on Saturday night. Which, by the way, is her only night, though she's going to change that—aren't you?"

"I said I was trying—and I am."

"Till then we'll share," Will suggested cheerfully.

"Yeah, all right. Except for special holidays. Or if I have a crisis and absolutely need her there."

"Let's define 'crisis,' " I heard him say as I headed for the nearest couch. A few seconds later they joined me there, flopping down on either side. Magda spilled some champagne on me.

"I really do adore him. It's so sexy that he knows first aid."

"That's why I learned it," Will replied.

Across the room someone had started playing the piano (which they must have had tuned, like, yesterday), and a blimp-shaped guy in a suit he was busting out of started singing some morbid song. Even if you couldn't understand the words, you knew some intense young Werther was coming unhinged in the forest and contemplating suicide. Magda moaned, then blew a few of the candles out to make us more invisible. We passed around a bottle of semiwarm champagne we found on the floor beside the couch. Just when we started to feel all right, small, sad Michael sailed over to us, an ancient woman attached to his arm, all decked out in leopard skin. He introduced her as "Glittering Jewel" and she did some fluttery stuff with her arms, staring at him seductively. It wasn't until they'd drifted off, talking about some wedding scene, that I realized she was Jewel LeBlanc, a prima ballerina of almost my mother's caliber.

Magda, however, was not impressed and said that she was a perfect example of a delusional ballet person. There ought to be a law, she said, against people moving their arms like that, dressed in anything leopard-print. Will said he didn't think Jewel was crazy, just sort of wistful and nostalgic because the best part of her life was over and nothing that happened afterward could ever compare with those brilliant times. "I give her a lot of credit for not just shooting herself," he said.

Magda said we were going to have to shoot *him* if he insisted on playing Mister B. Compassionate. She tipped the bottle against her mouth and a dismal trickle ran down her chin. "Dead soldier," she said disgustedly, dropping it onto the floor. Then after a yawn: "I think I'm ready to blow this place. A person can take only so much fun."

"I'll get more champagne," suggested Will.

"I bathe in champagne," she told him. "What do I care about champagne?" She rose from the seat with another, much more violent, yawn. Will got up too and said he hoped they would meet again sometime before the end of the world.

Magda said, "Ditto. *Ciao.*"

I told Will I'd be right back, and walked Magda to my bedroom so she could get her stuff.

She picked up her bag and started shoving crap inside. "He's yummy," she said. "If he were mine you'd probably never see me again."

"That's not true."

"I'd drop you like a dish."

I walked her out so that she could say goodbye to Carla and Marina, and waited for the elevator with her. After a million years it came.

"I'll give you a call tomorrow. And thanks for being here today."

"Don't worry, I'll get even. Ta." She made a face as the doors pulled shut. I stood there for a little while. She was a maniac, but I knew she would never drop me like a dish. If she did, I would shatter all over the universe.

Chapter 18

BACK INSIDE, the blimpy old guy was singing another morbid song ("Perilous darkness of night; Whirlpools and billows of fate!") and Jewel was attempting to dance to it—spinning Will along with her. He looked a little nervous yet managed to catch her, God knows how, as the music reached its climax and she flung herself backward into a dip.

"I'm sorry," I said when I got to him. "Don't say I didn't warn you."

"Forget it, Giselle. My grandmother's crazier than her. Luckily she doesn't dance." He smiled at me. "Anyway, I'm glad I came. And I'm glad I met Magda. She's really great. Listen, is there anyplace we could go to talk?"

"Yeah," I said, "I know a place." I led him from the ballroom and down the low-lit hall.

My room was kind of darkish too with only the tiny desk lamp lit. It felt chilly compared to the party room, and very quiet and far away. I closed the door and the silence boomed. Will looked around, his eyes moving slowly up the walls to the dusty plaster angels dancing around the high blue globe.

"Wow," he said. "Is this really where you get to sleep?" He started to walk around the place. Then, "God, you're neat. You're incredibly neat." His fingers grazed the big, old chair and the surface of my desk. He stopped at the shelf where I kept my pictures and other stuff. For a while he just stood there looking, then he picked up the bone.

"What's this?" he said. I told him, a bone. He said that he knew it was a bone. "But where's it from? What does it mean?"

"It's from the house we used to go to when I was small. I told you about it—the house on the lake."

"It's nice," he said and put it down. I gently pushed it back to its place.

"And the feather too?"

I nodded. "On our last day there I took it. I think I knew that we wouldn't go back." He brushed it over his fingertips.

"And you never did?" I shook my head.

He picked up the rock and laid it in his open hand. He rolled it a little from side to side, then set it down in the feather's place and put the feather next to it. His eyes continued to scan the shelves. "Is this the picture you told me about?" He took the photograph in his hands as I repositioned the feather and rock. "It looks like a place from another time."

"It was a place from another time."

He looked at the other pictures there. My father the Rose, my Bluebird father, flying through air. "You are definitely his," he said. He put down the picture and looked at me. Then after a second, "Aren't you going to move them too?"

"What?"

"The pictures. I didn't put them ex-act-ly pre-cise-ly where they were."

I lowered my eyes and they landed on the feather. "I'm crazy, I know. Obsessive-compulsive, Magda says. It's just that it means a lot, this stuff."

"Okay," he said, "but why does it matter where it is? An inch to the left, an inch to the right, what the hell difference does it make?"

"I just like to have them in their place. So they're there, you know, when I look for them."

"And if they aren't, what happens then?"

"Nothing happens. They always are."

He seemed about to speak again, then changed his mind and went back to walking around the room. From the top of my bureau, he picked up Hugo Junior, the monkey Frank had given me. He peered down at his fancy, gauzy pants, then touched his golden cap. He was still holding him when his eyes drifted up the balcony.

"Holy shit!" he whispered, stepping back as if he'd been pushed. In the semidark you only saw the eyes at first, but after a while the furry outlines came into view, ears and tails and beaks and wings, all along the balcony. I watched his gaze as it traveled the shelf. Finally he turned and stared at me.

"They're gifts," I said. "Like Hugo Junior was a gift."

"And you kept them all?"

"What's wrong with that?"

He took a step closer. "They're all so— Didn't you ever play with them?"

"I guess I just took care of them."

He blinked his eyes. As if he thought they wouldn't be there when he looked again. He shifted Hugo in his hands, then turned away from the huddled toys. Again he seemed about to talk, then something drew his eyes away. I followed his gaze and saw through the window the square of light burning in the courtyard's dark. He moved to the window and after a moment I followed him. There in the frame of brightness the Chinese girls, all three of them, and three tiny faces belonging to their black-haired dolls, peered out at the night, and us. One of the girls began to wave, but the others didn't see us there. I flicked on the light, and their faces broke out in smiles. The youngest one picked up her doll and made it dance. Then the one in the middle copied her, and after a while even the biggest girl joined in. The dolls looked like replicas of themselves with their shiny black hair and flowering robes.

Will made Hugo start to dance. First he sort of bobbed him around, then after a while got funny and made him dance on top of my head. The little girls laughed hysterically; I thought they'd fall through the window guards. Then the big one disappeared. She was back a moment later with a fancy dragon puppet, red and gold with tassels that swung when she made it dance. Will dropped Hugo onto the floor and ran back to my balcony. He grabbed a koala and threw it across the room to me.

"Make it dance!" he told me as if I didn't know how to play. Then he hurled a bunch of other toys—my red plaid pony, my Persian cat, a furry sloth that Otto and Jacinta had brought from South America. In the window across the courtyard, one girl came back with a fuzzy bear. She made it jump on the dragon's back till the puppet collapsed in a big red heap, which amused her sisters out of their minds. Meanwhile, Will kept throwing things. They were piling up beside me faster than I could make them dance. I glanced around to look at him, and as I did I saw him grab a little yellow animal.

"Don't!" I said in a really loud voice as he pulled back his arm to throw it. He hesitated—a second or two—and looked me in the eye. Then he threw it anyway. It landed almost soundlessly, and I quickly snatched it up.

"Why did you do that?" I screamed at him. "It isn't a toy! It's meant for show!" I held it briefly against my chest, then frantically started to brush it off. It was something special, a yellow velvet poodle, once a prop in a jewelry store in Paris—diamond bracelets had draped on its back—which my father had asked if he could buy. It had real mink ruffs, and a powder-puff tail, yellow mink, if you can imagine such a thing. It wasn't something you throw around. I glared at Will in disbelief. For a moment he glared right back at me. Then he dropped whatever was in his hand, jumped from the chair and came across the room. In front of the window he picked up the sloth and made it take a deep, slow bow. Then he reached to the desk to flick off the light. I stopped looking at the girls, their faces wide and waiting like the open blossoms on their robes. Will held my shoulders and pulled me close. Part of me wanted to yank away, but my other part refused. He drew me to the bed and we lay down.

"It's okay," he whispered into my ear. He was holding me tight, yet stroking my hair as if I were hysterical, even though I hadn't made a sound. I moved a little and the poodle slid into the sweaty slot between us. He lifted my face and looked at me. He kissed my cheek and an achy place above my eye.

"It's all right, Giselle. I swear to God."

"It's not all right. I'm not all right."

"Yes, you are. You're fine."

I laughed in his shirt. "You're out of your mind."

"Hey, everyone has crazy shit. Tell me what's going on."

"How can I tell you when I don't know?"

"You have a clue though, don't you? Does it have to do with your house and stuff?"

"It has to do with—I don't know. It's just how things keep going on. Even Marina's going on. First she has Blitz and now all those people are back again. They fixed up the room and soon they'll be having parties again. And growing flowers and everything else."

"But that's good, Giselle. Come on."

"It should be, I know. That's the thing that's wrong with me." I lowered my eyes and stared straight into the cloth of his tie. "You heard what Carla said to me. She said I was the only one—and it's true, I am. The only one who's stuck in place. She said that I was like a child."

"Does part of you still want to be?"

"A child?"

"Yeah. Safe inside your Realm of Ice."

"I don't know. I don't want to be weird like Amanda's weird, but I want to hold on to something, and it feels like everyone's trying to take it away from me."

"Don't let them then."

"But what if they're right? What if I remember wrong? I keep wanting to get some answers, but the more they tell me the less I really want to hear."

"You're talking about your father."

"Yeah."

"Believe me, Giselle, I understand. There were lots of things I wanted to know about my dad. Like what it was like in prison camp. Stuff about the war. But I didn't want to know everything. Sometimes he'd tell me horrible shit—things he'd done to stay alive, and I'd end up almost crying, begging him to stop."

"That's awful."

"Yeah. And it's not like I don't want to know the truth. But not all at once. And not just because *he* feels it's time."

"Magda says the truth is overrated. That it's better not to know it, since it only makes you feel like hell."

I sensed the smile in his voice. "She has a point. Anyway, maybe there isn't just one truth. My dad was brave, but he also was a bastard. He was strong but he also fell apart." His mouth brushed over the side of my face. "Just for now let's fuck the truth. Can you think it, Giselle? Just fuck the truth?" With the lightest touch, he kissed my ear. He kissed me again, this time lower, along my jaw. "Say it, Giselle," he whispered, but when I turned to answer him, his mouth on mine cut off the words. I could taste the champagne between us, faint and hot in our open mouths. After a while he slowly peeled away from me.

"Don't move," he said as he climbed to his feet. "I'm going to clean up everthing."

"I'll help you—"

"No."

"But you don't know—"

"Just stay where you are and watch, okay?" He went to the window and scooped up a pile of animals. Then, crossing the room, he dumped them onto the balcony, then hurried back for another batch. Wherever they landed, that's where they stayed, toppled sideways and upside down, some not even facing front. When that was done, he went to the shelf and rearranged my souvenirs, the feather, bone and rock. He repositioned the pictures too.

"Nothing bad will happen," he said. I didn't answer, and he came to the bed and crouched on his knees in front of me. He gathered both my hands in his, and after a while spoke again. "When do I get to see you again? How about next Sunday? Magda can have you Saturday night as a gesture of goodwill. But after that we have to take turns."

"And maybe soon I'll have Fridays too."

"Yeah, good girl. Keep working on that." He brought my fingers up to his mouth and kissed them bunch by bunch. I lowered my face and kissed his beautiful bean red hair. Then he got up and we forced ourselves back to the ballroom, where he said goodbye to Marina and Blitz. I walked him out to the hallway. The elevator, for once in its creaky, stinking life, didn't take ten years to come.

"I'll call you," he said, pulling me close to kiss him as the doors began to close on us. I stepped away and watched him go.

"Everything's okay," he said, and then he disappeared.

But once inside my room again, I climbed on the chair and started fixing my animals, sitting them up and putting them in their order, trying to make things right again. Then suddenly I stopped. I looked back down around my room. It was darker now, yet light fell over my rumpled bed, shadows in the blankets where Will and I had messed them up. I stepped from the chair and pushed it back against the wall. I tried not to look at the animals. "Fuck it," I said, though the word sounded false coming out of my mouth. I went to my shelf and looked at the feather, bone and rock. I didn't touch them, I swear to God. And I didn't move the pictures. Except for one, I had to, the one of my father and me, on the stormy day at the edge of the sea.

Chapter 19

CARLA SLEPT till Monday. That's when I saw her next, at least, an apparition in green striped pants and red plaid shirt.

"*Bonjour,*" she said as she came into the kitchen, where Marina and I were finishing breakfast, such as it was. She carried a beat-up suitcase, which she planted on the floor.

"What's this?" said Marina, glancing down. "I thought you were going to stay awhile."

"I thought so too. But after the party on Saturday I suddenly changed my mind."

"Was it really so bad?"

"It was wonderful. It made me realize I want to be home. I want to get on with the rest of my life." She sank to a chair and ran her hands through her splotchy hair. She looked somewhat better than she had, but still didn't look that great. And that outfit, God, even *I* wouldn't travel dressed like that.

"What are your plans?" Marina asked.

"I'm not quite sure. First I'll go back and see how it feels. Then, who knows? I was starting to think I could open some sort of restaurant. At the *casa,* I mean. Or maybe a bed-and-breakfast. Frank and I used to talk about that."

"Frank—a bed-and-breakfast?"

Carla smiled. "Of course, that couldn't happen. He'd want to hand-select the guests. Only beautiful people need apply."

"Are you really ready to be alone?"

"I won't be alone. I have very good friends in Old San Juan. Like the two of you, I burrowed away when Frank was sick, but now I'm going to reconnect. I decided not to wait ten years."

Marina smiled. "Our bad example inspired you."

"It positively frightened me."

"Well, I'm sure your friends will be really glad."

"And you also have to stay in touch. Not just with me, but with everyone else. Yvette and Flor and Stella. And sweet little Michael, he's such a love."

Marina smiled. "I'm having lunch with Yvette this week."

"Really? That's grand. And I'm all with Blitz—open up the house again. Air out the rooms. Redecorate." She had to be crazy. *Redecorate?* "As for you . . ." She turned to me. Her eyes were hardly pink at all now that she had slept. "You keep that Will. He's good for you. We don't want you getting carried off by some fifty-year-old Dane. Good luck with that girl," she added to Marina, meaning, of course, Amanda.

"I'll prevail," Marina said in a tone that made you know she would. The horny old guy didn't have a prayer.

"Thank you both so much again," Carla said as she picked up her bag. "I couldn't have done it without your help."

Marina and I escorted her down, then waited with her for a taxicab. It was a warm morning, the first this spring, and we talked about that—the weather—and how pretty everything looked in the park all feathery and green.

Carla said, "I'm expecting you to visit too. The house is gorgeous, thanks to Frank. Escape the cold next winter when you have a break from school."

"Sounds wonderful," Marina said as the doorman finally snagged a cab. Carla embraced her and thanked her again for everything. Then she turned to me.

"Good luck with *Snegurochka*. I wish I could have seen you dance." Holding me close, she whispered intensely into my ear, "Let go, Giselle. Get on with it!" She climbed into the car and rolled down the window to wave goodbye. I tried to find something in her face, some answer to what I'd never asked, but it was too late, she was already gone, taking it along with her, which I guess was what I wanted no matter what I told myself.

———

The next day, Tuesday, Magda showed up at our meeting place with yet another Fiona card—a glossy picture of a beach, on back of which she'd stuck a stamp.

"Tenerife," Magda explained. "They're heading home this week." She read aloud: " 'Wouldn't miss the end-of-year performance. Light of my life, I really want to see your lights.' "

The lights, by the way, really were improving; no one

had gotten a shock in days. The dancing was also shaping up, with everyone going the way they were supposed to go and remembering their steps. I was actually starting to love my role. The choreography was challenging, but at the same time it was fun to play my flighty Spring. I even kind of hammed it up, flitting around, waving my wand at the sparrows and clouds. And so, like that, the week went by.

The minute I entered the dressing room on Saturday, Liz pushed over and grabbed my arm.

"God, Giselle, what happened to you last weekend?" I told her about the memorial, and she said it sounded sad. Then breathlessly, as she pulled on tights under her towel: "We had to endure Eglevsky twice. It was absolutely heine-ous." Through a break in the bodies Sasha and Moira came into view (I knew they couldn't be far off) squeezed on a bench together, lattes in their laps.

"We missed you!" sang Sasha, peering between some arms and legs. "Did you and your mom jet off somewhere?" That was pretty funny. They'd freak if they knew we couldn't afford the tax on our apartment if it weren't for good old Blitz.

"Where'd you go?" demanded Eve, who I didn't even know was there.

"A fu-ner-al," mouthed Liz.

"Who died?" said Moira. You could tell she cared. And after I told her: "I guess he must have been pretty old." As if that made it okay to die.

In Madame Eglevsky's class I got a good place at the barre for once. She was in a lousy mood though, and limped

178

around while we did pliés, insulting people and poking them with her walking stick. To me she said, "Eet vas terrible news about dahling Frank." I nodded in my demi-plié and she walked away, not jabbing me.

I actually think that a Saturday off had been good for me. I was rested and strong and for once in my life, nothing was sore. I was good in Skouras's class as well and borderline great in Marina's class, which sometimes happens, even to me.

After class, the dressing room was hectic. A buzz of voices filled the air—moans and groans and noisy discussions of weekend plans. Sasha and Liz were having the usual argument that meant so much to the Western world—Café Europa or the diner on Fifty-seventh Street—while Moira pretended not to care, standing there like Lady Godiva brushing her hair. Somehow I managed to make my escape.

Out in the hall I bumped into Yumi, my mother's friend who actually isn't Japanese despite her name. I shouldn't be mean about Yumi, I know, since thanks to her we went to the garden store that day. But I just can't help it, she makes me crazy. She believes that rocks have magic power and that vegetables scream when you boil them.

"Giselle!" she cried on seeing me. "Where *is* your darling mother? It's lunch-and-leg-wax Saturday."

Marina, in fact, had just emerged from one of the studios down the hall. Amanda Reid was with her and crying fairly hysterically, using leg warmers for a handkerchief. They ducked back into the room again, and after what seemed like ages, Marina came out alone.

"Problems?" said Yumi, consulting her watch.

"Poor Amanda. She's been offered the place in Chicago Ballet."

"That's good, one would think—or wouldn't one?"

"It should be, of course, but her mother isn't doing well. Amanda's afraid to leave her now."

"Sickness is dreary," Yumi said.

"Amanda is the only child. Her father's been gone for years." Marina reached up and drew the ribbon out of her hair, releasing a mass of gold. She dropped her eyes to her manicured hands. "It's a choice she has to make herself. But I think her mother would want her to go. It's a brilliant opportunity that might not come around again. I think she ought to seize the day."

That, of course, is what Marina would have done. Without even thinking all that hard. She'd have left the mother in someone's "care" and gotten on with her gorgeous life. I started feeling queasy, and swamped with the need to get away. Nothing new, as you know by now. Fortunately, Marina and Yumi were on the verge of leaving too.

After I got away from them, I walked to Central Park. On the benches there, some bums and other lowlives slouched, but a few other normal pedestrians passed, and a couple of people were walking dogs. A group of young mothers came snapping along with their high-tech fold-up strollers. They looked so zippy and practical with their no-fuss haircuts and comfortable shoes, like people in astronaut training school. I had the feeling when I looked at them that, if asked for their opinion, they'd have told Amanda to leave her mother and take the job with the ballet. That life marches on. That really great jobs don't grow on trees. That her mother had already lived her life. One thing I knew was that none of them would think like me.

Sometimes I felt that nobody did. I could walk through crowds of people, millions of them really, and feel totally alone, like a Martian lobster from outer space.

⁓

On Saturday night Magda and I ate in our Mexican restaurant, and on Sunday I had my date with Will. Marina and Blitz were out, thank God, so we didn't have to chat with them or visit the plants or anything weird. He'd made a reservation at a restaurant across from Lincoln Center, and we walked there slowly, holding hands.

"I was really scared," he told me as we crossed Columbus Avenue. "I thought you might be mad at me for messing up your stuff."

"And I thought you might never call. That you'd realized how sick in the head I am."

"You don't know the meaning of sick in the head."

"Oh yes I do." Oh yes I did.

The restaurant was quiet. The matinee crowd was gathering up their *Playbill*s and slowly trickling out, and a peaceful lull was setting in before the later dinner hour. Will and I were led to one of the plush red booths, and a waiter set the menus down. Will ordered a couple of ginger ales, and then he said, "So when do I get my ticket?"

"What?"

"My ticket to *Snegurochka*." For once he said it not fooling around. "I really can't wait to see you dance. I think about it all the time."

"And I try *not* to think of it."

"Well, think of it now. What's the date?"

I stared at the menu, the words a blur. "If Magda's right, it's three more weeks. May twenty-fourth, Saturday night."

Will pulled out a pencil and scrawled the date on the edge of the paper tablecloth. He tore it off and stuck it in his pocket. Then: "While we're discussing big events, there's one I'd like to ask you to. But remember, Giselle, you're allowed to say no, like I could say no to the funeral thing."

"I owe you big for that one, Will."

"Believe me, Giselle, this invitation is right on par." He took a breath before going on. "See, every year we have this thing at my stupid school. They call it—don't laugh—Exchange Day. Anyway, the idea of it is to invite a guest who comes from another culture, but since nobody knows anyone from anywhere, everyone just invites a friend. So naturally I thought of you."

"Thanks, that's nice. But what does it entail?"

"Nothing. *Nada.* You just spend the day at my gorgeous school."

"You mean go to classes and stuff like that?"

"That's about it. So whaddya say? It happens next week on Friday."

"I'd have to get excused from school, but yeah, I guess. Maybe I could. As long as I don't have to talk and stuff—I mean, you know, in class."

"So you'll come? That's great! You won't have to say a word, I swear." Suddenly in the world's best mood, he popped his menu open and started suggesting things to eat.

When the waiter came back, Will ordered for the two of us. You'd think I'd feel shy or nervous, or worried again that something weird would get stuck in my teeth, but the truth of it was that Will and I were past all that. I don't know how it happened so fast, but somehow we were friends. Friends and something more.

It was after nine when we finally left the restaurant. It took ten years to reach my house; we kept stopping almost every block to lean against a tree and kiss, to press against a streetlamp or a Dumpster, a wall, whatever was there.

Chapter 20

PART OF ME never believed the day at Will's school would happen. I'd be struck by a bus, the world would end or I'd die in my sleep, the first known case of adolescent crib death in the history of the world. Even Magda thought it a pretty unlikely event. Marina wouldn't let me go, she'd grimly predicted as we trudged to school on Monday. Yet strangely enough, Marina didn't object at all. I mentioned it that evening as she and Blitz were heading out to dinner.

"A charming notion," Blitz declared. "East meets West and all of that."

"It does sound lovely," Marina said, "and you really should spend some time with Will. Starting next week, you'll have rehearsals every day. As a matter of fact, I doubt you'll be seeing him again till the night of the performance."

"That can't be right—" I quickly started to calculate. But of course it was true. Marina would know. In the final preperformance week there'd be daily rehearsals, sometimes two, including the weekend before the horrid week began.

"So of course you should go"—a slender smile—"and have a lovely time."

The week dragged on, horrible as usual, but despite my premonitions I woke on Friday still alive. At seven-fifteen Magda called to tell me what I shouldn't wear, and by eight o'clock there I was in Grand Central Station, ticket in hand, heading for my train. Unlike the night Magda and I had skated there on our make-believe lake of light, the station teemed with people now. A steady roar vibrated through the vast, bright space as streaming crowds poured from stairs and corridors into the central terminal. I increased my pace to stay in synch with everyone else, even though as usual I was going the opposite way. The lower level was a little more calm, though every few minutes another suburban train pulled in spewing new arrivals, swept away in a rushing, self-created wave.

After that, my train seemed very peaceful. There were hardly any passengers, and I settled near a window, my backpack beside me, *Nijinsky's Diary* on my lap. Even so, a loopty-doop of nausea made a circle through my stomach, so I guess I was pretty nervous too. I tried to read Nijinsky, thinking that would calm me down. But Nijinsky was psychotic, and it made me uneasy to read about some of the things he did. I closed the book and started to contemplate my clothes.

I stared at my knees and the toes of my shoes poking out from under my skirt. Magda had told me what to wear: this longish skirt, black of course, and over it a scoop-neck sweater, also black. The same jade earrings I wore to the museum that day. I also wore my gray all-purpose jacket, which Magda had told me not to wear.

Not that it seemed to matter to Will. The minute he saw me his face lit up like fireworks. I hopped from the train, and with just a couple of giant steps, he had me in his arms.

"Hey, Giselle, welcome to suburbia!"

"It's great to be here," I told his shirt, where my face was pressed deliciously.

"You say that now. We'll see how you feel in an hour or so."

"If I'm still with you, I'll still feel fine."

He drew me back and kissed my cheek. "You really looked great coming out of the train. Sometimes, you know, I see you and can't believe you're mine—not that I think I own you, but just that you're here, like, next to me." He wrapped his arm around me and we both began to walk. Ahead of us a plump old lady waved to a friend in a waiting car, and a mother shook out a stroller and stuck a little kid inside. A couple of railroad workers stood on the sidelines talking, but aside from them, there was nobody else. Delicate-looking, the tracks stretched on ahead of us, growing faint and small to a trailing-off line. The feeling of nausea stirred again, a ripple inside like a passing breeze that just as quickly floated off. Holding hands, we walked to Will's car, which was parked beneath a smallish tree shedding flowers crazily like something out of a haiku poem. He scooped up a mound of blossoms and I dunked my face right into them, all cold and wet and smelling like bark. The smell made me feel like crying, and then I felt like laughing as he tossed the petals into the air and they fluttered back slow motion, landing in our hair.

He opened the car and tossed my backpack into the back. Beside it on the seat was some other stuff that must have been June's—a Barbie Corvette, some dog-eared books and a muddy yellow boot. We climbed inside, but instead of turning the engine on, he reached across and pulled me close.

"I can't believe you're really here. I haven't thought about anything else. I mean it, Giselle, I'm losing my mind."

"Mine's already lost," I said, crushing my cheek against his shirt. It smelled of the soap they did laundry in, Tide or Cheer, whatever it was, and I clung there a while inhaling it. I hated when he pulled away and started up the car.

We left the station parking lot and drove through a town full of stores and stuff; then down some streets lined with smallish houses, low white fences hemming them. The scenery changed as we traveled along, and soon we crossed a wider road. After that, the houses were larger and more spread out, half hidden in the trees. Now and then a person crossed a wet green lawn, heading for a car.

Speaking of cars, I loved being in the car with Will. No one I know even has a car—except for Blitz and he doesn't count—and it seemed so sexy I thought I'd die. I realized that if we wanted to, we could pass Will's school completely and follow the road wherever it went, clear across the country to California even, and no one would ever know. I'd never felt so free before.

Will's school looked like a high school on TV, sprawling and low in the middle of a huge green lawn. Giant trees surrounded the lawn, and off to one side, beyond the rows of hedges and another stretch of bright green grass, dark brown bleachers rose above a pale brown field where groups of students jogged around. The parking lot, which was off to the other side of the school, was filled with about a million cars. Everywhere around us, doors were springing open and passengers were piling out, sometimes five or six of them.

"Wow," I said, "everyone comes to school by car?"

Will chuckled. "It's way uncool to take the bus. You might as well wear a Kick Me sign."

"Really?"

"Yeah. Even a goofy car like this is better than no car at all."

"Your car's not goofy."

"Compared to that one there it is." He pointed to a nearby car. "And this one here. And that one too." I looked at the cars. They were shiny and new and one was a convertible, but it didn't mean anything to me. I'm a total moron regarding cars. He turned off the engine and looked at me.

"Are you ready for this?" I nodded, but the funny twinge was back again. I guess I felt out of my element what with all the grass and trees and cars. Or was it the sight of the people emerging from those just-parked cars brandishing keys and cell phones, sunglasses flipped to the top of their heads? They seemed so—what? Adult, I think. They knew how to drive and park a car. They could probably read a map.

"Don't worry," said Will, "this place is a great big nothing, Giselle. There's nothing to be afraid of. And no one either. So just relax."

"I am relaxed," I told him. I sounded just like Carla on the verge of a cheese soufflé.

"Come on," he said, and reached in the back to grab our bags. He held my hand as we walked across the parking lot. A couple of people waved to him and Will waved back and yelled hello. When we'd almost reached the building, three girls came running up to us. Two were twins, blond and small and totally identical. The one in between was also blond but taller and sort of muscular, like someone who was good at sports.

"Wow!" said Will, laughing as he greeted them. "You brought Martha to Exchange Day?" He turned to me. "Martha's their cousin from down the block."

The taller girl laughed. "Yeah, so what? I go to another—much nicer—school."

"We can't help it," said one of the twins, "if we never go anywhere at all and never get to meet anyone." Pointedly she looked at me. I felt Will's hand against my back.

"May I present Giselle Parke-Vanova. Giselle—Samantha and Robby Dalwin and their exotic cousin, Martha, from five or six minutes away from here."

We all said hi, then the twin named Robby bubbled at me, "So you live in the city? It must be fun. We hardly meet anyone from there."

"And I never meet anyone from here—not, I mean, till Will."

"He's not a good example of us," the other twin, Samantha, said. "He's a total misfit really. We let him hang around with us because we're humanitarian."

"He likes to do crazy things with rocks," Robby said confidentially. "Has he taken you to the graveyard yet?"

"My rock construction," Will explained.

"When Mitzi dies—that's our cat—we're going to have her buried there." Will smiled, not seeming to mind, and

189

we drifted along in a cheery tide of people, everyone fooling around like that, smiling and even laughing as if going to school weren't hell on earth. Ahead of us, long low steps led to a bunch of open doors. WELCOME TO EXCHANGE DAY read a big cloth banner above the doors. Over it all, the American flag limply flapped.

The inside of Will's school was the complete opposite of the inside of Dante School. First of all, Will's school was bright, while Dante was dark like the dungeon it is. In Will's school, light streamed in through high clear windows along a hall lined with pale blue lockers shining in the sun. In Dante School, light eked through the grimy leaded portholes aided by flame-shaped forty-watt bulbs, so you practically had to feel your way to mummy class. We didn't have lockers either, which seemed like a really fun thing to have, not to mention useful.

To me, the lockers seemed like little rooms. One of them, for instance, was papered with flowered gift wrap, which gave it a sort of boudoir feel. A fancy mirror hung from the door, and its owner stood in front of it squirting hair spray all over her head. Another locker was plastered all over with glossy pictures of football stars and other football-related stuff. You knew the owner had OCD by how organized the pictures were and the way he'd lined his sneakers up, side by side, on the high top shelf. A little farther down the hall my eye was caught by an eerie-looking locker that must have belonged to some nerdball expert on World War II. Taped all over the inner walls were copies of ancient headlines announcing D-day and stuff like that, plus a really unnerving photograph of some parachute guys at an open hatch, just about to jump. Dead center on the open door was a poster of Winston Churchill slumped in a chair by a potted palm, smoking a fat cigar. I looked away from the weird dark hole, but some of the darkness followed me, a floaty shadow in all that light.

As we continued down the hallway, a lot of people greeted Will—athlete guys with rackets sticking out of their bags, punky guys and brainy geeks. Plus a lot of girls, who smiled over the piles of books pressed against their chests, all of which were bigger than mine. The speckled white floors, shiny as glass, stretched away forever through the endless, sunlit corridor.

We finally reached Will's locker.

"Give me your jacket. I'll stick it in here." He held my bag as I passed the jacket over. I felt his eyes graze over me. "I like your sweater. You really look nice."

"No I don't," I told him as he hung our jackets on two little hooks. I wanted to look at the pictures on his locker door, but a deafening bell began to ring, totally disconcerting me, so that all I recalled was a mass of notes and sketches like some madman might have made.

In Will's school they have this thing called homeroom. You may know what that is if you go to a normal school. Anyway, that's where we headed next. The place was packed with people, double the usual, I guess, but was even more chaotic due to the decorations—bright balloons and hanging paper streamers that tangled in your hair. An equal amount of streamers were lying on the floor. Will stayed close, his hand on my back as he introduced me to some of the kids: a guy named Paul with a guest from Someplace, Connecticut; a girl named Cindy with a guest from Japan who was living in Cindy's neighbor's house. A skinny girl

191

with green-streaked hair starting passing name tags out. They said, HI. MY NAME'S_____. WHAT'S YOURS? and we were all supposed to fill them out and stick them on our chest so everyone would know who we were. Will filled his name in as Ishmael.

After a while, an adult man's voice, obviously a teacher's, raised itself above the noise.

"All right, folks. Settle down. Grab a seat if there's one to grab. Ladies first is still an acceptable rule of thumb."

"Chauvinist!" yelled someone and everybody laughed. The hideous bell started ringing again, and after it stopped the room got pretty quiet and half of us were sitting down. Now I could see the teacher. He was Mr. Fitzgerald, his name tag said, and he looked like a teacher's supposed to look, in a tan tweed jacket, normal pants and a normal tie. Also his hair was normal and you couldn't see his underpants.

"Welcome, everyone," he said. "Sorry about the lack of chairs. One of these years we'll get this right." He said some Exchange Day–related stuff; why exchange was such an important thing, how even a small event like this was a broadening experience. You could tell that no one was listening, and Mr. Fitzgerald knew it too. Switching gears, he suggested that the "host students" present their guests, each of whom should say a few words about himself. I must have started trembling—Will promised I wouldn't have to talk—and he patted my shoulder, which didn't help.

The first person to get up said, "My name's Tom, in case you can't read. And I brought my buddy, Lloyd." Everybody started goofing on him, making rude noises and yelling stuff.

Mr. Fitzgerald looked at his watch. "We've got thirteen

minutes to do this, folks." He turned to Tom's guest. "I apologize for the manners of my students. Please, can you tell us a bit about yourself."

The guy, Lloyd, who had also been hissing at Tom, stood up. He was tall and huge with golden curls and a permanent smirk.

"So anyway, yeah, my name is Lloyd. I live in Hastings—" More boos and catcalls. "Yeah, I know, we trounced your football team this year. Forty-two to ten. I bring greetings from the Warriors—"

"Lloyd," said Mr. Fitzgerald, "can you tell us something regarding Lloyd?" Everyone laughed, including Lloyd.

"Oh yeah. I'm captain of the wrestling team and I'm also an ace at video games. Well, that's about all. The end." Everyone burst into loud cheers, and when Lloyd got back to his seat, Tom smashed his head with a chemistry book.

Next a girl named Janine introduced her guest, Melissa.

"Hi ya," said Melissa. She giggled and waved her fingers. "My name's Melissa but everyone calls me Lissy—except my dad, he hates that name. Well, anyway, it's really great to be here with my bestest friend, Janine." She waved to Janine. "Hi, Janine. We met playing tennis three years ago. We both love tennis, but totally. When we get old, like after college, we're going to open a tennis camp with our gorgeous tennis-pro husbands. Oh, and I live in Scarsdale." She giggled some more, the class clapped and Tom and Lloyd pretended to volley some balls at her.

Then suddenly it was my turn. You might wonder how I could be nervous following Lloyd and Lissy, but anyway, I was. I started to do my counting-backward-in-French routine as Will got up and said who I was. It helped a little, though not very much, that he stayed where he was beside me instead of going back to his seat. Everyone was quiet now, and staring like you can't believe. *Dix, neuf, huit.*

"Yes, I'm Giselle. It's great to be here. I've never been to a school like this. My school is like a dungeon—actually, it used to be a hospital."

"What school is that?" Mr. Fitzgerald wanted to know, and when I told him he looked impressed. He explained to the class that Dante was a school for "professional young people." As if that could be a profession. Janine asked if anyone famous went there. I told her about the few actually well-known students, two of them actors, plus Vincent Falco from Flinch, as you know, and Zora, the world-famous jeans model, which seemed to impress them out of their minds.

Then Mr. Fitzgerald said, "I think the most famous people Giselle knows are her own parents." He smiled at me. "Grigori Vanov. Marina Parke-Vanova, yes?" He turned to the class, a sea of empty faces. "The famous ballet dancers? Are all you people troglodytes?" He shook his head, seeming deeply depressed. "Are you going to be a dancer too?"

"It looks that way," I answered, which caused a ripple of sympathetic laughter. After that I wrapped things up. "So anyway, as Lissy said, it's really fun to be here. And as Lloyd said, that's about all, the end." Everybody laughed and clapped for me. Especially Will. I looked at him, and he gave me a smile that made me die.

After me, the rest of the guests got up and talked. Almost everyone came from a nearby town or just went to a different school, except for Misao, who as I mentioned was from

Japan. "I love America," she said, closing her speech, which inevitably caused a lot of crazed saluting and some off-key renditions of "The Star-Spangled Banner." Mr. Fitzgerald looked really relieved when the earsplitting bell blared out again and the thirteen minutes had run their course.

Chapter 21

A<small>T THIS POINT</small>, the class broke up and everyone went their separate ways. I went with Will and some of the homeroom people to chemistry, a subject I'd never studied. Mr. Bluth, the teacher, didn't give the regular class, nor the usual Friday-morning quiz. Instead, he gave a class on chemical reaction in honor of Exchange Day, which was, he said, a kind of social experiment in the mixing of human elements. He was quite a philosophical guy. The class was quite intriguing too, though I couldn't tell you what combinations caused what events to happen. I can say this: be very careful about what you mix together. Violent bubbling can occur. Ditto for noxious fumes.

After chemistry we went to what everybody called "World Civ," where we saw a film, I swear to God, on mummies. Will sat next to me, our desks touching because there were so many extra desks in the room. I loved sitting there with the shades drawn down and Will's kneecap grazing mine, as up on the screen they ransacked Tutankhamen's grave. Strangely enough, I did learn something during class. I learned what a genuine expert Mr. Lenox really was, never mind his underpants. Next to him, Will's World Civ teacher was a total mummy amateur.

Lunch was next. It took place in this giant cafeteria, all bright and cheery and washed with light. It was totally full of people and the noise was unbelievable—roaring voices, crashing trays and a throbbing bass of music that seemed to be coming from the walls.

"Hungry?" Will queried next to my ear as he placed himself behind me and steered me to a line. I nodded, my eyes roving over the steaming silver bins of food and piles of shrink-wrapped sandwiches. At Dante School we don't have food—you have to bring lunch or go out to eat—so the whole idea of an actual cafeteria was really an amazing thing. On the wall near the kitchen someone had hung a bunch of signs announcing the special Exchange Day fare. FOODS OF OTHER LANDS. EGG ROLLS FROM CHINA. PIZZA FROM ITALY. MEXICAN TACOS (with a pair of maracas dancing around).

"Pizza," Will marveled with make-believe awe as we took two trays and slid them along a silver edge. "What eez theez strange, mysterious food?" We took some other exotic stuff, which Will insisted on paying for, then roamed around trying to find a place to sit. Suddenly a voice yelled out: "Will! Strange girl! Over here!" We turned toward the sound and the skinny guy it came from, who was standing at a table with one long, thin arm and a snaky leg coiled around two empty chairs.

"Yo, Nick," said Will. And over his shoulder, "That's Nick, Giselle." We threaded our way to the table, and Nick released the furniture.

"Some zoo," he said in greeting. "Do you know what violence I had to commit to keep these for the two of you?" Then, "Hi," he added. "I be Nick."

I put down my tray. "I'm Giselle."

"The famous Giselle." Nick's head was long and bony with blue-black hair standing up in spikes. His lips were thin; they were hardly lips, and didn't seem inclined to smile. The smile happened in his eyes, which were dark, intense and warm.

"Sit," he ordered, pulling out one of the chairs for me. "Will, over there with your poo-poo plate." Nick sat down beside me and crossed his endless legs. He was smooth and graceful when he moved, with hands as dainty as a girl's.

"So where's your guest?" Will asked him.

"Oh, didn't I tell you? Really? So totally insignificant I guess I forgot to mention it. I've been what's commonly known as dumped." The thin mouth managed a mangled smile.

"You're kidding."

"Right. My kooky humor knows no bounds."

"Shit," said Will. "When did it happen?"

"The e-mail arrived sometime last night."

"She broke up with you by e-mail?"

"She thought it would be 'kinder.' Why torture ourselves with an ugly scene?" Nick turned to me. "I'm always making ugly scenes. You can't go anywhere with me."

"Anyway, that sucks," said Will.

"Distinctly. On the other hand, she was driving me kind of crazy. Not only that, I was starting to neglect my fish."

"Nick has fish," Will told me.

"What do you mean by fish?"

Nick furrowed his brow and stroked his chin, a chicken

leg poised in his other hand. "A fascinating question. Yes, what do we really mean by fish?" He turned to Will, who told him I was deep. Then he explained, "Nick raises fish, the tropical kind. They're so happy in his El Caribe fish tanks that they reproduce like crazy and he sells them to pet stores all over town." Nick pulled out a card from the saggy pocket of his shirt. It read SOMETHING FISHY, his address and telephone underneath.

"And now it's back to business," he said. "No more chicks. Only fish." He raised his can of Diet Sprite. "To fish!" he toasted. "And to Will and Giselle. May they never break up. At least not out in cyberspace." We watched him gulp from the tilted can. When he surfaced for air, he regarded his plate, which was piled high with mismatched food—chicken legs, a taco, some fried brown rice and an ice cream sandwich melting through its paper wrap. He picked up a fork as if he were going to stab himself.

Suddenly from somewhere, Robby, Samantha and Martha appeared, exhausted-seeming and out of breath, reminding me vaguely of you-know-who from ballet school.

"Hi, Will."

"Hi, Giselle."

"Hi, weird Nick."

They had only one tray among them, which was heaped with bags from some of the many vending machines lining the walls. They plunked it down and looked around with big wide eyes.

"Like, hey, you guys, do you think you could maybe, like, get us some chairs."

Nick asked if they looked like the Great White Chair Hunters or something, but he and Will got up to search.

Robby and Samantha quickly filled the vacated chairs and started to tear at the bags of chips.

"So how was the morning?" Samantha asked.

"Fun," I said. "Chemistry was interesting—"

"Did Bluth do his little magic show?"

"Personally," said Martha, "I found that disgusting. And dangerous."

With a scrape of chairs Will and Nick were back again.

"You're angels," said Martha, flopping down. Trays slid as the seating rearranged itself.

"Just for that," Samantha said, "we'll let you come to our party tonight."

"What party is that?" Will queried.

"The one we just decided to have. Exchange Day and all. Won't it be fun?"

"Yeah," said Nick, "like a broken arm."

"Nick," said Robby softly, "a party's exactly what you need."

"We heard about Lauren," Samantha said.

"How in hell—she doesn't even go to this school!"

"We have our sources, stupid. The point is that we're sorry. We think she's a total bitch."

Robby agreed, "She was always a bitch."

"All this time you thought I was going out with a bitch?"

"They're just trying to be nice," said Will.

"Yeah," said Robby. "We're being nice. And Lauren's not invited. So you'll come, all right? We're inviting practically everyone and all the kids from the other schools."

Will looked across the table at me. "What do you think?"

"I don't know. With Saturday class—"

Samantha popped a soda can. "You go to school on *Saturday*?"

"Not to school. I have ballet classes, three of them."

"Three?" yelped Robby, assaulting a bag of corn chips. "Isn't that kind of—much?"

"It's normal," I said. "When you dance, I mean." They were listening politely as they chewed their chips and pretzels and little packaged cheese ball things. I realized I probably couldn't explain to them. I couldn't explain to anyone who didn't actually do it too. Sometimes I couldn't explain to myself.

"I guess you love it," Robby said when after a moment I didn't go on. "It just sounds like kind of a drag to me. I mean, every single Saturday. When do you get to sleep?"

"Did you ever hear of night?" said Will.

"She doesn't mean that kind of sleep," Samantha answered patiently. "She means quantity sleep. Like the kind that lasts till it's time to get up for dinner."

"What does it matter anyway?" Robby said with a giant shrug. "The party's tonight, not Saturday."

That, I certainly couldn't explain even if I had a month. *My mother won't let me.* They'd laugh themselves sick.

"We'll try to work it out," said Will.

"They'll be there," Samantha said so it sounded like a threat. She made a pile of the empty cellophane packages, then they all got up and went off to invite the rest of the world.

"What the hell, let's go tonight," Will suggested cheerfully.

"I'd like to," I said, "but it'll be late."

"What if I drive you home?"

Nick leaned forward and tapped my arm. "I'll go if you go. But only if."

"And if Nick doesn't go, he'll sit at home and pine," said Will. "Already he has ceased to eat." Grinning, Nick chomped the taco, then shoveled some chicken into his mouth. We watched him devour the pile of rice and soon after that the ice cream soup. When he was finished, we went outside.

We stood around with a bunch of other people in a kind of cement patio hemmed with hedges and rows of shrubs. The sun felt good and the air had the smell of fresh-cut grass. But my stomach was feeling really weird. All that food from other lands, I guessed.

Calculus, which happened next, was a total blur. I had no idea what anyone was talking about, and the elaborate mathematics scribbled on the blackboard might as well have been the hieroglyphics Mr. Lenox likes to draw next to his mummy cats and mice. On top of that, I was feeling queasy in the extreme. Only now I'd figured out what it was.

By the time I got to a bathroom, the blood had already seeped through my tights and was starting down my leg. Thank God I'd worn black. And thank God Will's school had dispensing machines. At Dante we don't have any equipment like that, as if we're all nymphs from the forest glade. I feel I should explain to you that the reason I was so surprised is because, like a lot of skinny dancers, as I think I mentioned earlier, I have very irregular periods. I hadn't had one in quite a while and I guess I'd forgotten the warning signs. The good news was that now a lot of things made sense. Like the way I'd felt like crying all day without really feeling sad. And the twinges in my lower parts.

As I dropped the money into the slot, some girl came in and dug for nickels of her own. "I wish I was a guy," she said. I smiled at her, thinking of Magda, who unlike most girls loves when she gets her period. It makes her feel like a goddess, she says, in synch with the moon and cosmic tides.

I tried to look normal when I came back out. Will was standing there and I got the feeling we were late since not many people were walking around.

"Are you okay?" he asked me.

"Yeah," I said, and we hurried down the hall to French.

Mademoiselle Arlen was one of those perky, fun-type teachers you sometimes read about in books. She wore red high heels and a little red skirt, and half the guys were probably in love with her. Anyway, she made us pretend that the classroom was a café—Le Chat Blanc—on the Rive Gauche in Paris. Everybody got a role to play by picking a paper out of a hat—*garçons, jeunes filles* and *jeunes hommes*. Will ended up being a waiter and Nick, who was finally in a class with us, was a *jeune fille*. Another guy had to be the *jeune homme* at the table. The guy told Nick he was yellow and pretty and had a monumental nose. They ordered coffee, snails and grapes.

In English, the class pored over a Gerard Manley Hopkins poem, which they'd apparently been poring over for quite a while to no avail. It was about a "darksome burne" in a brook in Scotland called Inversnaid, only you had to know from the outset that "burne" meant "small waterfall" instead of burn like with cigarettes. It was the only class all day long where I had any clue what was going on.

From there we went to gym, where we were supposed to play volleyball. I have no idea how to play any kind of ball games, so I was allowed to sit and watch while a student with a broken tibia explained what was going on. This was good, since I didn't feel much like jumping around. Then that ear-crushing bell sounded again, and school was over for the day.

Everyone was suddenly in the world's best mood. Will

and I went to his locker to get our stuff, then let ourselves be swept along in the one-way wave toward the exit doors. Outside, the day was still its gorgeous self. Shadows were long and deep on the grass, and a breeze was rustling through the trees. There was a mad rush to the parking lot, and almost at once the sound of engines and slamming doors.

Nick loped by. "Tonight," he threatened. "Eight o'clock or die."

"We'd love to, *jeune fille,* but we've got to see if Giselle can come."

"If she can't, you bastard, call me. This fête would be de trop alone." Nick turned to me. "I really hope you can come, Giselle. I'd love to have a chat with you about what you see in this ugly mutt." He made an exaggerated bow. Then, "Later, mutt," he said to Will and galloped off toward the parking lot.

When we got to Will's car, he came to the passenger side with me. I thought he was going to open the door, but instead he stood there looking at me. Then he leaned in and kissed my mouth. "I've been wanting to do that all day long. I thought I'd lose my mind. Stay," he whispered. "Stay and come to the party tonight. I really want to be with you."

Chapter 22

WILL'S HOUSE WAS just as I remembered it, if maybe a bit more shabby in the brighter light of day. The white of the shingles seemed grayish now and dark green paint peeled around the window frames and chipped from the backs of the wicker chairs. The wooden steps sagged gently from people going up and down. One of those people, June, emerged from the house as we parked the car. Solemn and still, she stood at the rail like a child queen, watching with her grave green eyes. From behind the door, Smiley's yelps grew high and shrill.

"Hey, bug," said Will as we mounted the steps.

"Hi, Giselle," she said to me.

"Hi there, June. I like your dress."

"It isn't really a dress, you know. It's a sweatshirt of my mom's."

"And it isn't a belt, it's a sock," said Will.

Still looking at me and not at him: "It isn't a sock. It's a bathrobe sash."

"And it goes with the dress—shirt—great," I said. She beamed at me, then glanced at Will triumphantly. As if I had a fashion clue.

When we got inside, Mrs. Brooks came out of the hall to the living room. I was struck again by how young she looked. She wore khaki pants and a polo shirt and cradled some schoolbooks in her arms. A pencil poked out of her ponytail. "Hi, you guys," she greeted us. She kissed me first, then pecked at Will. "So how was the day? How did you enjoy Will's school?"

"It was great," I said. "And the school's so pretty, it really is."

"So you met the gang? And Nick, of course."

"Yeah, I did. They were really nice." My command of the English language must have really dazzled her.

"Speaking of that," Will started, "Samantha and Robby are having one of their parties tonight. They invited Giselle and we'd like to go—"

"How fun. That's great."

"Giselle has ballet tomorrow, so I thought if I could drive her home—"

"Oh, Will. I'm sorry, I need the car. We've got our study group tonight. I'd ride with Jill, but her father's in the hospital and—"

"It doesn't matter," I quickly said. "It's probably not a good idea. What with class in the morning and . . ."

"Or else, you know . . ." She pulled the pencil out of her hair and touched it to her cheek. "You could stay and spend the night with us. Nick can pick you up tonight and Will, you're off tomorrow. In the morning you can drive her home. June, I'm sure, will give you her room and she can bunk with me."

"Yippee!" yelled June, who had followed us in and was jumping all around the place.

"Could you?" Will ventured softly.

"I don't know." The panic quivered in my voice as I instantly started mumbling stuff—like how hard it would be to get to Manhattan by ten o'clock. How I had to get eight hours of sleep. I heard myself go on and on. I even mentioned the scholarship, which I swear I never brag about, and how scholarship students *especially* are never late or lousy in class. All of it was true, of course, but it wasn't the reason really, the one I could never, ever explain. Even June would think it infantile that I couldn't sleep away from home.

"Well, think it over," said Mrs. Brooks, clearly sensing that something was wrong. "We'd really love to have you. I'd be just as thrilled as June."

"Thanks," I said, not meeting her gaze. I looked at Will, sure he was going to pressure me. Instead he suggested we go to the kitchen and get a drink.

"I know," he said when we were alone, "you want to get the hell out of here. I guess I can't really blame you for that."

"Can I have that drink you offered me?"

"I mean why in hell would you want to hang out in a place like this. I'm sorry I put you through the day."

"Stop it, Will. I loved the day."

"What is it then? I know it can't be your ballet class."

"Classes," I said. "There are three of them. And because of that—I know it sounds insane to you, but I'm not allowed out on Friday night. I have to, you know, sleep."

He looked at me blankly. "That's totally lame."

"I know it is, and like I told you the other day, I'm working on my mother—I am."

"That's bullshit, Giselle."

"You don't understand—"

"That's right, I don't."

"Well, I can't explain."

"Just be honest. You don't want to stay."

"I *do* want to stay. It's just, I—*can't*."

"What are you afraid of?" He was staring at me really hard. "Do you think I'm going to, I don't know—*attack* you in your sleep?"

"Of course not, no." The blood was hot as it rushed to my face. I looked away as if that could keep him from seeing the blush. "I'm sorry, Will, I guess I'm just not ready."

"Not ready for what? Not ready to have a boyfriend?"

"Don't say that, please."

"It's true, though, right? If you have a boyfriend—for real, I mean—you can't keep being a little kid. And that's what you're afraid of." He was like some guy with a fishing pole, perking up as he reeled it in. "It's the same with the stupid animals in your room. If we move 'em around, if we mess them up, you think your life is going to change. And you're totally scared to death of that."

"I let you move them, didn't I?"

"You probably put them back in place the minute I was gone."

"I didn't, Will. I swear to God!" My voice sounded crazy, even to me, and I took a breath before speaking again. "I started to fix them, but then I stopped."

"Why?"

"Because . . . I wanted to. And it isn't true that I like my life the way it is."

"Really? Well, if you don't, then the thing you have to do right now is call your mom and tell her you're going to stay tonight. If that's what you really want, that is."

"You know it is. Don't you, Will?"

"I'll know it when you do it." I turned from his gaze and ran my eyes along the kitchen counter. Scenes began to play in my head: Will and I together at a party; laughing and acting normal, talking to the kids from school. I imagined the place where the party would be; it looked like a party you'd see on TV with big soft couches everywhere and hardly any light. I imagined dancing slow with Will in some shadowy corner of the room. Then I imagined him taking me home, home to here, the place he lived. Kissing me in a doorway. Taking me up the stairs. And suddenly, from out of that daydream I heard my voice. It sounded like my voice, at least, though I hadn't told myself to speak. Then Will was lifting me off the ground, yelling yippee hooray like June, so I knew I'd said yes, though I didn't know how and didn't fully believe I had.

"You can call from my room," he told me, pulling me from the kitchen and through the cluttered living room, quickly, quickly as if afraid I'd change my mind. We followed a pale blue runner up the stairs and through the upper hallway, which was light and bright and filled with watery-looking sun. There were rooms on either side of the hall, all doors open except for one. That, of course, was Will's room.

It was dark inside in contrast to the sky blue hall, thanks in part to the windows being blocked with plants—giant mutant-looking things he'd rescued, he said, from the Dumpster at Patio & Pool. The floor was completely cluttered with stuff—rocks and wood, cans of paint and plaster, and messy heaps of tools. All around were piles of books and, occupying one side of the room, a scaffolding he must have built that sagged with the weight of a million CDs and a broken statue of a saint, probably from the Dumpster too. A normal-looking bureau dribbled sleeves and pant legs from halfway-opened drawers. Then it happened, this really weird thing.

Out of the chaos, the mbis poles began to emerge. At first you didn't notice them, but suddenly, everywhere, there they were. The first one I saw was on the shelf separating *Moby Dick* and the poems of Ezra Pound. About twelve inches high, it was a rougher version of one of the totems in his book. After that, I spotted one on the windowsill, half hidden in a vine. Then two on a chessboard on top of a crate. How many others were there, staring out of the dark at me?

"You can pick them up," Will told me.

And so I did, taking one of them in my hands. "I can picture them huge," I whispered. "They're so powerful-looking, even small." I was on my knees beside the crate, and his hand dropped softly into my hair. Reaching up, I took his fingers in my own. Weirdly, I wanted to put them in my mouth; they just seemed so special, these fingers and hands that carved such tiny amazing things. From a pile of junk he excavated a telephone. I moved to the bed and he set it heavily on my lap. Then without a word he left the room.

The phone was an ancient rotary type and weighed about a ton. For a while I just sat and stared at it—at the oversized receiver and the big white numbers in the circles of the big black disc. I wasn't ready to dial yet, and I let my eyes go drifting off, to the soft and saggy mattress and the thin, worn cover on the bed with its tie-dyed pinwheels of purple and gray. I stared at the dizzy circling shapes, then let my eyes roam up the walls. The ceiling, I saw, was painted with cryptic marks and signs that looked like the symbols in calculus. I studied the images for a while, following arrows and dots and swirls. Then my eyes fell down to the phone again, and the horrible wave of terror hit. I knew I couldn't stay at Will's. How had I ever thought I could? I would wake in the night and be deathly sick. I would lose control and have some sort of episode where I'd gag on my tongue and vomit, then have convulsions on the floor, my swollen face gone blue. I pushed the telephone off my lap and sat there in a slump.

I stared at Will's pillow, a silent mound. Then I pulled the cover away from it and pressed my face to the place where his would lie at night. It was cool and soft, the pillowcase worn and thin, like silk. I closed my eyes and pictured him. I imagined how he'd look asleep. Smooth white eyelids, tranquil mouth. I imagined the sound of his dreaming breath, slipping softly in and out. I pulled myself up and stared at the telephone again. But the sight of it almost made me sick. I folded forward and pressed my head between my knees. I was hot to the touch and cold inside. Or maybe it was the opposite. Whatever it was, it felt all wrong. I breathed for a while upside down.

What if I just went home right now? I could catch a train and by five o'clock I'd be stepping into the dark foyer. Marina and Blitz would be having drinks in the reading room, the way they did each evening, and of course they would invite me in. How was the day, they would want to know, as they offered me a ginger ale and some slippery hors d'oeuvre. Nipper would assault me and soon it would be time to eat. After that I'd go to bed, and in the morning I'd get up and go to ballet class like every Saturday of my life. For a moment I let the scene sink in, then very slowly I eased back

211

up. I ordered my finger to dial the phone. The metal disc spun slowly, scraping as it turned. On the seventh ring Marina picked up. My mouth was dry as wood.

"Hi. It's me." My voice felt weird coming out of my throat.

"Hello, darling. How was the day?"

"It was really great."

"I'm glad you enjoyed it." She sounded glad.

"There's a party tonight. And I want to go."

She paused for a moment. "It's Friday, you know."

"I know it is."

"And there's class tomorrow."

"I know that too. Mrs. Brooks invited me to spend the night. Will said he could drive me home early, in time for class."

An even longer, stiller pause. Then her voice again, strange and light: "You want to spend the night, Giselle?"

I swallowed drily. "Yes."

"That's"—Her voice was soft and breathless because, of course, *she* knew. She and Magda and Dr. Sloop. She finished the phrase—"just fine."

The panic uncoiled like a waiting snake. What had I done? Oh God. How could she *let* me? *How?*

"Remember, Giselle, you can always call. . . ."

I sucked in air. "Why would I call?"

"If you change your mind. Whatever."

"I won't," I said, fixing my gaze on a tie-dye swirl that started to spin like a crazy top.

"All right then, darling. Have a good time. And thank Mrs. Brooks for inviting you." Then she added softly, "You know, Giselle, the world wouldn't end if you missed a class."

"What?" I couldn't have possibly heard her right.

She said it again in different words: "It's all right if you miss Eglevsky's class."

"It is?"

"It is. I'll tell her. I'm happy you're doing other things." For a couple of seconds I couldn't speak. If I wasn't already sitting down, I would've had to find a chair.

Finally I murmured, "I'll skip it then. If you're sure it's okay."

"I'll see you afterward."

"Yeah. Okay."

"*Bonne nuit* then, darling."

" 'Night."

I hung up the phone and sat there, stunned. There was a soft tap on the door and Will poked his head in. I breathed, I stirred. I covered up the pillow so that he wouldn't see that I'd tried it out.

"So how'd it go?"

"Okay."

He came inside. "I knew she wasn't going to freak. I know you don't believe it, but I think she wants you to have a good time. Be happy, you know, and shit like that."

"Be happy?"

"Yeah. Happy and seminormal. Like everyone says we're supposed to be." He sat beside me on the bed, pushing the telephone away. She wanted me normal, that I knew, though not in the way Will meant it, but truly normal, not sick in the head like the way I was.

Mrs. Brooks was pleased when we told her I'd stay. She insisted on getting me "settled in," and took me back upstairs again.

"Here we are," she said with a smile as she brought me

into June's room. Everything was blue and white—the gingham curtains, the fluffy rug and the ruffled pillows all over the bed. I looked around at the toys and games, clustered into little groups, strangely neat and organized compared to everything else in the house. An army of dolls stood in line on a narrow shelf very much like my balcony, while a lower ledge held dozens of small stuffed animals arranged in order, as I could tell. White-framed pictures of puppies, seals and other baby mammals dotted the pale blue walls.

"June's quite neat," said Mrs. Brooks. "Unlike someone else we know. She got it from her father."

"I'm that way too. It's like a disease."

"Not at all. It's a wonderful trait. I wish I had a bit of it." She pulled back the bedspread, also light blue gingham, and started yanking off the sheets.

"I can do that—"

"Don't be silly—I'll do it later anyway. I'll show you where the bathroom is." Along the way, she stopped at a hallway closet and pulled out a bunch of towels and sheets.

"How about a toothbrush? I've got a whole supply."

"I've got one in my bag," I said. "I'm kind of a nut about brushing my teeth." My eyes ran over the cluttered shelves loaded with health and beauty aids, but I didn't see what I needed most. I guess I was pretty obvious because she asked me softly, "Anything else?" I know it sounds really immature, but I felt embarrassed to ask for what I needed. I probably wouldn't have asked at all and just used toilet paper wads if June's bed wasn't such pale celestial blue.

"Actually," I mumbled, "I got my period today. It was kind of a surprise."

"Isn't it always?" she said with a smile. "Don't give it a thought. I'm well equipped." Postponing the scheduled bathroom tour, she took me to her room. It was big compared to June's, with a huge brass bed that she shared with her husband, I supposed, before he lost his mind. She'd probably redone the place after he moved to the firehouse, because everything was rose or pink or covered with flowered chintz. I can't say the room was a total mess, but it also wasn't neat. You could tell she was pretty busy and always in a hurry because of the things that were lying around—handouts from school, grocery lists, store receipts she was probably meaning to put somewhere.

"You can see who Will takes after," she said as she opened a bureau drawer. "Here, Giselle, take what you need."

"Thank you," I said. I took a few tampons and some pads.

"Take these too," she said, pressing some underpants into my hand. "I really can't use them. They're much too small." I looked at them dumbly. I really didn't know what to say. No one had ever given me underpants before. She glanced around, and after a minute found a little shopping bag. We dropped the articles into it, and she smiled again and asked, "All set?" I told her yes and thanked her, and after that we went downstairs.

June and Will were fooling around in the kitchen, and when June saw us she started yelling all over again, "Hooray! You're sleeping over! And I'm sleeping with my mom!" She turned around to Mrs. Brooks. "Can we have popcorn in bed tonight?"

"Sure we can. If you're good for Kim."

"Kim? But—" Kim, I surmised, was the babysitter, and

215

judging by June's stricken face, she had just discovered that all of us were going out. She froze like she did when doing her Enemy Statues thing, and her eyes filled up with tears. She bit her lip till the blood drained out, but the tears plopped over anyway. They were really huge, each the size of a champagne grape, slithering down her cheeks. To cheer her up, Will told her we'd play with her awhile. We went out in the yard and played hide-and-seek, and after that drew some pictures in the sand encircling Will's rocks. We tried to play catch for a little while, but Smiley kept intercepting the ball, refusing to give it back. But it was fun and it got June into a better mood.

After a while Mrs. Brooks came out to say goodbye. She had changed into white jeans and a blazer, and looked like a total college kid. She told Will and me to have a great time. To June she said: "I won't be late. And we'll have that popcorn in bed, okay?"

Not long after that, Kim, the babysitter, came. She was about fourteen, I guess, but she looked more like forty with all the makeup she was wearing and her piled-up, dyed hair. She was chewing a wad of gum about the size of a golf ball. From her big pocketbook she pulled out a bunch of gum packets, which she used to lure June into the house. "I'm allergic to grass," she told us, "and trees and nature and stuff like that."

After they went inside Will asked if I wanted to do anything to get ready for the party, like wash my face or something, and I said that yeah, I did. Upstairs in June's room, I saw that Mrs. Brooks had turned down the bed and had left a nightgown there for me. It was clean and white and smelled like Will's shirts. If I woke in the night I could smell it, I thought, and I wouldn't be afraid. *Don't think of that.*

Don't think of the night. I snatched up a towel and headed for the bathroom, where I splashed cold water onto my face. I looked at myself in the mirror on the cabinet. I could have looked better, that was for sure, but there wasn't much that I could do. I brushed a little mascara on and smoothed some lip gloss over my mouth. Then I hurried back to June's room. Ten seconds later Will peeked in.

"Ready?" he said, stepping inside. He was wearing a black shirt and black pants and he looked very dark and good. He glanced around the room. "My mom gave you towels and stuff, I guess. And something to wear—to sleep, I mean?" I pointed to the nightgown. He came over to where I was standing and kissed me. "Can I see you in it later on?" I didn't say anything and he kissed me again. I felt his tongue at the edge of my mouth.

"You taste like—what is it—cherries?"

"It's lip stuff," I mumbled. I couldn't tell him passion fruit.

"Lip stuff, hmm. I like it." He pulled me close against him. My breasts were sore, but the hurt was soft and gushy and melted in the heat of him. Below, outside, an engine revved. An impatient horn began to beep.

June hollered up the stairs, "Skinny Bones is here for you!"

"Like we couldn't hear him!" Will yelled back. He pulled away and smiled at me. "Ready?"

"Yeah." I smiled back. I was ready, oh yes. Like those parachute guys were ready—the ones in the picture taped inside that locker door—on the brink of thin, gray air.

Chapter 23

"YOUR CHARIOT AWAITS," said Nick as Will and I emerged from the house. At curbside, a grimy heap of metal sputtered softly and gave off smoke. Nick opened the passenger side for me. "Let the muttface sit in back." We followed his orders and climbed inside, Will squeezing in with a bunch of cardboard boxes piled on the seat. Nick slammed the gas pedal and we lurched away.

"So," he said when the wheezing and sputtering faded out. "You haven't yet explained to me what you see in this mangy mutt."

"She likes me for my mind," said Will.

"Well, I think she ought to be warned about that. Forewarned is forearmed and all of that."

"Yeah, but who needs four arms?" I dizzily quipped.

Nick agreed. "Just two's a responsibility."

"I'd like to have four arms," said Will.

"And I know what you'd use them for."

"You ought to be spayed," Will told him. The conversation went on like that, the two of them sniping back and forth, exchanging insults cheerily. As for me, once we were really driving, I hardly even talked. I was too enthralled about being where I actually was—in a car with two guys, heading for a party somewhere in suburbia on an actual Friday night.

The car thing alone—the sense of escape and freedom of that—made me feel almost drunk. As we flew along, the world outside my window unfurled itself like a paper scroll, and I lost myself in the dark, exotic scenery—the driveways and lawns and houses nestled distantly. We crossed a few small bridges—a "burne" went rushing under one—and soon we turned onto a smaller road, its entrance marked by two enormous pillars. After that, we seemed to be in a separate place, as if we'd entered a huge pale tent. Through the branches of trees you could see the houses here and there, all spread out and big and bright. In one, golden light beamed in every window, so it looked like a giant lantern hanging in the sky.

"Chez Twins," said Nick as we nose-dived into a parking space. Other cars were parked in the vicinity, though elsewhere in the neighborhood there were none in sight, sealed, I supposed, in the massive garages attached to the homes. Nick flicked off the engine.

"I hope I don't get towed," he said. "In places like this, they'd take my gorgeous car for scrap."

"That could happen anywhere," Will said lightly, reaching over to squeakily open the door for me.

The house didn't look like a lantern up close. It just looked like a humongous box with a lot of holes cut into it. Floodlights hidden in some bushes beamed on its coral-colored stone. We climbed some steps to get to the door, which was not in the front but on the side, and was twice the size of a regular door. The bell made a long, elaborate chime that was still sounding when a plump blond woman greeted us. Deeply tanned and shimmery in a peach-colored caftan and lots of golden jewelry, she glowed like a setting sun. She looked like she'd be hot to touch.

"Welcome, Will. Hello there, Nick!" You'd think she'd been waiting all day for them. Her bright blue eyes beamed onto me. "And you're the ballerina. Sam and Robby told us all about you." The other half of "us" appeared, a towering man, also tanned and friendly, who extended his hand to Will and Nick. We entered a light-filled living room, vast and pale, the color of sand. A gigantic sand-toned sofa curved around a low glass table, its surface covered with drinks and hors d'oeuvres and a petrified cactus center-piece. In the plush surrounding cushions another sun-tanned couple lounged, sipping from enormous globes.

"Pardon us for not getting up. We're exhausted," said the woman. "We've been up and down like jumping beans."

The man nodded and waved at us as if from a great dis-tance. Nick waved back and I said hi.

"Jim and Betty Molson," said the twins' father. "Our sea-faring companions with no sea legs." Whatever that meant. The twins' mother explained that they had just returned from a Caribbean cruise. We made a bit more small talk, then headed down a stairway cut into the floor like a huge trapdoor.

The downstairs looked a lot like the upper floor, though it felt like a basement. Which it was not. Through the slabs of slanting windows you could see the spotlights hidden in the bushes, so you knew you weren't underground, despite the feeling of being deeply buried like an unexploded atom bomb. The only light, aside from the spotlight beams, came from zillions of chili pepper lights hanging all over in flame red loops. Despite that it was darkish, you could see that the place was really packed. Still more people gathered on a porch outside, visible through some open doors. Kids I recognized from Will's school started saying hello and stuff and how great it was that I could come.

Martha appeared in a sexy black dress with rhinestone straps. "Hi, everybody," she greeted us. "Stuff to drink is thataway. Food's over there and there's more to come. Nick, you angel, tell me you brought us something good."

"That's why I'm here, babe, isn't it?" From somewhere on his person, Nick pulled out a pint. "But let's be a little discreet, all right?" Martha moved closer and held out her glass.

"Don't be stingy either. I'm sure you've got more in that hideous Batmobile outside. What the hell is this anyway?" She could've been someone's mother, that's how old she seemed to me, as she jiggled her glass and a slender strap slipped down her arm.

"Vodka, of course. Like I said, discretion counts."

"Discretion my ass. My aunt and uncle couldn't care less. We could be drinking turpentine. They've been at it themselves since five o'clock." Nick poured a quantity into her cup. "Thank you, Nicolai." Then to us: "Go get a drink and Nick the nurse will fix it up." We ambled to a table and helped ourselves to some purplish punch. Nick offered a splash of vodka, but we told him we'd rather wait awhile. As we drifted slowly out to the porch, one of the twins ran over to us. She was wearing a tiny orange dress, not seeming to feel the chill.

"So glad you could come!" she said to me.

"Thanks a lot. The party's great."

"Except nobody brought very much to drink." She glanced at Nick. "You did, I hope. Put a drop in this Kool-Aid shit. My mother calls it pookah punch. Would you believe she had an extra ice ring just waiting for a night like this?"

Nick tipped the bottle over her cup. "An ice ring being?"

"Where were you born? It's a big ring of ice with fruit and shit stuck into it."

"Sounds delicious." Nick stared at her. Then to me: "Are you sure you won't have a little drop?"

I'm not opposed to alcohol, I just wasn't in the mood right then. I already felt really floaty, thanks in part to the hormone thing. Will and I drifted away from the twin and Nick, and down to the end of the wooden deck. More hidden lights beamed up from bushes and landscaped shrubs, giving the scene a stagelike glow. A comma-shaped swimming pool filled the center of the yard, covered in a gently flapping tarpaulin. Farther back, the grass sloped into darkness, fringed with ink black trees. A sudden gust blew over the porch and Will encircled me with an arm.

"Do you come here in the summer?" I asked, settling back against his warmth.

"Funny, I was thinking that. Yeah, we do. We did, that is. Though I guess it's pretty much over now. Maybe one last summer, then life as we know it ends." He paused for a moment. "Though actually, life as I knew it ended the day that I met you."

"Same with me," I told him. More than he could know.

"Everyone says that once you go to college, you drift

222

away from the people at home. But that can't happen with us, Giselle—"

"We only just got started."

"Yeah. And Cornell is not that far away. I'll come home some weekends and sometimes you can visit me."

Another gust swirled over the deck, scattering fallen leaves, and people started going inside. Will and I just stood there, watching the trees at the edge of the yard swaying slowly from side to side, dipping low in the rising wind. A chilly dampness tinged the air and after a moment Will suggested we go inside.

The air in the house felt warm and thick. The noise was intense, voices over voices competing with the music, throbbing, loud and bass. At little café tables, groups of people huddled, their words a blur, their laughter lost in the general din. Another group had draped themselves on some sand-colored couches against the wall and a few of them were kissing as if they were alone. Will and I got some food and found an empty table in the glow of some chili pepper lights. Misao, the girl from Japan, who was sitting nearby with a couple of guys, said with awe that she'd never been to a party like this; it was just like in a movie.

"The twins give awesome parties," one of the guys yelled back. "You should've been here last Fourth of July. We all got shitfaced and jumped in the pool with the beer and the food and everything."

"This, by the way, is Tim," said Will. "And this other clown is Paul."

"Yo," said Paul. Then, grinning with the memory: "The twins' parents said that was it. The last damn party we'd ever have. But here we are. And isn't it sweet?"

"They're party mongrels themselves," said Tim. "They

probably forgot the whole thing ever happened. They probably forgot they even cared." In earnest, Misao asked him what a mongrel was, and when Will said "dog," Tim looked totally mystified. The twins came over in their tiny orange dresses, sandwiching Nick between them and making him spill some pookah punch.

One of them regarded me with sympathy. "If only we'd known, you could've borrowed something to wear."

"Samantha, really, she looks just fine."

"I didn't mean that. Of course she does. I meant, you know, for fun."

"Yeah," said Nick, "borrowing clothes is a major laugh."

"He's so depressed," said Robby. "It's pitiful to watch. What's wrong with Lauren anyway? I mean, couldn't she wait until after the prom?"

"It's the cruelest blow of all," said Nick, his delicate fingers tapping his heart. "All my life I've dreamed about the senior prom. Wrist corsages. Cummerbunds. And she leaves me just before the Night."

"You're just trying to act like you really don't care. You don't fool us," Robby said. She plunked herself down on top of Will. Scarlet light rippled on her thighs. "Don't worry, Giselle, he's just like some kind of brother to me. I don't even think of him as male."

After a while some slowish music started up and Will managed to get her off his lap. He took my hand and pulled me into the sweaty dark where people were sort of dancing. They were actually more like standing there swaying slowly back and forth, due to lack of space. But I didn't care if we moved or not, as Will's warm arms encircled me and I pressed my face against his shirt, nose just north of his hearable heart.

At a certain point, disturbing sounds began to intrude on my beautiful trance—violent thumps and banging as if someone were throwing things around. Vaguely I wondered if the twins' parents were having a fight with Jim and Betty Molson upstairs, though that didn't seem too probable considering their mellow state. I opened my eyes and as I did the doors to the porch flew open too, and a violent gust of wind blew in. Leaves and napkins swept into the room and some plastic cups skittered lightly across the floor, with a sound like tiny claws. It was maybe just a moment, but it seemed forever before someone sprang forward and shut the door. Will took my hand and we went to the window to look outside.

Above the deck, more white napkins swarmed in the air like a flock of frantic butterflies, while out in the yard, the trees and shrubs jittered in the spotlights' beam.

"It looks like a goddamn hurricane," Paul declared as everyone drifted over and pressed against the glass. For just a second he cracked the door, and the wind, rushing in through the narrow slit, made a human-sounding howl. Right after that, the lights went dead. The music too, as if someone had flipped a giant switch. Out in the yard, the lights in the bushes went black as well and the world plunged into darkness, toneless and complete. Then it began to rain. It was not a normal rainfall, but a drowning wall of water that turned the windows white. Everyone gasped, and sounds of commotion and running feet came from up above. The twins' father clomped down the stairs.

"Power failure. Just stay calm." He roamed a flashlight over us. I turned from the beam and glanced around behind me. I pulled myself closer next to Will and tried to remember when it was that I'd felt like this. But whenever an answer started to form, it would melt and slip away from me as if the rain were taking it, sweeping it just beyond my reach.

"It's just no fair!" whined a startling voice, and I spun around to see one of the twins wringing her hands hysterically. "Our first real party in over a year and what do we get—a cyclone!"

"All nature conspires to wreck her little world," said Nick, who was suddenly there beside us, his red eyes close to mine. Will opened his mouth to answer him and as he did the downpour stopped. As abruptly as it started, like a giant faucet shutting off. A stunning silence filled the room. Somebody opened the doors to the deck, and cool, wet air blew in like a breath.

"Wow," said someone, possibly Tim. "It looks like a damn tornado hit." We stepped outside to the drenched back porch, now littered with branches and sopping leaves and the tortured remains of garden chairs. In the yard, dark without the floodlights, the swimming pool gaped, a huge black hole, its tarpaulin twisted and wrenched away.

"My dad's gonna freak," said one of the twins. "The pool will be filled with leaves and crap." Then some of the guys started worrying about their cars, and suddenly everybody wanted to go out front to check on things.

"Don't you think my parents would have told you if your cars, like, suddenly blew away?" one of the twins wailed woefully. But nobody paid attention to her in the stampede up the stairs.

It was stunningly bright in the living room where the twins' mother and Betty Molson, still ensconced on the curving couch, seemed to bob and float in a bath of light. Brandy snifters glowed on the table like drifting lamps.

"Wasn't that exciting?" A flush of red colored Mrs. Dalwin's face, but her large, peach body didn't budge.

"Like being on the *Titanic*," said Betty Molson, her eyes ablaze.

"Yes," said Nick, "it does feel like that."

"A really great party," Will declared, urging us toward the door.

"What a lovely boy," said Betty as if he were a vase.

Outside, the twins' father and Mr. Molson were clearing branches and other debris out of the driveway and off the cars. Four guys were hauling a big limb that had just missed the house, and girls were gathering flowerpots, garbage can covers and other small objects scattered around. Everything looked strange and flat, eerie in the flashlight beam. The motionless trees seemed stunned.

We headed down the sloping drive. At the bottom, Samantha and Robby were yelling at their father, "Why do you have to do that *now*? Everyone thinks they have to leave!"

Samantha announced that a lot more food was coming, including hot dogs and popcorn shrimp. A portable CD player too. Nick was in favor of melting quietly into the night, but Will insisted we say goodbye. Predictably, the hostesses went crazy and Samantha accused us of maliciously starting a leaving trend.

"We're very trendsetting types," said Nick.

"Shut up," said Martha loyally. "I hope your car got scrunched by a tree." Somehow we managed to find said car, guided through the inky dark by the flicker of far-off candles in windows along the street. Nick's car was plastered with soppy leaves and a cardboard crate had lodged beneath a fender, but aside from that, it seemed okay. As he opened the door, Will snatched the keys away from him.

"Sit in the back and talk to Giselle."

"What the hell—"

"You're shitfaced, Nick."

"And you're a fucking ass."

The back of the car was cold and damp, and the smell of fish food rose in wafts from the cardboard boxes on the seat. As we drove, I tried to get Nick to talk to me. It seemed to calm him down a bit, and his mood was a little better by the time we reached his house.

"I'll return your wheels tomorrow," said Will as we pulled into a muddy drive. "Do you need a key to get inside?" Nick said no. He kissed my cheek and slid toward the door.

"It was really great to know you." And then to Will: "I'll get even with you for this, you know."

"I'm scared shitless," Will replied.

Even drunk, Nick had a lithe and graceful walk. He balanced himself with winglike arms as he climbed the steps and entered the house, which was bigger than Will's but more run-down and falling apart, like everything in his neighborhood. Once inside, he must have found a flashlight. We followed the tiny glowing beam as it drifted past windows and disappeared through rooms and unseen corridors.

"Come on up here," Will said to me, and I climbed from the back right over the seat, getting all tangled up in my skirt and stuff and practically landing on the floor. It was pretty stupid and both of us started laughing. He pulled me close and we laughed some more. "Nick's kind of depressed right now," he said. "He's really a fantastic guy."

"You don't have to say that. I know he is." I pulled away and looked at him. He was just about to kiss me—or so I thought and hoped—when a banging sound distracted him. We looked toward the noise, to a small, square window high in the house. Ablaze in the dark was Nick's red face, the flashlight stuck in his open mouth so he glowed like an apparition in the blacker-than-normal night.

Chapter 24

NOTHING STIRRED as we drove back to Will's in the soggy car. It looked like a twister had struck, he said. *But how could a twister happen here?* Twisters came from the Plains, I thought, from faraway fields and prairies— from Kansas and Nebraska, places remote as Oz. *How could a twister happen here?* Not that I knew where I actually was. Nothing looked familiar now, even though we were travel-ing back the way we'd come. I didn't even know Will's street till we'd pulled in the drive beside his house, close be-hind his mother's car.

Smiley began to whine at the door, and we hurried in so he wouldn't bark. We petted him till he got a grip, then set-tled ourselves on the saggy couch in the dark, chaotic living room. Small red numbers pulsed on the face of the VCR, letting us know that the power had gone off here too. The flashing numerals softly blipped, strobing in the dark.

Will put his arm around me and we sat in the gloom

with the sounds of the blips and Smiley's quiet snores. A wearying ache nagged my breasts and stomach and whined along my thighs, and I wondered for a moment how it would feel to live inside Will's body, all lean and loose and simple, always the same from day to day. Moon Goddess Magda wouldn't like it very much, but I thought that it might feel quite calm. Calm in a way I wished that I could feel right then. Even when Will kissed me, leaning close and briefly blotting the eerie blue, my insides churned and I felt unsafe. Crazily, I wished I had brought an animal—like Hugo Junior, he was small. Or if I'd known, I could have brought a photograph so that if I woke I would find it there and wouldn't feel alone.

"You're cold," said Will as he let me go. "We ought to get you up to bed." Weakly I resisted as he pulled me to my feet. Smiley stirred and shook himself, and I smelled his sleep-warm fur. He bounded up the stairway, waiting and wagging at the top. When we got to June's bedroom, Will reached in and flicked on the light.

"Anything you need?" he asked, and when I said no, he murmured, "I guess you know where the bathroom is." I pointed across the hallway, which caused him to semi-smile. "I'll be back to say good night, okay?" I said okay and forced a smile. But it really wasn't okay at all. And watching him go away from me, walking backward down the hall, a hundred thousand miles away, I knew how un-okay it was. He paused at the door and waved to me as Smiley nosed into the lightless room. Absurdly I waved back to him, and then he disappeared. Instantly my throat went dry. Then something loosened, and panic burst inside me. I felt as if I were full of birds—tiny, crazy, frantic birds, beating their wings on my inner walls. *Oh God.* I heard my murmur. Soon I wouldn't be able to breathe. I pushed inside the room.

For a moment I felt better with the cozy gingham all around and the pictures on the sky blue walls. The sight of the nightgown calmed me most, clean and white and folded in a perfect square. What could go wrong with such a nightgown folded in such a perfect square? I picked it up and pressed my face against it, inhaling its cool, clean scent. The bird wings slowed and I breathed again. Maybe I would be all right.

I gathered my things and ventured into the hall again. In the bathroom I put the nightgown on as if it were a talisman. I washed my face, avoiding it in the mirror, looking instead at the pale green tiles behind me. The shower curtain was also green and patterned with dark green turtles that seemed to be flying through the air. There were turtles on the hand towels too, and crawling across the oval rug. They made me uneasy, I don't know why. But I needed to get away from them. I hurried with what I had to do, then horror struck as I realized I'd flushed the tampon. You can't in certain toilet bowls, like the ones we have at ballet school. What if it broke the plumbing, and plumbers came and found it there and everyone knew it was all my fault? I stared at the bowl, awaiting the surge. Then out of the corner of my eye, I saw a living turtle, small and dark, wagging its tail on the ledge of the tub, and I bolted out the door.

Optical illusion, I told myself, safely back in June's room—from the greenish light and all the turtle-patterned things. I draped my clothes on the gingham chair, arranging them compulsively. I was suddenly wide awake again, and started to walk around the room. There was a dressing table I hadn't noticed earlier, and I sat on the little heart-shaped bench, my knees poking into the gingham skirt. On the mirrored top was a purple plastic treasure chest and a satin box in the shape of a heart. I peeked inside the treasure chest and found June's stash of jewelry and all those ornaments for her hair. Behind the chest, a pair of china angels posed, a water-filled globe between them with a big red rose crammed into it. In a nearby bin were some beat-up lipsticks that must have been her mother's, and some little kid cologne. Unscrewing the cap, I took a sniff. Little kid perfume has always smelled the same, I guess, from the time that they invented it. I touched a droplet to my throat and it flooded me with memory. Maybe it would help me sleep.

After that, I went to the window and looked outside. Down below I could see the tail of Nick's black car and a portion of the sagging steps. A plastic bag, crumpled and wet, rustled along the front yard hedge. Beyond the hedge, the street lay silent, slick with rain. On the shelf above me, June's dolls from around the world sat there staring into space. Unlike my stuffed animals, you could tell they'd been played with quite a bit. Miss Switzerland was armless and Miss Haiti's head with its basket of bananas clung to the neck with reams of tape. I glanced at the weird-looking cat-shaped clock. It was not electric, so I knew it was the actual time: a quarter after two. I went back to the bed and climbed inside. I lay like a board, with the overhead light shining directly into my face. How had I thought I could bring this off?

A little while later I heard Will in the bathroom. There was the sound of running water, which I very much liked and wished would never end. Then I heard Will pee. I liked that too; it made me calm. A few seconds later there was a tap, hardly even a sound at all, and Will peeked in the room. He came inside and closed the door. He crouched on his knees beside the bed so his face was next to mine. His skin was cool and slightly damp, with the lingering scent of soap.

"Are you okay?" he whispered.

"Yes, I'm fine."

"Well, you don't look fine. You look . . . real weird. Are you nervous about my being here?"

"No," I said, and that was the truth. I was nervous about him *not* being here. He climbed to his feet and turned off the light. I reached through the dark to find him, and he caught my hand and brought it quickly to his mouth. He turned it over and kissed my wrist. I wondered if he felt the birds, thrashing to get out.

"Do you want some water?" he whispered then. The question seemed absurd to me and I didn't try to answer him. I felt him move, shifting now to the edge of the bed so his body towered over me. I could see his blurry outline, and inside the face, just shadows and shapes. His lips were warm and gentle, hardly even a touch at all, drifting across my forehead to the dent beside my eye. They rested there, then skirted my cheek. Delicious chills ran through me as the warmth brushed softly over my ear and along my turning jaw. And now his mouth was on my throat, so firm and clear I could feel the top and bottom lips, distinct and separate parts. Heat burned through the nightgown's cloth where his body pressed on mine. The wings began to beat again, but I realized it wasn't only me. Will was also full of birds, stronger, wilder ones than mine. Trembly, he pulled away. I could see his eyes in the circle of white as he eased back up, drawing the blanket to my throat.

"I love you," he said in a voice so low I thought I had imagined it. Before I believed it, he was gone.

———

Later it started to rain again. A rushing, crushing downpour that woke me from my sleep. It masked for a moment the other sound, the sound that wasn't human and came, I knew, from the pitch-dark lake. It could never get me, my father had said. The beast was footless and couldn't walk. It needed water to stay alive. But its howling scared me all the same, and I climbed from bed in the humid dark.

The floor was cold beneath my feet as I ran from the room and through the house, skittering on the scatter rugs. I pushed through doors, but all the rooms were empty, and when I tried to call his name, no sound came out of my open mouth. I tried and tried, but I had no voice. And then I reached the Chinese door with its carvings of boats and twisty trees. I pushed at the door and the hideous howling got very loud, and before I saw it with my eyes, I knew that the beast was in the room.

It was my father howling, sitting up in the big black bed with the headboard that looked like dragon wings. His robe had fallen open and inside the gap I saw his ribs and the swollen mound where his stomach was, lumpy and blue, a strange pale bag attached to it. Like a vacuum cleaner bag, I thought, though it made no sense and I wondered vaguely who'd put it there. I wanted to take it off him, and I started running toward the bed. It was strange, this room; three shallow steps led up to the place where my father slept under the Chinese carvings on the poppy-colored walls. He must have heard my footsteps. He turned to me and I met his eyes. Rimmed with sickly yellow, they glittered inside like hard black jewels. He started pushing from the bed, trying to get up. At first he couldn't lift himself. This made him angry, I could tell, and the anger seemed to give him strength. He tore through the covers one by one and struggled to his feet. Then, bellowing, he lunged at me.

———

That's when I woke with the scream I couldn't scream before, clawing my way through layers of sleep, wall after wall, like fragile, gray-black eggshells till at last there was natural air. I struggled from the blankets and pulled away from the hot, damp bed, plunging toward the window, that frame of light that somehow seemed the place to go. Something was caught around my leg, the twisted nightgown maybe, and I felt myself tripping, flailing out for something to hold. A horrible crash and everything went crazy, as I toppled down in a rain of tiny objects. I didn't know where on earth I was.

Time went by. It must have. I realized at some point that someone was there beside me. Someone was there and holding me, a hand cupped firmly around my head as if I were having that fit I feared.

"It's Will," said the person. "You had a dream." The sound of his voice made me start to cry. How long I went on, I couldn't say. I only know that after a while there were no more tears and everything was dry inside. I opened my eyes on his hot and soggy T-shirt. A gila monster silkscreened on the front of it stared at me through sleepy lids.

"It's okay, Giselle." For one demented second, I thought

that the lizard had talked to me. "Everything's fine. You had a dream."

"It wasn't a dream." I heard my voice as if from very far away. "My father did awful things to me."

I turned my face from the lizard shirt, and saw Mrs. Brooks standing in the doorway. She was dressed in an all-white jogging suit, like a strange athletic angel. In her hand was a glass of orange juice, glowing like a flame. That's when I realized that night was over and day had come. How long had I been rocking there in the circle of Will's arms? Buttery sunshine flooded the room, and glittery leaves rustled at the windowpane. I looked at the mess of June's room. I had crashed into her vanity, knocking down the mirror and all the boxes and knickknacks there. A million barrettes were scattered around, and the water-filled globe had shattered, spewing the soggy rose. The big oval mirror was cracked in half.

"God," I groaned. "I'm sorry—"

"You are not to apologize for this," Mrs. Brooks said firmly.

"But Junie's stuff—"

"Nothing is irreplaceable." She knelt on the floor beside me and offered me the orange juice. I took a sip mainly because she wanted me to. "I tried to call your mother. Then I remembered she's teaching class. Can you tell me how to reach her at school?"

Marina. Oh God. I hadn't even thought of her. And now, in one overwhelming moment, I understood the story and why she had sent my father away.

"Don't call her, please. She'll want to talk and I don't know what to say to her." I looked at Will. "At Otto's house, my father pushed me down the steps. It wasn't just then; there were other times." I picked up his hand and led it slowly up to my head and into my tangled hair. I searched with my fingers, as Carla had done, and halted when I found the place. "I had stitches," I said. "I think it was then."

"Your mother can explain, I'm sure," Mrs. Brooks said gently.

"It was only after he was sick. It made him crazy—being sick."

"That happens to people," said Mrs. Brooks.

"Not most people," I answered her. Will tightened his hand around my own.

"Your father was not most people, Giselle."

"I know he wasn't. He was . . . less."

"He was very sick. You said it yourself. He'd never been bad to you before."

"*Your* father survived a prison camp. He didn't come home and—beat you up." I burned with shame as I said the words.

"Will's father was a soldier. He was trained to endure all sorts of things. And yes, he was brave," said Mrs. Brooks, "but he couldn't compose a gorgeous ballet. Or write a brilliant book."

"Besides," said Will in a quiet voice, "he did kind of beat us up in a way."

"Come on, Giselle," said Mrs. Brooks, pretending she hadn't heard Will's words. "Let's get you on your feet." They helped me up and she told me she would run a bath. To Will she said, "We'll see you downstairs in a little while."

In the bathroom, she hung my things from some plastic hooks, then started to run the water. She perched on the edge as the tub filled up, and I wondered if she was planning to stay in the room with me, worried I might drown myself. But after a moment she moved to the door.

"There are blueberry pancakes downstairs," she said. I looked at her—it seemed such a crazy thing to say. What did that have to do with me?

"June won't start without you. She's really very fond of you. As we all are, Giselle, I hope you know." I swallowed a lump, unable to talk. "Just relax and enjoy the bath." As she closed the door, I saw the living turtle again, small and dark on the edge of the tub. I realized now that it was a soap. Two more floated in the suds into which I slowly sank, weighty as a whale.

They all looked up when I came into the kitchen. They were sitting at the table, empty plates in front of them, bright blue cups and saucers all set out on a blue-and-white-checked tablecloth like a picture in a magazine.

"You shouldn't have waited. Really."

"It's okay," said June, " 'cause the pancakes are in the oven. We put them there to keep 'em hot."

"That was really nice of you." Will got up and pulled out a chair, and limply I plopped down. I looked around the sun-filled room. There were potted plants hanging in the window, which I hadn't noticed there before, and stained-glass sun catchers catching the sun of which, as I said, there was quite a lot. Just beyond the window a perky bird sat on the clothesline singing, though luckily we couldn't hear his happy tune.

June tried to cheer me up by telling me that she had nightmares all the time. She described a recent one she'd had where her teacher turned into a giant worm and started devouring the school. I guess I'd woken everyone. I probably gave them a heart attack. While June talked, Mrs. Brooks served the blueberry pancakes. They looked pretty on the blue glass plates, golden yellow circles with runny purple polka dots. When I started to eat I realized how fatigued I was. And the more I ate the more fatigued I started to feel. I probably said about seven words. Pretty soon, breakfast was done. I thanked Mrs. Brooks and told her I felt much better now.

In truth, I had stopped feeling much of anything. I had turned into a big, numb lump, like a giant human pancake blob. As we got up to leave, June started wailing about wanting to come in the car with us, but Mrs. Brooks bribed her off with the promise of making cookies, and finally we got out of there.

It was almost pleasant to ride in Will's car in my zombie state, even though the sky was a lot too blue and bright, and the trees a blinding green. Everything, really, was way too bright, as if the world had been viciously scrubbed. Cleanup crews were out in force, sweeping up stuff that was strewn on the street; and in front of houses, ordinary citizens were gathering garbage and raking lawns. Will, thank God, didn't try to make me talk. He knew, I guess, that I'd tell him everything when I could. Just right now it seemed unspeakable to me.

When we got to Manhattan everything seemed normal, as though the storm had happened in another world. In front of my building it looked like any Saturday. Paki was loading piles of weekend bags and a bunch of stuff from

Zabar's into the Yamagoris' Volvo, and Mr. Stein, in coffee-splattered jogging pants, was heading out with his beagle, Clark. Will pulled me over close to him.

"Everything's going to be okay."

"I know," I said. Which I didn't at all.

He kissed my hair where it lay near my eyes, flat and undoubtedly horrible. "I'll call you later on, okay?"

"Yeah, okay." I raised my face to take his kiss, then somehow managed to pull away and separate from the car. I paused for a second and closed the door. I found his eyes and held them.

"I love you too," I murmured. And then I turned and ran.

Chapter 25

I T W A S B R I G H T and sunny even in my room. I yanked
down the shade to make the place more bearable. Then I
walked to the shelf and gathered my things—the pictures of
my father, the feather, bone and rock. I settled cross-legged
on the bed, holding them in my lap. Then from out of
the jumble I plucked the rock. It would have felt good to
hurl it at the window, but knowing my luck it would land
kerplunk on the janitor's head and further wreck my life. I
slammed it instead on the picture glass, then threw it
against the wall. After that, I heaved the bone. I tried to
hurl the feather too, but it just kept floating back to me. So
I broke it into pieces till the pieces were too small to break.
I curled into a ball, as I had last night, and started to cry
all over again. I cried and cried, then tumbled into a black-
hole sleep.

I woke in the dark and at first I didn't know where I
was. Then with a twinge of vague relief, I recognized my
room. The sun was gone around the edge of the window

shade. What time was it? What day was it? I rolled onto my side to look at my clock, and saw with a chill that someone was sitting in the chair. It was Marina. She shifted forward slightly, though she hadn't really been sitting back.

"You scared me," I said.

"And you scared me." She paused a moment. "Can we turn on a light?"

"The one on the desk. It's not too bright."

She got up and turned on the lamp, and when she came back she sat on the bed instead of the chair. She didn't touch me, but she looked as if she wanted to.

"I talked to Mrs. Brooks," she said. "Can you tell me what happened last night, Giselle?" I looked at her face, and knew that she knew.

"I remembered the night at Otto's house." I pulled myself up to sit on the bed. The air felt cold, and I clutched a pillow in front of my chest. "I remembered the storm and waking up. The wind was howling really loud, but then there was this other noise, this different howling from somewhere else. It made me scared and I went to find—to find him. And I found him in the Chinese room." I heard Marina's breath draw in, and I looked away from her shadowy face. "I came inside and I saw that the noise was coming from him. He was lying on that big, carved bed and his robe was open down the front and I saw his stomach sticking out and I saw that awful bag. I know what it was, but I didn't know then. I wanted to get it off him. And I wanted the terrible noise to stop." I still wouldn't meet Marina's gaze. It was bad enough to feel her there, a hardly breathing ghost.

"At first he didn't see me. But when he did . . . it was horrible. Everything just twisted up—his face, I mean, it didn't even look like him. He got out of the bed—he was swaying around and shaking. I remember his eyes, how I didn't recognize his eyes, the whites were so yellow, they looked so wild, and then he just sort of—came at me." I heard Marina's nip of pain as her hands flew up to cover her face. Long seconds passed before she dropped them back to her lap. Slowly she began to speak.

"We were late getting back, Jacinta and I. We left you with Otto but apparently he fell asleep. We'd gone to town, but a storm came up and had flooded the roads. He was hours late for the morphine shot. He was half insane with pain."

"That was the night. The night you decided to send him away."

"He was the one who wanted to go. But I agreed. I wanted him gone." She paused a moment and drew a breath. "It should have been much sooner. It should have been the very first time he hurt you."

"The old hotel."

"You remembered that too?"

"And then I remembered other times."

Marina touched my fingers where they pressed the pillow against my chest. "I denied it at first. I told myself it couldn't be true. No matter how sick Grigori was, he never could have done those things. You had dropped the teapot and scalded yourself. You had tripped and fallen once again. I couldn't admit it to myself. Until that night we found you there."

"What happened to me?"

"You fell when he pushed you, and hit your head. You weren't conscious and I thought for a moment that you

244

were . . . dead. I gave Grigori the morphine shot—quite a bit more than usual—and rushed you to the hospital." She paused and swallowed heavily. "It was only a concussion. A serious one, but no permanent damage, thank God for that. Your father, of course, in the aftermath, was totally distraught. It was always that way after one of his fits; but this time he was desolate. He told me he wanted to go away so he couldn't hurt you anymore."

"I don't understand how I blocked it out. How I didn't remember anything. It makes me think I'm crazy."

"You aren't crazy—"

"Will's father did the same, you know. He blocked out his memory of the war."

"And why do you think he did that? He did it to survive, Giselle. You aren't crazy, you're utterly sane. And blocking out the trauma was a way of maintaining that sanity. Dr. Sloop explained it all to me."

"But how do I know—if I don't remember certain things—that the things I remember or *think* I remember are true at all?"

"Don't do that, Giselle."

"Then tell me. How?"

"Because I was there. I can vouch for all those years. Those lovely years when he was well and reveled in your company."

"Carla told me he never wanted to have a child."

She uttered a brittle-sounding laugh. "He *thought* he didn't want a child. He *said* he didn't want a child. But once you were born, the sun rose and set on your bassinet. And later on—don't you remember?—he took you out of nursery school to keep you at home with him. I thought, my

245

God, he's lost his mind. How could he work with a three-year-old at his side all day? And yet he did. The two of you thrived. Whenever I peeked in on you, you were busy doing something—drawing pictures, looking at books, playing underneath his desk.

"But the most amazing time of all was the day I came in and found you at the barre with him. You were four years old and following him perfectly. I think of that day quite often when I see you working in class. If you ever doubt your past, Giselle, just look in the mirror—you'll know the truth."

"Half the truth," I murmured. But Marina shook her head.

"The things you remember are true and real. Nothing can change the fact of that."

Slowly I let my eyes find hers. "I don't understand why you never told me anything. Sometimes I really hated you. I thought you were just selfish and didn't want to take care of him."

She nodded faintly. "That hurt at times. But when you were small, it seemed like such a blessing. I knew Grigori loved you, and if you remembered only that—well, that was the most essential truth."

"But what about you? All these years I've been so horrible to you—"

"I wasn't blameless, darling. I didn't protect you. That was wrong."

"But you didn't know for certain."

"I should have though. I should have been stronger inside myself." Her narrowed eyes seemed tired and hazed. "When I met your father, I was sixteen and he was nearly forty years old. We were married two years later. You know the story, you've read the books. Grigori choreographed for me, my career took off, and as you said the other day, everything was wonderful—"

"That was stupid to say."

"It was true in part. But in marrying Grigori, I also lost a piece of myself. He was like a father in many ways. He managed our life, took care of me, exactly as a father would. Sometimes he told me what to wear. I never questioned anything." She paused for a moment, releasing her breath. "There was just one point where I couldn't let him have his way. I wanted to have a child." A rush of warmth, something that felt golden, swept through my body at her words.

"I wanted you so very much. I should have taken care of you."

"I never knew."

"That I wanted you?"

"I thought I drove you crazy. I thought you only wanted to dance. I didn't believe it when Carla said it wasn't Grigori who wanted a child."

"Your father had this strange idea that ballerinas weren't really women. They were spirit creatures like the corps de ballet in *Les Sylphides*. He thought it would change me to have a child." The thinnest smile crossed her face. "And he was right. It did. Once you were born, all I wanted to do on earth was stay at home with you."

"And it's true he wouldn't let you retire?"

"He wanted to do a new ballet. What he made, of course, was the wonderful masterpiece, *Avila*. Not long after that, he learned he was sick."

"*Avila* is beautiful. I think that it's my favorite one."

"I think mine too," Marina said. "Though I couldn't bear to see it now."

"It was the last one, wasn't it?"

Marina nodded. "When he was sick, I wanted him to choreograph another work. Just one more dance, like a parting gift. I thought it would help him also, would give some kind of hope. Oscar agreed to play piano, to work with him. But something had happened to him, Giselle. It shocked me to learn how weak he was—or maybe I mean fragile. He was so aesthetic, so sensitive to everything; he couldn't rise above being sick. While others fight an illness, he just gave up; it swallowed him whole." She was prodding my fingers gently now, opening them one by one. "I think, Giselle, that you've been stronger than both of us. I'm sorry we failed you the way we did."

"You didn't fail me. I was a jerk."

"You weren't a jerk—"

"Yes, I was. Sometimes you tried to tell me things. Carla tried to tell me too. Even Will thought there was something I didn't see. I was just so stubborn. I wouldn't look." Marina's fingers pried some more, and the comforting pillow fell away.

"It's not for me to ask you to forgive him. That's for you to decide yourself. But please, Giselle, keep the best of your memories too. Maybe someday the good will overcome the bad." She was holding both my hands in hers, pressing them tight, insisting that I look at her.

"I believe that a life is a sum of everything. No one on earth is perfect, and if in the end Grigori lost his dignity, it doesn't mean the rest of his life was meaningless. His contributions were huge, Giselle. He gave the world sublime ballets. And all those brilliant books. Certain ballets have been saved from extinction because of him. It was so important, the work he did. But more important than all those things—more important than history and fame and dance—is the fact of *you;* that you exist. You are his greatest work of all. And he knew it, Giselle. He told me so on the very last day."

As I looked at her face in the shadowy light, for the first time ever I saw her age. Spidery lines trailed from her eyes and over the cheekbones faintly, and deeper indentations marked the corners of her mouth, tilting with her slender smile. I suddenly wanted to hold her tight, to wrap her fiercely in my arms. But I didn't know how; we had never done that sort of thing. So I moved a little, the way I had when I first kissed Will. Then she moved too, clumsily, as I'd never seen my mother move, lurching forward toward me as I opened my awkward arms. I heard her sigh and felt the soft collapse of her. Thin shoulders. Fragile bones. I couldn't believe how small she was, this woman who seemed to fill a room.

I held her close for a pretty long time, then little by little we drew apart.

"So what happens now?" I asked her.

"What would you like to happen?"

"Start over, I guess. Something like that."

"Something like that sounds good to me." She lifted a strand of my dampened hair and kissed my forehead underneath. "Shall we start with dinner maybe? I'm sure there's something of Carla's left." She smoothed back my hair and rose from the bed. As she started to leave, she picked up one of the photographs. Her smile was faint, a shadow, and her voice was like a shadow too as she rested the picture against the lamp.

"God, what a beautiful Rose he was."

But I turned my face away from him.

Chapter 26

POOR MAGDA. She was frantic to know how Friday had gone, and had started to lose her mind when she didn't hear from me. She had called six times while I was asleep, but after Marina and I had talked, I couldn't talk to anyone else—not even to my life's best friend. Then it was night, and time to sleep all over again. I actually didn't speak to her till late on Sunday morning, by which time she was nearly insane.

She insisted that we meet for brunch, and though I felt exhausted, I knew I had to fill her in. At least the place she chose was dark, with tables set into tiny nooks like a place where you'd have your fortune told. Over cappuccino and a spinach omelette I didn't want, I told her what had happened. She didn't say a single word until I was totally finished, and even then, she didn't talk for a very long time. She was probably thinking, Holy God, even her lousy father had never done stuff like that to her. Finally she said, "I guess we had Marina all wrong."

"You might say that," I answered. "I didn't know who she was at all. And I didn't know my father. I've lived in a fog for half my life." Magda told me it wasn't my fault, but I knew it partly was; I'd made up my mind and shut the door. I'd refused to consider anything else.

Late in the day I spoke to Will. Once again, I heard the story pour out of me. He understood completely, of course, since the same thing had basically happened to him with his father going crazy and his mother having to make him leave. Our lives were so weirdly parallel. Sometimes it scared me just how much.

On Monday the countdown to *Snegurochka* began. Five more puny rehearsal days and then it would be Saturday. Panic hit as the fact sank in. But the panic became hysteria when I got to rehearsal that afternoon and found that I couldn't dance. All of a sudden, nothing about my role made sense. When I started flitting around the place, acting all gay and flighty, I felt like a total jerk. I couldn't even do the steps. Which caused Mrs. Turock to go berserk. After rehearsal she ordered me to her "office," the wardrobe closet really, where, perching on a dusty trunk of costumes, she gave me a little "talk." The jitters was what I had, she said. Everybody got them, a perfectly normal phenomenon. What I needed to do was focus: relax, breathe deep, *self-actualize*. Repeat to myself like a yogic chant, "I am Vesna-Krasna. I am Vesna-Krasna."

"Try it," she ordered. "Close your eyes." And so I did. Or I'd never have gotten out of there.

It was not only me who was falling apart. Everyone was nervous and having blackout episodes. On Tuesday during my adagio, Yarilo forgot that I had to do penché after my promenade and let me go just as I was heading down. Luckily

I was in an unusual state of alert or my understudy, Delia, would have had her dreams come true. The lighting people were screwing up too. At one point, a big plastic color screen crashed to the stage, barely missing a sparrow's head. Mrs. Turock lost it, then ordered some wretched stagehand guy to get her a glass of water, which she downed with some prescription drugs excavated from her purse.

By the time she let us out of there, it was almost ten o'clock. Magda waited while I changed, and together we schlepped out. We stopped off for pizza at a place on Columbus Avenue, and while we ate we chuckled over how really bad rehearsal had been and what a psycho Turock was. Then suddenly she dropped the bomb: Fiona wasn't coming back. She'd called that morning to explain that she and Leif had reconciled and needed time to "work things out."

"It was Sonia who took the phone call," Magda said, staring at her barely eaten pizza slice. "I could hear her screaming from way upstairs. It was hard to believe it was even her. It was like she couldn't stop herself, yelling at Fiona, saying what a lousy mother she was and what a crummy human being for leaving me the way she did to run away with *Haircut Boy*. She kept calling him that— Haircut Boy." She paused for a moment, drawing a breath. "It was really awful the things she said. She never said stuff to my dad like that—and he deserved it a whole lot more. I ended up feeling sorry for Fiona."

"Did you talk to her?"

"No. By the time I got down to Sonia's room she had slammed down the phone and was crying like a maniac. Then I started to worry for *her.* She's old, you know, and I thought she might have a heart attack."

"God."

253

"I know. Plus the whole thing's my entire fault."

"What do you mean?"

"That photograph. That picture of Agrippina pregnant in the bathing suit. It drove Fiona over the edge. I never should have shown her that."

"Maybe not, but Fiona was screwy way before that. So what are they going to do?" I asked. "Just roam around forever?"

"Who the hell knows? Or cares." She sounded so pathetic that I squirmed from the booth and went to her side to hug her. She endured me for longer than usual before she shrugged me off.

"Sonia loves you a lot," I said. "That's why she stuck up for you."

"Yeah, I know. Sonia's great. I just thought Fiona would—what the hell." She slid from the booth, dragging her bag along with her. "She doesn't know a thing about lighting anyway. So what the hell difference does it make?"

Limp and exhausted, we headed out. Too morose to wait for a bus, Magda hailed a taxicab. I blew a kiss that she didn't return and started walking north. No one was home when I arrived. I could tell by the sense of stillness as I stepped inside the dark foyer. I paused as always to breathe the scents and let the echoes swirl around. I stood and waited. Nothing. I closed my eyes and listened with every part of me. And soon I knew that something had changed. The music had stopped inside my head. The ghosts were gone and slowly the living were coming back, opening the doors and rooms.

I went to the kitchen and made some tea, then brought it to my room. I took a shower, and when I came out, I sat by the window sipping the tea. Suddenly a light went on in the window across the courtyard. As if on a little movie screen, I could see a man dressed in blue pajamas cross the room and scoop up one of the little girls. You could tell that she was crying—she must have had a nightmare. She hooked her arms around his neck as he pulled her from the sheets. Then, holding her close, he lowered himself to the edge of the bed and started to rock her back and forth. For a minute or two the other girls watched, then one by one dropped back to sleep. But the man kept rocking the little one, gently, evenly, back and forth, till I almost felt I was rocking too in a cradle of cool and silky sleeves that smelled of deep black soap.

I set down the teacup and went to my shelf where I used to keep my special things. They weren't in their places now; they didn't have places anymore. But the photographs were lying there, facedown on the shelf and shattered. I didn't move to pick them up, but I knew by their shapes which was which—my father the Bluebird; my father the Rose; my father and me at the old hotel, that place like a ship on the wide gray sea.

I walked to the door and went out of the room. The hallway was dark, and the air felt thick, alive with night. The floorboards creaked beneath my feet as I headed toward the ballroom. Deep blue light flooded the floor from wall to wall. I entered the room and crossed the sea. At the terrace door I paused for just an instant, then turned the handle and stepped outside. As always, the high cold air was startling. Over the edge, the dazzling city glittered, white and gold and in the distance shimmering, pale like dying stars. Whenever I look at lights at night I almost drown in my own desire. I don't even know what it is I want, but I want it so much it makes me ache till I almost can't bear the feeling, the sense of possibility and equally wild loss.

I turned at the sound as a gust of wind rattled through the dried-up stems. I walked to the old frame boxes, where the white gardenias used to grow. Remembered fragrance dizzied me as I started ripping out the weeds. They were easy to pull and I wrenched them free, moving quickly from box to box. From an old clay pot I yanked the skeleton of a shrub. This gave way with the faintest tug, this ghost of a stalk dead so long it had hollowed out. More dead stalks and up-pulled weeds piled in mounds on the terrace floor. I have no idea how long I worked, but when I was done the boxes and pots were emptied out, ready to be filled again.

In my mind I could see my father's drawing, delicate green and olive, terra-cotta and faintest pink, depicting the garden row by row and pot by pot, the Latin names penciled lightly along the edge. I knew where it was, this hand-worked plan, folded into a smaller square on a shelf in the shut red room. I would go there with Will. After *Snegurochka*. I would take him to that place I hadn't been in years. Will would be thrilled to see that plan. He could help us decipher the Latin names, and then we'd re-create it— Will and I and probably Marina too. And Blitz, I supposed, since Blitz was here and part of our life. Probably forevermore.

The following day, Wednesday, we had two rehearsals back to back. It was almost eleven by the time I was changed and ready to leave, but Turock wanted another chat, and dragged me into her "office" again. It was total chaos in there now, half-sewn costumes strewn about and bags of tu-tus hanging from the ceiling, banging you in the head.

"Tell her it shows, Giselle," she said, a knowing look on her rabbitlike face.

"What?"

"The coaching. Tell her it shows."

I looked at her blankly. "What do you mean?"

"Isn't your mother coaching you? Your dancing's completely different now. Your character is—" She narrowed her already slitty eyes. "Or maybe the exercises helped. . . ." She waited a moment, and when I still had nothing to say: "Just keep it there. Whatever it is. Wherever it is you got it from."

———

Dress rehearsal on Friday night made the other rehearsals seem polished by comparison. Mizgir actually fell on his butt and Snegurochka came pretty close. The sparrows stank, the Berendeys' scarves kept falling off and the sound system stuttered steadily—b-bad news for my f-first variation, act 1. Mrs. Turock was oddly calm. Almost eerily calm, it seemed to me.

"That was horrible," she told us, injecting wit into the curious pep talk that followed. The gist of it was that dress rehearsals are always bad. If we'd been good, she'd be worried now. And as we could see, she was quite serene. "You'll be beautiful," she told us, tapping out another pill.

Chapter 27

T HE NEXT DAY I slept until nine o'clock, then lingered in bed, thinking of *Snegurochka*. And Will. And how soon I would see his face again. But that was *after,* a long way off, at the end of this just-beginning day. The sun pressed hard on the window shade, and I turned away and closed my eyes, imagining it was night again and this day not here, not quite, not yet. An hour later I was heading for the studios.

It really felt weird traveling in the cab alone for the single class I would take today—Marina's, of course—so as not to overtax myself. And it seemed a moment later I was heading home in yet another taxicab, Marina there beside me, telling me how well I'd done and what excellent shape I seemed to be in. A bath, a rest—I'd be brilliant tonight.

"Let's hope so," I said, gazing from the window at the regular people walking around, doing regular, normal Saturday things.

At home we had lunch together, sitting in the reading

room. It felt so strange, our new and friendly relationship, and I hoped to hell I'd get used to it soon—the touches and smiles and quiet chats we seemed to be having all the time. After our plates of pasta, she said (with a smile, touching me lightly on the arm) that I ought to take a nap. I told her I couldn't possibly sleep and she answered "Try" in a normal voice, which after all our whispering was almost like a reprimand. Strangely enough I did fall asleep. A floaty, watery, dreamless doze she actually had to shake me from.

"I've run a bath," she told me as I pushed myself out of bed. "You have twenty minutes, no more than that. Then we'll do your face."

I have a bathtub of my own, but Marina had prepared the bath in her giant, lion-footed one. It seemed a long time since I'd entered that inner sanctum, since my date with Will when she'd lent me Martha Graham's black sash. Now as always, it felt like a place apart from the world, serene and white, like a realm of clouds. In the marble bathroom, huge white towels as thick as furs lay folded on the counter, and a massive bar of pearl-like soap gleamed in a golden dish for me. I sank into the water, mountainous with bubbles, and wished I could float away.

Thirty minutes later I was seated in the hard-backed chair as she opened the giant makeup box and set it on the vanity. "Don't move," she said as she started her work, swabbing my face with pale foundation, greasy and thick. Next came powder, dabbed and brushed, and spots of rouge almost roughly smeared. Her hands dipped back to the makeup box and now she started on my eyes, tracing first with a liquid brush. The coldness felt strange, half pleasant, and told me the shape of my own dark orb, before traveling out to some distant point beyond the natural edge. After that, eye shadow, applied with cotton then blended with her fingers, layer on layer up to my brow. My eyebrows heavily reinforced, a crayon dragging over the arc. Then tepid glue, the artificial lashes, and another sweep of liner till I almost couldn't lift my lids. A warmer pencil drew my mouth, its waxy tip like a sculptor's tool cutting into clay. Heavy lipstick precisely applied. For a moment she stopped to appraise her work. "A touch more rouge," she murmured, and ruthlessly started to swab again. More stares, more frowns and finally, oh finally, a slow grave nod. My entire face felt plastered. Moving my eyes from left to right, I could see the spidery web of lash.

Now for my hair. As she brandished the brush, she glanced with contempt at the flower wreath I had to wear. "They should have put finer combs," she said, "and better grips for hairpins. Don't they realize you're dancing in this?" Then she began to brush my hair. Gone was the new Marina, gentle and solicitous; she was suddenly all business, raking my scalp with violent sweeps that left the surface tingling. She pulled it taut and raked some more, tugging it tighter with every stroke, till I felt my eyebrows stretching and thought my makeup mask might crack. With a quick and expert motion, she snapped a band around it, then wound it several times again, pulling tight and tucking, creating a knoblike bun. She sprayed without mercy, shielding my eyes, then slicked my skull with the flat of her hand. I imagined my head, smooth and sleek, shiny as a billiard ball. She picked up the wreath.

"We'll put this on now. Just to be safe."

"But I'll feel like an idiot walking to school—"

"You're not walking. Blitz is taking you in the car."

"The car? No way. I'll get a cab."

"You're going with Blitz. Not another word."

"But I hate that c—"

"There's no discussion, darling." She suspended the flowers over my head, then the combs descended, piercing my scalp. I opened my mouth to argue with her, but the ring of the telephone intervened. "Don't move," she said, extending an arm to answer it.

"Hello? Oh, yes." Her Will voice. "I'm afraid she's occupied right now."

"Is that Will?" I rasped. I tried to jump up, but she held me there, impaled with pins.

"He just wants to wish you good luck tonight. Which is very bad luck to say, you know."

"Let me talk to him!" I wailed. I must have seemed mildly dangerous because after a second she let me go. Hairpins clattered to the floor as I vaulted from the chair.

"Just for a moment—and take it here. No one's going out of this room." She smiled faintly as I ripped the phone away from her.

"Will?" I whispered.

"God, Giselle. Did I break some kind of ballet law?"

"It isn't any law of mine."

"Good, I'm glad. What's going on?"

"Makeup and hair. You wouldn't recognize me now."

"I'm sorry to interrupt and all. I just wanted to call to say—"

"Don't say it, Will."

"I won't. I wanted to tell you something else."

I bit my lip. "What is it?"

"I can't wait to see you. I love you, Giselle." And then with a click he wasn't there.

Marina detached the phone from my hand.

"Look at you now. You've got lipstick all over your two front teeth." She grabbed a tissue and did something violent to my mouth. It was slightly refreshing, I had to admit, to have the old Marina back. She barked a list of orders then: "Try not to talk. Don't touch your face. Wear something that closes down the front. Don't smile until you're on the stage." Then, "There. That's it. Come take a look."

I moved to the mirror cautiously. Over the gleaming bottles and jars and the fat white roses from you-know-who, I met my face in the circle of glass. The makeup was a thick, pale mask, yet I saw myself behind it—saw myself somehow shining through—and unable to hold it back, I smiled.

From habit, I guess, I took the backseat in Blitz's car instead of sitting up front with him. As it was it was weird enough. The car felt so huge and empty, and whenever we turned a corner, I went sliding across the wide expanse. It was also strange just to be alone with him. Especially with the odd way he'd been acting ever since he picked me up. Like he didn't believe it was really me. Not that I could blame him. I totally didn't look like myself. Plus my head didn't go with my lower part in the crummy zip-up jogging suit.

As we sailed the few blocks to Dante School, he hummed very lightly under his breath. I think it was "The Polish March." Now and then I would see his eyes in the rearview mirror over his head. It was all I could see and I realized I'd never looked at his eyes, except to notice how blue they were. They were narrowed slightly and somewhat bright. If his mouth were in the picture, I felt sure there would be a nervous smile to go with those shiny, nervous eyes. At least he didn't try to talk. I give him points for that.

Around the school, cars and taxis were all backed up. I recognized people piling out, one of them being Mizgir, twitching and smoking a cigarette. I told Blitz to pull over and leave me at the corner, and surprisingly he obliged. He turned off the engine, but didn't spring up to let me out. Probably only seconds passed, but they felt intensely long to me. I slid myself to the nearest door.

"Wait," he said as my fingers touched the handle. I looked to the mirror, but nothing was there. And then I saw that he'd turned around and was passing something back to me.

"What is it?" I asked.

"A little something for tonight."

"What do you mean?"

"Just take it, Giselle."

It was a small box wrapped in golden paper. It actually looked like a cube of gold. I sat there dumbly and stared at it.

"I consulted with your mother, if that makes you feel more comfortable. She said it was something every ballerina needs."

I looked at the box and back to Blitz. He nodded again. *Please open it.* And so I did, tearing the paper gently, baring deep black velvet underneath. A black velvet box: a jewelry box. My fingers were stiff and clumsy as I lifted the tight-hinged lid. I took a breath, but it caught in my throat, which was suddenly tight and dry. I tried to speak but nothing came out, though God only knows what I would have said. Next I tried to look at him, but that didn't happen either. Somehow I couldn't seem to move. I could only sit there, frozen, staring down at the open box and the two fat orbs of diamond light.

Finally something stirred inside, some foggy call to action, and I heard myself whisper, "They're beautiful." I touched them with a fingertip; they were cool as chips of ice. "Do you think I ought to put them on?"

"That's what they're for," he answered, a trace of heartiness coming back. "Have you got a mirror somewhere there?"

"Yes," I said, fishing for my makeup box. My fingers shook as I set the box on top of my lap and opened the mirrored lid. Slowly I put the earrings on. They glistened fiercely, flanking my face and causing my eyes to shimmer too. Blitz met the shimmer, eye to eye. "I'm Vesna-Krasna." I heard my voice in the silence of the darkened car. "That's my role tonight, you know. It means Spring. I play the part of Spring." I think that was the first time I had ever said anything to him about myself, about who I am. He nodded, his gaze unblinking, watching mine.

"Thank you," I said, "for the beautiful gift. The most beautiful things I've ever owned." I leaned forward and kissed his cheek, then, not looking back, I grabbed my bags and flew from the car.

Chapter 28

INSIDE CRAZY DANTE, I tried to find a quiet place away from all the nervous wrecks and their pre-performance hysteria. I ended up in the Michelangelo Parlor, which was empty and dark, the noise from below muffled to a distant hum. I approached the massive mirror and looked at the earrings once again. They glinted with light whenever I moved, and even when I didn't, they seemed alive with their own white fire. Then I looked at the face between them. It seemed so pale, almost luminous, in the barely lighted parlor, the shadows shapes of blackness, so it looked like a face in a photograph. It shocked me for a moment. The way it had shocked my father's friends, Carla, Michael and Glittering Jewel, how very much I looked like him.

I moved from the mirror and set down my bags. I pulled off my shoes and, choosing a place on the gritty floor, settled on my back. I stared for a while at the grimy ceiling high above. Then, closing my eyes and turning out the distant sounds, I reached my arms straight over my head and, pointing my toes, stretched myself to my longest length. I let out my breath, felt it course to my fingers and toes, and imagined it flowing out of them. I flexed my feet and pointed them, then turned them at the ankle, rotating in and out again. Then I raised a leg in front of me, bending the knee and straightening, pulling it to my chest. I did the same to the other leg. Then, sitting up, I stretched to a split, dropping forward against the floor. My body was loose and supple, yet strong, not tired as it would have been had I taken more than Marina's class. I drew deep breaths, blocking out thoughts of the ancient germs I probably was sprawling in. Other thoughts too, I tried to crowd out. Of Will, for instance, watching from the audience. And Marina, of course, with her expertise.

Not to mention everyone else who'd be sitting there, their avid eyes devouring me. *Dix, neuf, huit. Sept, six, cinq. I am Vesna-Krasna.* I blocked out the faces. Saw just myself. My breath flowed in, and through and through, and finally I found the lake inside, hidden behind the thickets where nothing and no one else could go.

When I went down to change into my costume, the atmosphere was crazed. Half-dressed people were running around in circles, having psychotic episodes. Mrs. Turock was worst of all, borderline hysterical, clinging to the costume rack, a clipboard on a ribbon hanging from her neck. She shrieked when she saw me come into the room.

"God, Giselle! Where have you been? What are you trying to do to me?"

I wanted to smack her, sort of. But she looked so bad—her hair was standing straight on end, and she'd spilled some coffee all over her blouse—that I said I was sorry and tried to explain:

"I can't be around when everyone's going out of their mind. I need to keep my calm." She stared at me as if I'd said something deeply profound. Or maybe it was my diamonds that had put her into an instant trance. Still staring at me, she murmured, "You really look superb." Then, turning to the clothing rack, she riffled through the few remaining garment bags. She passed me my costume and put a check on her crazy-looking clipboard list. "Here," she said. "Go wherever you have to go. But please be back at a quarter of eight. I'll need to see everyone's face by then. I know I can count on you, Giselle."

I took the bulky bag from her. Through the foggy, crinkled plastic I could see the sheen of the satin top and the wide stiff tutu of the skirt, robin's egg blue, layer over layer, and sprinkled with violets and deep green leaves. Suddenly, I couldn't wait to put it on. I wanted to dance, to be onstage. I wanted to be Spring.

Magda found me in the group just before eight o'clock. By now, Mrs. Turock had come unhinged. Still wearing her clipboard necklace, she was shouting roll call and counting heads as if we were on a field trip somewhere in the bush. Magda crept in and tugged my tutu from the back.

"Wow," she said when I turned around. "You look amazing. Incredible. Who the hell are you anyway?" I smiled at her and felt a hairline fracture crack my spackled face. Then, "God," she breathed as she noticed my ears. "Where'd you get the rocks?"

"Blitz."

"For real?"

I nodded.

"I'm speechless," she said. "I'm absolutely without a voi—" That's when Turock spotted her. Her eyes popped totally out of her head, and her hair, I swear it, smoked. Babbling sounds came out of her mouth, but before she could form them into words, Magda had long since gone. I felt a twinge of sympathy, though she really did need to get a grip. She was making things worse for everyone, the Berendeys in particular, sweating in the babushkas nailed to their heads with fifty thousand bobby pins.

A few minutes later I stood in the wings. It was airless and hot in that dusty space in between the curtains—the panels to either side of us and the heavier velvet wall in front. From beyond that wall, the hum of voices filtered through. You could tell the theater was totally full. You could sense the warmth of bodies and smell the crowded air. Somewhere near, not far at all, Marina, Blitz and Sonia sat. And with them, Will, his green, green gaze awaiting me.

"Ready?" said Mrs. Turock, appearing, panting, at my side. With her were Moroz and Snegurochka, he already sweating in his feathery white fur cape. We glanced at each other, no more than that, as the buzz of voices suddenly stilled. The house lights were down. The silence that fell was palpable, expectant as a breath. Then music shattered the stock-still air.

"Merde," said Moroz as he strode onstage to be there when the curtain rose. Snegurochka made the sign of the cross, then tiptoed behind him and took her pose. Rope raced on a pulley, quick and dry. *Whoosh!* the curtains parted, velvet sweeping swirls of dust. And suddenly— light, the blinding glitter and filigree, the silver-white of the Realm of Ice. Moroz extended a curved white arm, and his little daughter began to dance. Over the footlights, the ghosts of faces began to appear like bits of flotsam surfacing

in the black sea of the audience. I turned from that blackness into the light. I rose *en pointe*. I drew a breath. Then I glided into the snow white heat.

———

Afterward, no one had to tell me. I knew it as it happened. I felt the moment clearly in the middle of the pas de deux. It's hard to describe a thing like this. It's like slipping past some see-through wall into another world. The calmness and sureness surprised me at first. And the way it happened all at once, almost like a click. I was suddenly altered yet deeply myself, perfectly clear and free of fear. And in this place, I knew with simple certainty I could do far more than I'd ever done. I could balance longer, enlarge my penché. I could do an extra pirouette in the same clear space of time. The music seemed liquid and part of my blood, and full of living music, I knew myself as Spring. My joy was complete at the sight of my creations—the flowers and clouds and the little brown sparrows flitting around. But my arms grew tense and tremulous as I watched my little daughter dancing toward her death. I felt it still, this wild calm, even as we took our bows and cool, damp flowers filled our arms—mine and Snegurochka's—ghost gardenia overlying the heavy rose.

———

Alone, Marina came into the dressing room. Our eyes cut through the chaos of bodies and cast-off clothes. She came to me, and caught me tightly in her arms. I held her too, feeling again her thinness and no longer surprising warmth.

"You were glorious," she whispered, her mouth against my ear. "I've never been so proud." She held me another moment, then slowly let me go. Her gray silk dress was splotched with sweat in the places where my skin had pressed. "There's someone who wants to see you," she said. "But you ought to know, he's really quite beside himself."

"Will? Where is he?"

"Out in the hall." She motioned for me to follow her, and we wove through the jam-packed dressing room into the jam-packed hall. There he was, leaning up against the wall, a bouquet of flowers in his hands. He looked at me and didn't move. I took a step and very slowly he came to me, the flowers clasped in front of him, a clump of deep red hearts.

"Will?"

He stopped. He lowered his eyes. And when he looked up they were bright with tears. I pushed the flowers out of the way and pressed myself against him. "Will, what's wrong?" I whispered. A second passed. He was holding me in the weirdest way as if he were afraid I'd break. I held him tighter, as tight as I'd held Marina.

Finally he whispered, "Nothing's wrong. You're . . . just so . . . fucking beautiful."

Magda came in and waited while I showered. Afterward, she helped me chip off the last remains of makeup. When we were through, my face felt like something newly hatched. Though she hadn't been able to watch the whole performance, she'd made a point of catching the adagio.

"I couldn't believe it was you," she said. She was wrapping up my pointe shoes, winding the ribbons and tucking them in. "I knew you were good. And I knew at rehearsal that something big was going on. But tonight you were truly awesome. No one was breathing, I swear to God."

"Thanks," I said and smiled at her. "The lights were really awesome too."

"Screw the lights," she answered. "Nobody cares about the lights."

We gathered my bags and the fat bouquets. I carried the one from Will, of course, dipping my face into the weird wax hearts, breathing the scentless air of them. We made our way through the long dim hall, yelling goodbye at some of the people still hanging around, such as Mizgir and Frost, still in his furry headpiece, and Mrs. Crazy Turock, who flew to my side and hugged me. She wouldn't be surprised, she said, if after tonight I was asked to try out for "some very major company." Weird how I actually didn't care. How all I cared about just now was the night right here in front of me, this night with Will and the people that mattered and made my life.

We all packed into Blitz's car; Marina in front with all the bouquets, Will and I with Magda and Sonia in the back. They all kept saying how great I'd done and how wonderful the lighting was.

"I was so impressed by the Realm of Ice," Sonia said, clasping Magda's arm. "The snow effects were wonderful. I was shivering in my seat." Will remarked that he also liked the forest scene and the way the light filtered so naturally through the trees. He asked her how she'd done it, and she cheerfully explained. It was really nice seeing her so happy, which she hadn't been in quite some time.

We were all pretty happy really, which you wouldn't think would be the case, what with all the things that had just gone on. Sitting there, I had this urge to hug them all, even horsey Blitz. I can't explain it really, but that's how I felt in the crowded car, all of us crammed together, sailing through the night.

As Blitz pulled into a bright garage, he told us he was taking us someplace Russian and elegant in honor of Tchaikovsky and his beautiful ballet.

"Divine," said Sonia dreamily.

The night was warm, and we ambled slowly eastward, our strange, connected group. I held Will's hand and in the other clutched my clutch of hearts. Ahead of us, Blitz walked beside Marina, a constant hand against her back. Next to them, Magda and Sonia strolled along, not quite touching but keeping in pace, laughing every now and then.

Everything seemed ablaze with light. It streamed from cars and taxis, and spilled from windows and opening doors. In the Redeye Grill on the corner of Seventh Avenue, the light burned hot and orange, and a singer in the balcony flashed sparks of red from her sequined dress. Although we couldn't see them, I felt that the sky must be full of stars, millions and zillions of diamond specks just beyond the arc of light that cupped us like a lid. A crystalline glow beckoned from Petrossian. We regrouped in its beam at the restaurant door, and Blitz stepped into his role as host.

"Head count, please. Is everyone here?"

"He sounds like crazy Turock," Magda said with a roll of her eyes as Sonia led the way inside. Blitz held the door for Magda and Marina, and Will and I came next. I started to enter, and suddenly I remembered another Russian restaurant. It was long-gone now, but suddenly I was there again, at the Russian Tea Room's small, bright door.

In a gleaming window off to the side I see the silver samovar. Its polished belly shimmers, and in the curve of mirrored light, I see a slender, graceful man. "Make a wish," he whispers. *That we'll live in the woods at Otto's lake. That you'll never go away from me.* He laughs out loud and hoists me suddenly high in the air, over the hats and tall men's heads, and through the chilly, falling dusk into the warm, dark taxicab with its scent of candy Easter eggs.

Now it is now. Someone says my name aloud. It is Will, of course. He presses my hand, and the dream of silver fades away. We push through the door to a space of ice and candlelight. Marina smiles as if she knows. As if she has felt the sweep of silk and can see him there beside me, my delicate father, my Bluebird, the Rose.

Celeste Conway
is a writer, an artist,
and a lifelong devotee of ballet.
She is the author of the picture book *Where Is Papa Now?*.
She lives in New York City.